DEATH LIES BENEATH

Recent Titles by Pauline Rowson

TIDE OF DEATH
IN COLD DAYLIGHT
IN FOR THE KILL
DEADLY WATERS *
THE SUFFOCATING SEA *
DEAD MAN'S WHARF *
BLOOD ON THE SAND *
FOOTSTEPS ON THE SHORE *
A KILLING COAST *
DEATH LIES BENEATH *

* *available from Severn House*

DEATH LIES BENEATH

A DI Andy Horton Mystery

Pauline Rowson

Severn House Large Print
London & New York

This first large print edition published 2015
in Great Britain and the USA by
SEVERN HOUSE PUBLISHERS LTD of
19 Cedar Road, Sutton, Surrey, England, SM2 5DA.
First world regular print edition published 2012 by
Severn House Publishers Ltd., London and New York.

British Library Cataloguing in Publication Data

Rowson, Pauline. author.
    Death lies beneath. – (A DI Andy Horton mystery)
    1. Horton, Andy (Fictitious character)–Fiction.
    2. Police–England–Portsmouth–Fiction. 3. Detective
    and mystery stories. 4. Large type books.
    I. Title II. Series
    823.9'2-dc23

ISBN-13: 9780727897954

Severn House Publishers support the Forest Stewardship Council™
[FSC™], the leading international forest certification organisation. All
our titles that are printed on FSC certified paper carry the FSC logo.

MIX
Paper from
responsible sources
FSC® C013056

Typeset by Palimpsest Book Production Ltd.,
Falkirk, Stirlingshire, Scotland.
Printed and bound in Great Britain by
T J International, Padstow, Cornwall.

*With thanks to the captains and crew of the
Wightlink car ferry and especially to John
Monk and Paul Marshall for my wonderful
trips across the Solent on the Bridge.*

One

'Anything?' Detective Superintendent Uckfield asked hopefully.

Inspector Andy Horton shook his head and pulled at his black tie. Loosening his collar, he stepped into the shade of a tree in the crematorium gardens hoping to find some relief from the burning sun and wondering what Uckfield, head of the Major Crime Team, and Detective Chief Superintendent Sawyer of the Intelligence Directorate had expected they'd gain by a police presence – a weeping confession from the killer of Daryl Woodley over his coffin? That would have been nice but Horton knew that Woodley's handful of mourners would sooner have their private parts tattooed with a blunt and dirty instrument than confess to a crime. And grassing to the police was only one step below being a paedophile in their code. They'd got nothing out of them during the investigation into Woodley's death and they'd get nothing now. And neither would the crime reporter from the local newspaper, Leanne Payne, he thought watching her slim figure move amongst the mourners as they stood blinking in the bright sunshine like miners released from deep underground.

She addressed a shaven-headed, skinny man with tattoos up his hairy arms. Reggie Thomas,

1

like Daryl Woodley, had been released from Parkhurst Prison on the Isle of Wight in March. When questioned, Reggie claimed to have no knowledge of why his former fellow inmate had been assaulted just off the Portsmouth waterfront eighteen days ago, or why, after three days in hospital, Woodley had risen from his bed and somehow ended up dead at the marshes to the north of the city three miles from the hospital. No one claimed to have driven him there, it was inaccessible by public transport and he could hardly have walked that distance.

Despite Uckfield's public appeals for information no one had come forward with any sightings of Woodley, either where he'd been attacked or where his body had been found by a man walking his dog. Exasperated, Uckfield had declared, 'Someone must have seen him; this isn't the Starship bloody *Enterprise*, he couldn't have been beamed to the marshes.' But it was almost as though he had been.

The pathologist, Dr Gaye Clayton, had said that Woodley had died from his earlier injuries, a violent blow to the head and hypothermia. Hard to believe with the temperature soaring to equatorial heights, thought Horton plucking at the shirt sticking to his back, but a fortnight ago it had been as cold as December.

Uckfield sniffed noisily. 'Can't think what they're doing here, anyway. None of that lot had a good word to say about Woodley when he was alive.'

Did anyone? thought Horton. Even the chaplain had struggled to find a kind word for the man

2

who had lied, cheated, robbed and assaulted his way through his forty-seven years.

'Probably wanted to get their picture in the newspaper.' And he'd witnessed some heart-breaking performances by them worthy of an Oscar, put on for the benefit of the local press photographer, Cliff Wesley, who'd been snapping away on their arrival.

'This is a waste of time.'

A sentiment shared by Horton. DCS Sawyer was going to be disappointed, he thought. Sawyer's department was also responsible for gathering prison intelligence and Sawyer believed that the attack on Woodley had been carried out on the instructions of big-time crook Marty Stapleton, currently in Her Majesty's Prison Swansea, where he'd been transferred after Woodley had attacked him in Parkhurst in September. Horton had ventured the opinion that a crook as big as Stapleton wouldn't bother himself with low-life scum like Woodley only to be told he would because Woodley had humiliated him, and Stapleton, with a record of robbery, violence and extortion, wouldn't allow that to go unpunished.

Horton guessed there was something in that, but watching Woodley's mourners shuffle off, he thought that Sawyer's hope of apprehending and gaining information from Woodley's assailant on where Marty had stashed the proceeds of his robberies was too optimistic.

'Perhaps we should send Marty Stapleton some of Cliff Wesley's photographs,' he said.

'Yeah, and while we're at it we'll send him a

3

signed copy of the video Clarke's shooting. Marty can watch that and have a good laugh.'

Clarke, the forensic photographer, was under Sawyer's orders, filming the occasion in a van with darkened windows under the trees in the car park at the front of the crematorium. Horton wouldn't have wanted to exchange positions with him in this heat. He saw DC Marsden cross to Leanne Payne, who had lingered to jot down the words of condolence on the labels of the few floral tributes laid out on the cold slabs beside the aisle. They exchanged a few words and smiles before Leanne Payne moved off in the same direction as Woodley's mourners.

'At least she didn't ask for a comment,' Uckfield growled.

'Unless Marsden gave her one.'

'I'll have his balls for doorstops if he did.'

But Horton knew it was easy to get caught out, especially when the reporter was experienced and keen, and the copper, despite his degree and being on the fast-track entry system, was inexperienced in handling investigations and the media.

Marsden straightened up as they drew level. 'There are no flowers from any anonymous source, sir, or from anyone we don't know,' he said with disappointment.

'His killer's hardly likely to send a wreath and sign his bloody name,' Uckfield snapped before striding off.

'It's the heat,' Horton tossed at Marsden before following Uckfield through the aisles and past the courtyard where he stepped aside to allow a sombrely dressed elderly man to pass. But Horton

4

knew the temperature had little to do with Uckfield's foul mood but more to do with the fact that ACC Dean had been constantly on the Super's back carping about the lack of progress in the Woodley investigation.

'Just look at them with their bling, beer guts, tattoos and tits,' Uckfield exploded. 'Bloody villains the lot.'

Horton didn't think he was referring to the small crowd of mainly elderly mourners gathering outside the waiting room for the next funeral, or the attractive suntanned woman in her mid-forties in the figure-hugging black dress, high-heeled court shoes and a wide-brimmed black hat standing a short distance away from them. He watched her scan Woodley's mourners with, he thought, an air of puzzlement, but then, as Uckfield had pointed out, they were enough to cause anyone bewilderment.

'And what's that bloody press photographer still doing here?' Uckfield continued, as Wesley turned his camera towards them. 'Hasn't he got enough pictures by now?'

Horton would have thought so. Leanne Payne crossed to Wesley and they huddled over his camera, obviously examining the digital images Wesley had shot. Horton turned his gaze on Woodley's mourners as they made for their cars. With surprise he saw Wayne and Maureen Sholby climb into a new Mercedes and Darren Hobbs into a new Audi. Either benefit payments had increased massively or they'd won the lottery, and as he considered neither was likely he was curious to know how they could afford to drive such expensive new motors.

5

Uckfield turned to Marsden, '*If* you can tear yourself away from ogling Leanne Payne's tits it's time we got back to solving crimes that deserve it.' He stomped off leaving Marsden to scurry after him.

Horton decided to follow suit. There was nothing more to see here, though he took one final look around. His glance again fell on the woman with the large-brimmed black hat. She hadn't joined the elderly mourners congregating outside the chapel entrance but stood for a moment looking at them, then Leanne Payne caught his eye and seemed about to make a beeline for him. It was definitely time to leave.

Horton climbed on his Harley and headed back to the station, mulling over the attack on Woodley, as he'd done many times during the investigation. Several things about it bothered him. For a start Woodley had been miles off his patch, drinking at the Lord Horatio, a rundown pub just off the Hard and more than five miles from his usual haunts in the north of the city. And if the landlord, and those they'd managed to question since, could be believed, Woodley had been drinking alone. He'd left at closing time and had been attacked a couple of streets away heading north but he hadn't been discovered until one in the morning by two students staggering home after a night out in a club at the fashionable waterfront complex of Oyster Quays. On the house-to-house they'd drawn the 'three monkeys' syndrome: nobody had seen or heard anything and even if they had they certainly weren't saying anything. The occupants in that part of town were as closed-mouthed as Woodley's associates to the north. So what had Woodley been doing there? How had he got there? He didn't have a car and none of the bus or taxi drivers questioned claimed to have seen him. His mates swore on all they held sacred, their plasma TVs and mobile phones, they hadn't driven him there, but Horton didn't set much store by that.

He halted at the traffic lights to Horsea Marina and thought back to the beginning of the investigation. He had believed Woodley had been at the pub to meet a fellow crook with a view to planning a job. Maybe the other villain hadn't shown, or had decided that after telling Woodley his plans on a previous occasion he was too stupid to risk involving and thought it wiser to remove him from the scene. The weapon used on Woodley had most likely been a sap, more commonly known as a billy club or blackjack, and favoured by bouncers, street gangs, thugs, the military and the police. And although three-quarters of the station considered Woodley's death retribution for all the harm he'd caused to innocent victims in his evil miserable life, and the other quarter said they'd willingly give the person who had attacked Woodley and left him for dead a medal for doing so, Horton knew that no police officer would go so far as to clobber him, or bother to transport him to the marshes to die. Horton's money was on the villain. The blackjack was small enough to fit in a pocket and powerful enough to knock a man unconscious, which it had done. Whoever had attacked Woodley hadn't finished the job, either because they never

7

intended to or they were disturbed. That didn't explain how Woodley had ended up dead at the marshes though.

The lights changed and Horton made for the motorway leading into the city. The other theory, one that Sergeant Cantelli had favoured, was that Woodley had been attacked by a mugger who had been disturbed before being able to rob him of the fifty pounds benefit money he had in his pocket. Horton recalled his conversations with Cantelli before the sergeant had gone on holiday. After Cantelli had consulted his wife, Charlotte, a nurse, he'd suggested that Woodley had staggered out of the hospital in a dazed and confused state, keen to go back to the time before the attack, a common factor in head-injury cases though they very rarely picked up their bed and walked. Once outside Woodley had been given a lift by a lorry or van driver or a passing sales rep to the marshes where he had passed out and died.

'But why drop him at the marshes?' Horton had asked.

'Because whoever picked him up soon realized he was trouble and said that was as far as he was prepared to go,' Cantelli had answered.

Then Sawyer had weighed in with his bright idea about Marty Stapleton being behind Woodley's murder. As Horton pulled into the station car park, he thought that whichever theory might be correct, they seemed fated not to get a result on the case.

He made his way to the overheated CID operations room where he found DC Walters, perspiring and jacketless, munching his way through a

8

packet of crisps staring at a computer screen. It smelt like the back of a bin lorry. God alone knew what Walters had been eating but Horton caught the faint smell of curry, vinegar and eggs, which turned his stomach over.

'Don't you ever open any windows,' he said in exasperation, crossing to one on Walters' right and pushing it wide. It made little difference. There was no wind and hardly any air.

'Sorry, guv, got caught up watching these videos, trying to spot our metal thieves on the Hard,' Walters replied with his mouth full. 'Nothing doing. I've been sifting through the CCTV footage for so long that I wouldn't spot a masked robber if he stood in front of the camera and waved at me. Extra patrols around the area would stand a much better chance of catching the buggers.'

And Horton had about as much hope of getting that as he did of being able to walk across the Solent to the Isle of Wight. It had started with the theft of a bronze statue from a garden in Old Portsmouth and a fountain from a nearby wine bar eighteen days ago. Five days later two memorial plaques had been taken from benches in the museum grounds and two days ago two brass plaques had been removed from the wall of St George's Church, just off the Hard. It must have taken a hell of a lot of muscle not to mention noise but no one had seen or heard anything. The fact that there was no forced entry meant the thieves either had a key or an accomplice had let them in, or they'd entered the church during daylight hours when the door was unlocked. But no one had come forward after appeals in the local newspaper for witnesses. Uniform had interviewed the clergy and the regular parishioners without joy. It was hardly big time but the thieves were getting bolder and with the spiralling prices in metal, Horton knew it could escalate, as it had done in other cities across the country, and it might not be long before someone lost their life by trying to steal live cables from electricity pylons or cabling from the railways or the telephone company.

Walters said, 'Uniform's done the rounds of the licensed scrap-metal merchants but they all swear blind they've not bought any statues or plaques and they're worried they're going to be next in line to be targeted by the thieves.'

'Contact the Environment Agency; see what intelligence they have on any illegal and unlicensed scrap yards.'

He relayed to Walters what had happened at Daryl Woodley's funeral, which took two seconds and one word, 'nothing', and asked Walters to check out the vehicles Sholby and Hobbs had been driving when the video came over from Clarke. 'Find out how long they've had the cars, where they bought them and how they paid. Check if there is any finance on them. I doubt even they'd be stupid enough to drive stolen cars to a funeral, but you never know your luck.'

Horton pushed open his office door wishing that Cantelli wasn't on holiday. DCI Bliss had only grudgingly let the sergeant go after Horton had lied saying he was needed in Italy for a big family celebration. Cantelli had said, 'I only hope she doesn't decide to go camping in the New

10

Forest.' Knowing Bliss's desire for status and her almost pathological obsession with neatness, cleanliness and order, Horton thought camping was the last thing their CID boss would ever dream of doing.

His office was like an oven. Wrenching back the blinds he shoved the window open as wide as it would go but only the sounds of bad-tempered traffic filtered in. Slinging his jacket on the back of his chair his hand brushed against the letter in the pocket. For the last hour he'd forgotten about it. He had no need to read it again. Every word was ingrained on his mind. In six weeks' time he and Catherine would be officially divorced. The decree absolute would be granted and his twelve-year marriage would be finally and legally over.

His eyes flicked to the photograph on his paper-strewn desk of his eight-year-old daughter and his heart felt heavy. He desperately wanted to spend more time with her but now that she was at boarding school that looked less likely than ever. And Catherine seemed determined to keep them apart during the school holidays.

He turned to stare out of the window seeing nothing but the day spent with Emma last Friday with a brief smile which turned to a scowl as the memory of how it had ended encroached on his thoughts. Catherine had agreed to reasonable contact time, only her idea of reasonable was turning out to be different to his. One day at the beginning of the half-term holiday was not enough. And it had not been what they'd agreed. Catherine had conveniently found a reason to

11

take their daughter away from him yet again. At Christmas it had been with her parents to their villa in Cyprus. At Easter it had been a holiday with one of Catherine's friends and last week she and Emma had gone sailing to the Channel Islands on Catherine's father's yacht. He'd protested. Catherine had accused him of being unreasonable in trying to deprive Emma of her grandparents and vice-versa.

'Have you ever stopped to consider how you're depriving me,' he'd hissed, not wanting to upset Emma, who was climbing into Catherine's car.

'Emma loves her grandparents. And they deserve to see her. She and they were all we had when you were too busy getting drunk.'

He'd been stung to retort, 'If you had stood by me during my suspension instead of believing those ridiculous rape allegations I might not needed to have got drunk!'

'That's it, blame me. If all you can do is argue and shout when I collect Emma then it's obviously for the best that she doesn't come very often.' Catherine had turned towards the car but Horton had grabbed her. She'd spun round and he'd seen the glint in her eyes. God! He'd played right into her hands. As though stung he'd let her go. With a supreme effort, though his gut was churning with fury, he had leant into the open car window and kissed his daughter, forcing a smile. He didn't look at Catherine again.

'I'm glad you've got time to gaze out of the window, Inspector.'

Horton spun round to find DCI Bliss on the threshold. Dressed in her customary black skirt

12

and white blouse, with her hair scraped back in a limp ponytail off her pinched unmade face, she looked as cool as though she'd just stepped out of a refrigerator. He stifled a groan.

'Why did you attend Woodley's funeral without clearing it with me?' she snapped.

Horton wondered how she had heard. He didn't think Walters had mentioned it, because Walters for all his faults would have forewarned him, and he was very good at acting dumb when asked questions by those on high. Probably because he was dumb.

'I couldn't find you, ma'am,' Horton lied. He hadn't even looked for her, because he'd known what she'd say; it wasn't his case. 'Detective Superintendent Uckfield thought it might be helpful to have me there as I've been working on the investigation.'

'Not any more,' she replied crisply. 'We have enough of our own outstanding cases and I want an update now including what you are doing about these metal thefts.'

She plonked herself down opposite him. He sat and swiftly relayed where they were on several investigations, which clearly didn't please her because they all seemed to be going nowhere, finishing off with what Walters had reported about the metal thefts. That drew a deeper frown from her and a pursing of thin lips. 'That's simply not good enough. Make it a top priority. I want whoever is responsible caught and I mean soon not within days or weeks.'

Didn't she think that was what he also wanted?

'And I want a full report on it by six o'clock

this evening. I have a meeting tomorrow morning with Inspector Warren, Superintendent Reine and senior executives from British Telecom and the British Transport Police. Copper wiring and cabling thefts would mean a severe disruption to businesses.'

'Ma'am.' He watched her march out before he let out a sigh. Stuffing his tie in his desk drawer he turned his attention to his computer and located Clarke's email. Clicking on the link, he began to play the video he'd shot at the crematorium.

Woodley's mourners drove into the car park and congregated outside the waiting room. Cliff Wesley and Leanne Payne arrived separately. She moved among the mourners with her Dictaphone; Wesley with his camera. Horton had seen all this from his Harley. The hearse arrived. No other funeral car followed it. Woodley had no living relatives and none of his so-called friends had arranged the funeral or chipped in to pay for it, despite their flashy cars and gold jewellery and the latest gizmos in their homes. Woodley hadn't owned anything of value, or left any savings, the state had taken care of him during his life and the state had buried him.

The mourners filed in to the chapel behind the coffin and he followed them. No one entered after him, and Clarke's video showed no one hanging around outside or arriving soon after Woodley's short service started. The next thing Horton saw was Uckfield's BMW entering the car park and Uckfield and Marsden climbing out. They went to the rear of the crematorium. Nothing further happened. Clarke had kept the camera rolling but

Horton fast-forwarded it until cars began to pull in for the next funeral. Then Woodley's lot emerged from the rear of the chapel. They stood talking in the hot June sunshine for a while, the press photographer again snapping away. Where was Wesley while they were in the service? Horton hadn't seen him go into the crematorium gardens so he guessed he'd probably sat in his car for a smoke. Leanne Payne broke into the Woodley crowd and then a few minutes later he, Uckfield and Marsden came into view.

Clarke's video swung back to the Woodley mourners and to their right where Horton caught sight of the woman in the black dress and wide-brimmed black hat before the camera followed the Woodley crowd climbing into their cars and driving away. Then Uckfield's BMW almost collided with the next hearse arriving. Next up was him leaving on his Harley, then Leanne Payne and Cliff Wesley.

Horton sat back letting the video play as Clarke swung the camera back to the chapel entrance and waiting room opposite it. The mourners for the next funeral, about fifteen of them, were going in. Horton looked for the woman in the black hat but there was no sign of her. Perhaps she'd answered a call of nature. Whoever she was and wherever she had gone, Horton thought, forwarding the video to Walters, she clearly had nothing to do with Daryl Woodley, and neither did he any more, Bliss had made that perfectly clear.

He switched his attention to the metal thefts, trawling through reports across the wider area looking for similar patterns, and paused when he came to a brass propeller stolen from an old boat being renovated in a boatyard in Fareham creek. That was about twelve miles from Portsmouth. Could it be the work of the same villains? It seemed a little off their patch. The theft had occurred last night and Sergeant Dai Elkins of the marine unit had filed the report. Horton rang him, but got his voicemail. He left a message asking Elkins to call him in the morning to discuss it. He then spent the remainder of the afternoon finishing the report for Bliss and attempting to clear the backlog of paperwork that had piled up while investigating Woodley's murder. It was a couple of hours later when Walters knocked and entered.

'The cars driven by Sholby and Hobbs are registered in their name and bought from the same source, a garage near Waterlooville.'

Which was six miles to the north of Portsmouth. 'For cash?' asked Horton.

'Looks like it. Can't find any finance on them.'

Horton wondered how they had got hold of so much money. Both had no formal occupation, they spent most of their lives claiming benefit and the remainder inside after being nicked for theft or receiving stolen goods. Did their newly acquired wealth have something to do with the robbery on Mason's Electricals three weeks ago, which thankfully Bliss hadn't mentioned? There had been no progress on that either. A black van had been recorded on the CCTV cameras pulling up outside the store but they hadn't been able to get the vehicle licence number or any adequate footage of the two men seen like black shadows dressed in hoodies emerging from it. Their build could fit Sholby and Hobbs but equally it could fit a third of the male population of Portsmouth. One of the two security officers had been knocked out and tied up, the other had been in the toilet suffering from eating too much curry, though he claimed it was food poisoning and that he shouldn't have been at work anyway. By the time he'd emerged, the black shadows and their dirty black van had vanished along with a quantity of televisions, hi-fis, computers and anything else that wasn't screwed down.

Horton said, 'Do we know this garage owner?'

'No. Officers at the station close to it might.'

'Talk to them tomorrow, find out all you can about the proprietor.'

Walters took that as a dismissal for the day. Horton decided to followed suit soon afterwards, noting that Bliss had already left. As he headed along the busy promenade towards the marina where he lived on his yacht, he wasn't surprised to see that the pebbled beach was still packed with sunbathers. It was a glorious cloudless evening, still hot but not with the intensity of the earlier heat of the day, and he toyed with the idea of getting a couple of hours' sailing in before sunset. He might have done except there was hardly a breath of wind. Instead he ate on deck, enjoying the quiet of the evening and watching the sun set, trying to shut out thoughts of Woodley and work. But as the lights came on in the houses on the hill slopes across Langstone Harbour to the north, Woodley refused to budge from his

17

thoughts. Below the lights, and bordering the harbour, were the marshes where Woodley's body had been found.

Something nudged at the back of Horton's mind. Was it something one of Woodley's mourners had said in the interviews during the investigation? Most of it was lies, including the fact that Sholby, Hobbs and Reggie Thomas had all given each other an alibi for the time of the attack on Woodley. They'd been drinking at Sholby's house and watching football on the telly. Had thinking about Sholby and Hobbs jogged at an elusive fact tucked away, which they'd missed in the investigation? Or perhaps it was something the chaplain had said during Woodley's short funeral service?

The thought of funerals took him back to another he'd attended four weeks ago, that of former PC Adrian Stanley. It had been very different to Woodley's. Horton had recollected it while in the chapel but had pushed it aside to concentrate on Woodley. Now he focused his full attention on it, or rather on what Adrian Stanley, the copper who had investigated his mother's disappearance just over thirty years ago, *hadn't* told him about Jennifer Horton's disappearance. When he'd visited Stanley in April, the ex-copper could throw no light on why Jennifer had walked out of their council tower-block flat on a chilly November day in 1978 leaving her ten-year-old son to fend for himself. There had been no reports of her carrying a bag or suitcase and her clothes had still been in the flat. A witness, their neighbour, had claimed that Jennifer had been dressed up, wearing

18

make-up, and had been happy. She never showed up that night at the casino where she worked, and no one had seen or heard of her again.

Horton sipped his coffee, feeling the familiar jag of emptiness in the pit of his stomach which the memory always conjured up. He tried to ignore it and instead thought back to Stanley's last words to him, uttered from his hospital bed after suffering a stroke following Horton's visit to his flat. They had been about a brooch, or at least Horton thought that was what Stanley had managed to utter before dying. It tied in with the fact that a photograph of Stanley's late wife, wearing a brooch when her husband received his Queen's Gallantry Medal for thwarting an armed robbery, had vanished, along with the brooch itself. But how that connected with his mother's disappearance Horton didn't know except he suspected Stanley had either stolen it from her belongings or had been given it as payment to keep quiet about something he'd discovered.

He'd questioned Stanley's son, Robin, after his house had been broken into the day his father had died. Along with the family photograph albums, jewellery belonging to Robin Stanley's family had been taken. It was the neatest burglary that Horton had ever come across. No prints, no mess. A double-glazed kitchen door lifted off its hinges, no witnesses, not even a report of a car or van. A highly professional job.

Robin didn't remember the brooch and said he hadn't really noticed it in the photograph. And so far Horton had drawn a blank tracing the missing photograph of Adrian Stanley's wife wearing it.

He wished he could remember what the brooch had looked like but he hadn't realized its significance until too late. So with that line of enquiry a dead end, did he go back to the beginning of Jennifer Horton's life and try to trace her movements from a young girl until the day she vanished in the hope that somewhere along the line he would find the answer? That would take months, though, years even and could result in nothing. Alternatively should he take up DCS Sawyer's offer and work with the Intelligence Directorate who believed his mother had connections with a wanted criminal they'd codenamed Zeus? That would be far the quickest and easiest option. He'd already refused Sawyer's offer twice, not because he was afraid of Zeus, but because he was afraid of what he might discover about his mother and what others, especially his colleagues, might learn in the process. Besides, he had told himself several times, if Jennifer had been involved with this Zeus then in all probability she was dead.

A police siren caught his attention but gradually it faded as it headed along the seafront westwards. It was still hot. What little breeze there had been had died completely. The flags outside the marina office hung limp. He swallowed the remainder of his drink and surveyed the marina a moment longer before going below. All was quiet. As he lay on his bunk Woodley's funeral again came to mind and along with it that nagging thought that something he'd seen or heard today was significant but try as he might it refused to surface. Perhaps it would come to him in his sleep.

Two

The trilling of his mobile phone woke him. Scrambling to answer it, he registered it was daylight and six twenty-three. A call at this hour could only mean one thing: work.

'We've got a suspicious death, sir. PCs Somerfield and Seaton are at the scene.'

'Where?' asked Horton, fully awake and heading for the shower.

'The former Tipner Boatyard.'

That was on the western shores of the city and the opposite side of town from his marina. It was a stone's throw from the commercial ferry port, ten minutes from the police station by car, and about fifteen on the Harley before the rush-hour traffic. He remembered reading that the boatyard had been sold for re-development a couple of years ago and that a salvage operation had only recently begun. They were clearing a Second World War munitions barge from the seabed and he wondered if a skeleton had been discovered during the clearance operation. He asked for more details.

'Sorry, sir, don't have them,' came the unsatisfactory answer. Horton didn't waste time enquiring why.

'OK, tell them I'm on my way.'

21

He ran an electric razor over his chin and was on his Harley heading there within ten minutes, mentally preparing himself for what he might see and hoping that it was a long-ago fatality rather than a recent one. He headed west and then north and soon was turning off the main road and travelling through the narrow streets of terraced houses, which reminded him of Daryl Woodley because this was where he had lived and where Reggie Thomas and the rest of Woodley's associates still did. Again he considered what was nagging at the back of his mind about the Woodley investigation. It hadn't surfaced during sleep. As he turned off by the allotments and rode under the motorway bridge onto the small peninsula that butted out on to the upper reaches of Portsmouth harbour, he again tried to conjure up the elusive thought but it refused to come. No matter. It might occur to him later.

He pulled into the boatyard and parked beside the police car. PC Kate Somerfield broke off her conversation with a suntanned, muscular man in his late forties standing beside a van, and headed towards him. There was a frown of concern on her fair face and he thought she looked paler than usual, which didn't bode well.

'The body's on the wreckage, sir,' she greeted him sombrely.

Body, not bones then, so a recent death. That certainly wasn't the news he had wanted. His eyes travelled across the yard to the far side of the quay, where a blackened rotting wooden hulk rested. It was still attached to the large yellow crane perched on a floating barge. Clearly the

22

wreck wasn't the Second World War munitions barge. It looked as though it had been a small yacht. PC Seaton was standing beside it. Two men were some distance to the right of him, one reading a newspaper and the other doing something on his mobile device.

Several thoughts rapidly ran through Horton's mind as he made towards it. How long had this wreck been submerged? How long had the body been on it? How did it get there? Were they looking at suicide or an accident? Or was it an unlawful killing? He sincerely hoped it wasn't the latter, the first two were bad enough but the third would stretch their resources even further and wouldn't be good for the victim's relatives either, he thought caustically.

Walking beside him, Somerfield continued with her report. 'The crane operative, Bill Shoreham, that's him reading the newspaper, spotted the body as he was setting the wreck down onto the quay. The other man on his mobile phone is Ethan Crombie. He's the boatman.'

'I hope he's not calling the press.'

'Seaton told them they weren't to.'

But Horton knew people didn't always do as they were told.

Somerfield added, 'Mr Crombie, and another man, piloted the floating crane around from the Camber yesterday on tugs. Mr Crombie returned in one of the small tugs this morning at five thirty and moored up just behind the crane barge.'

Horton could see the black and orange tug boat.

'The crane operative drove here from where he lives in Fareham. That's his blue saloon car parked beyond ours. He arrived at about the same time as Mr Crombie,' Somerfield continued. 'And Kevin Manley, the man I was talking to when you arrived, sir, who's in charge of the salvage operation, got here with his team at first light at about five a.m. Mr Manley called us.'

Horton glanced back to see Manley's crew of three sitting on the ground beside the van. Their diving suits were peeled back to their waists and they were watching the proceedings with interest. Not so Manley, who was pacing the ground impatiently with a frown of irritation.

By now they had reached the hulk. Horton tensed in preparation for what he was about to see.

'She's lying face down, sir, sort of wedged into the corner of the wreck. Seaton and I haven't touched her and neither have the others, or so they claim. It doesn't look as if she's been dead very long.'

A woman, then. He steeled himself and leaned forward to study where Somerfield indicated but no amount of prepar-ation could have primed him for the sight that greeted his eyes. With a shock he swiftly took in the figure-hugging black dress; the suntanned bare legs, the black high-heeled shoe on one foot, and the wide-brimmed black hat that was, remarkably, still lodged on the dark hair by a tangle of seaweed. Too late he knew what had been bugging him last night and he was angry he hadn't seen the significance of her appearance at the crematorium sooner instead of being sidetracked by thoughts of Sholby and Hobbs and their flash new cars. But

24

even if he had sat up all night wracking his brains he might not have thought of her and even if he had he couldn't have done anything to prevent her murder, because although he was no doctor it didn't need a medic to see the bloody wound in her back.

Sawyer had been right, someone had shown for Woodley's funeral, only no one had expected a woman, and no one had paid any attention to her because he'd assumed, probably like Uckfield, that she was there for the funeral following Woodley's. She still might have been, he rapidly thought, reaching for his phone, but that didn't explain why she was here, dead. But if she was connected with Woodley then had she been sent to his funeral by Marty Stapleton? Why though, unless Marty really wanted to check that Woodley was dead and cremated, and even then she had arrived too late.

Uckfield cursed vehemently and loudly on receiving the news before emphatically declaring, 'She can't be Woodley's killer.'

'She might not have been his attacker but she could have picked him up outside the hospital and left him for dead at the marshes.' On Marty's instructions? he wondered. Only she didn't look the type, but then what the hell did he know about her anyway?

Uckfield rang off after saying he'd be there within forty minutes. Horton called Trueman and quickly relayed what had happened, instructing him to notify the police doctor and mobil-ize the circus.

'Is Walters in yet?'

'He was in the canteen when I was there a few minutes ago.'

'Tell him to skip breakfast. I know it will break his heart but I want him to check around the county for any reports of missing persons.'

He hadn't seen a ring on the third finger of her left hand, but that didn't mean anything. Someone might have expected her back last night.

He said, 'Ask Walters to get the details of the funeral following Woodley's and we'll need photographs of the victim from Clarke's video for circulating to all units.' He hadn't needed to tell Trueman that but he said it anyway.

Uniform arrived within minutes and began to set up the outer cordon just beyond the motorway flyover and the inner cordon at the entrance to the boatyard. Horton instructed Seaton and Somerfield to take initial statements from the crane driver, boatman and Manley and his crew. While he waited for Dr Price and the scene of crime officers to arrive, he surveyed the boatyard.

Its isolated position made it an ideal place to leave a body or to commit homicide. Except for the small sailing club next door there were no neighbours. The sea surrounded it on three sides. The fourth was the only road to it. This was the end of the line, which it certainly had been for their lady in black, and if she had driven here then where was her car? And why come here? It was several miles away from the crematorium, but not he had already noted from where most of Woodley's associates lived.

There were no gates at the entrance to the yard

26

and Somerfield had told him no security patrols. But there must have been people in the sailing club last night; the weather had been too good for there not to have been. And if so then someone might have seen something. He recalled seeing a CCTV camera at the front of the small timber-clad building as he'd driven past it before pulling into the boatyard. There was also one over the dinghy park; perhaps they had recorded the victim's car arriving, and the killer's. He crossed to one of the PCs on the inner cordon and asked him to get the contact details of the sailing-club secretary and commodore. As Horton headed back to the body, Manley pigeonholed him. Somerfield threw Horton an apologetic glance.

'When can my men get back to work?' Manley demanded irritably.

'Not for some time, sir.'

'How long?' he pressed.

Horton explained they'd have to wait until the police divers had been down to retrieve any evidence and that could take a day or two.

'I shouldn't think they'll find anything. We didn't even see her when we went down this morning to attach the lines, and she certainly wasn't there yesterday when we did a thorough check of the area, including that wreck and the others.'

'Others?' Horton asked surprised.

'There's another wreck on top of the munitions barge. And before you ask we didn't find anything on that either, and only shells on the munitions barge, which we cleared with the help of the Royal Navy.'

'What time did you leave last night?'

'Just after seven thirty.'

'Did you see anyone when you left?'

'No. There were a few cars outside the sailing club, though: a Range Rover, a Mercedes, a Ford and a red Mini.'

'Can you remember the registration numbers?'

'My days of collecting car numbers are long gone,' Manley said with disdain.

No matter. They'd get them from the club.

Horton managed to extricate himself from a disgruntled Manley, leaving Somerfield to soothe him, and headed back to the rotting hull. Had the killer hoped the body would sink and then float later and wash up miles away too late to help them track him down? But only if he hadn't heard or read the local news. Either the killer was stupid, which Horton sincerely hoped because it would make their job easier (and that fitted the profile of many of Woodley's so-called mates), or he wasn't local and that would make it far more difficult to trace him. Or perhaps the killer simply didn't care if the woman's body was recovered.

He thought of the propeller theft in a boatyard further up the harbour to the west. That had occurred on Monday night, and he wondered if the thieves had been out and about last night. They might have believed there was valuable metal lying around. The victim had arrived and surprised them and they'd killed her and made off in her car. But that didn't answer why she was here, why she had been at the crematorium and why she was still dressed in her funeral clothes.

Horton arrived at the hulk at the same time the SOCO van drew up inside the inner cordon with Dr Price in his battered Volvo behind it. It took Price a couple of minutes to wriggle his bony frame into a scene suit, a couple more to climb gingerly onto the wreck and one more to declare in his usual alcoholic fug that life was extinct, probably from the knife wound in the back that Horton could see.

Horton had then called the pathologist, Dr Clayton. He wasn't sure what she'd be able to tell them with the body in situ but he knew it would be a darn sight more than Price even sober could.

'Fortunately you've caught me early, before I'm deep into a cadaver,' she said brightly. 'I'll be there in half an hour, traffic permitting.'

He rang off to see Uckfield's car pull up.

'So who the devil is she?' Uckfield bellowed as he stormed across the boatyard towards Horton.

No idea wasn't the answer Uckfield wanted but it was the only one Horton had to give. He recalled she'd been carrying a small black handbag with a gold chain on the video and he hoped that it was lodged under her body and contained some ID. He said as much to Uckfield, adding, 'Did you notice anything suspicious about her on Clarke's video?' He hadn't except for that fact that when Clarke's camera had surveyed the crematorium after the Woodley crowd had left there had been no sign of her.

'I haven't even seen the bloody video,' Uckfield exploded. 'Too busy wasting my time reporting to DCS Sawyer and Wonder Boy.'

Horton interpreted that as Assistant Chief Constable Dean.

Uckfield continued, 'I haven't told Sawyer yet and Dean's going to roast my balls over a slow heat if this is connected with Woodley's murder.' He leaned over the wreck without touching it and peered at the body, frowning. Straightening up he said, 'No woman is mentioned on the files I've seen connected with Stapleton?'

'Perhaps that was why she was sent.'

'*If* she was then why show up late? And why come at all?'

Exactly. But Horton had been mulling both questions over and now expressed one of the two ideas that had occurred to him. 'To pay off whoever attacked Woodley and took him to the marshes.'

Uckfield brightened up at that. 'Reggie Thomas.'

'He doesn't own a car, or have a driving licence, but we both know that wouldn't stop him stealing a vehicle. But his alibi for then is rock-solid. When Woodley left the hospital, Reggie was with his probation officer. His alibi for when the assault occurred though is definitely suspect.'

'Yeah, lying for the likes of Sholby and Hobbs is as natural as breathing.'

'One of them could have attacked Woodley and one of them could have taken him to the marshes in his shiny new car. On the other hand,' Horton swiftly continued, 'there is the possibility that she was at the crematorium for the funeral following Woodley's. Perhaps she recognized one of Woodley's mourners as the person who left him for dead at the marshes.' He recalled her slightly puzzled expression. 'She might have been walking her dog in the area where Woodley was found.'

'We interviewed all the dog walkers.'

'Only those the mobile incident unit picked up over the following week,' corrected Horton. 'She might have been on holiday when you gave your appeal for witnesses. She was suntanned. Then seeing Woodley's mourners something clicked with her. Woodley's killer, or rather the person who left him for dead, recognized her and couldn't take a chance that she might eventually be able to identify him.'

'Bloody bad luck for her then to attend a funeral at the same time,' scoffed Uckfield, leaving Horton in no doubt what he thought about that theory. OK, so it wasn't brilliant but it was possible. Clearly though Uckfield favoured the Reggie Thomas version.

'We'll re-interview all Woodley's mates and this time we won't be so ruddy soft on them.'

Horton didn't think they had been the first time but he agreed they needed re-interviewing, whether they'd get anything out of them was another matter altogether. 'They'd certainly know this boatyard,' he said. 'But if the victim was Marty's paymaster then why agree to meet whoever killed Woodley here? Where's her car? What did she do between the time she was at the crematorium and the time she was killed? Why is she still wearing her funeral clothes? And why kill her?'

'How the bloody hell should I know? I'm not psychic,' Uckfield exploded. Horton remained silent. After a moment Uckfield added more

31

evenly, 'We'll ask the scumbags when we re-interview them. Get a unit over to the crematorium to check for any cars left in the car park overnight and ask them to collect a copy of their CCTV footage. About time,' Uckfield declared as Clarke's estate car pulled in through the inner cordon. The photographer unfurled his six foot four inches and crossed to them. Before he'd even drawn level Uckfield was on to him. 'What time did she arrive at the crematorium?'

Clarke peered across at the body, clearly confused. Horton quickly explained who it was while Uckfield waited impatiently. 'Er, I don't know, sir,' Clarke replied.

'Did you see her park a car?'

'Cars were arriving just after Woodley's service began but I wasn't filming them or taking any notice of them.'

'Pity,' Uckfield sneered.

With an injured tone, Clarke said, 'I was looking at the chapel entrance for anyone who might have slipped in after the service had begun, and then I was waiting for Woodley's mourners to emerge from the rear, as instructed, Superintendent.'

'OK, no need to get your underpants in a twist. Do the business.' Uckfield jerked his head in the direction of the body. He stepped away and reached for his phone, presumably to call Dean. Horton saw the uniformed officer he'd instructed to check out the sailing club return and crossed to him while Clarke slipped into a scene suit and began to film the body. His SOCO colleagues, Taylor and Beth Tremaine, waited patiently nearby.

'The club secretary's details were on the door; a Richard Bolton, sir.'

Horton jotted them down. He rang Trueman and relayed Uckfield's instructions and the club secretary's details, then he called Walters. 'Is DCI Bliss there?'

'Just left, guv. She muttered something about seeing Superintendent Reine when I told her where you were.'

And Horton could guess why she'd gone running to their boss; to complain about his total disregard for proper procedure. He should have reported the incident to her and not Uckfield. But that would only have prolonged matters and besides the victim was connected with one of Uckfield's investigations. Reine wouldn't see it like that, though. Both he and Bliss were sticklers for procedure.

A red Mini pulled up and Dr Clayton climbed out. He returned her wave as she made for the wreck.

'Did you find out whose funeral was after Woodley's?' he asked Walters.

'Yes. The deceased is Amelia Willard, aged seventy-three. Her funeral was arranged by the Co-op in Fratton Road and it was the last funeral of the day at the crematorium. Want me to contact them for the address of her next of kin?'

Walters was thinking for once. Horton wasn't sure that was a good sign. 'Call me when you've got it. Any reports of missing persons fitting the victim's description?'

'No.'

It was early days yet. He rang off wondering

if he should have asked Walters if there had been any further metal thefts, not because of Bliss's meeting but because of Sergeant Elkins' report of the propeller theft from the boatyard near Fareham. He looked across to the hulk where Dr Clayton, now in a scene suit, was climbing onto it. Uckfield was still on the phone. Clarke had finished taking his photographs and was talking to Taylor and Beth Tremaine. He called Elkins.

'Sorry, Andy, I was just about to phone you. Do you need us at Tipner Quay? I heard about the body.'

'No. What do you have on metal thefts from boatyards?'

'That's why I'm late getting back to you. I'm at Northney Marina, Hayling. Two alloy propellers were stolen from boats laid up in a small compound overlooking Chichester Harbour last night and a brass bell has been taken from an old clipper. It looks as though it's the work of the same thieves who stole that brass propeller from the Fareham boatyard on Monday. No one in the marina office saw or heard anything, but the thieves didn't need to drive that far because the compound is several hundred yards before you reach it. There are no CCTV cameras over this compound, and there's no one in the office complex overlooking the boatyard at that time of night. Ripley's asked at the nearby hotel but the night shift have gone off duty. If a vehicle was used then it would have driven past the hotel but I doubt anyone would have taken any notice of it going towards the boatyard. We're putting out a notice to all marinas and boatyards.'

'OK, keep me posted, especially if you hear anything about robberies or boats seen heading for Tipner quay last night.'

He rang off, wondering if the boat thieves were the same culprits as those responsible for stealing the bronze statue and the plaques in Old Portsmouth. They were different methods, one set of thefts on land and the other on water, but maybe they'd extended their operational range. Perhaps he should call Bliss and update her for her meeting. But he didn't.

He made his way back to the body. The stench of the petrol fumes from the motorway seemed to be sinking lower over them in a smog as the morning grew hotter and more sultry.

He arrived as Uckfield came off the phone. His mood hadn't improved.

'Dean's informing Sawyer. I said it would help if he let me have DI Dennings back instead of allowing him to ponce about on the Isle of Wight at that ruddy music festival with the Border Agency trying to sniff out illegal immigrant workers, but he said that was *impossible*. Anyone would think I'd asked for Sherlock bloody Holmes.'

Dr Clayton straightened up. 'Do you want me to turn her over?'

Uckfield nodded leaving Horton to instruct Taylor to assist her. Horton waited eagerly. It was difficult to see the victim's face until Dr Clayton brushed away the seaweed. Beth Tremaine dropped it into an evidence bag. Horton didn't think forensic would get anything from it but they couldn't take any chances. He studied the dark lifeless eyes, the dirt-smeared face with its high cheekbones, the shoulder-length black hair now free of the hat, which Tremaine had also put into another evidence bag, and although death had stripped the personality from the victim, Horton got confirmation of what he already knew: that it was the woman he'd seen at the crematorium yesterday.

Extricating herself from the wreckage, Dr Clayton said, 'Stab wound to the lower back, but I can't confirm that was the cause of death until I do the autopsy. There are no other obvious signs of physical assault, no marks visible to show that she turned and struggled with her attacker, but I need to examine her more closely on the slab to be certain of that. And there's no identification on her or under her. No handbag I'm afraid, Superintendent, and there's no sign of the missing shoe on the wreck.'

Horton said, 'Any signs that she was brought here under duress?'

'Not on the surface. I'd say her killer came up behind her while she was standing on the quayside, thrust the knife into her back, then pushed her into the water. At a rough estimate she's been dead between ten to thirteen hours; some time between nine thirty p.m. and twelve thirty a.m. I can be more precise when I do the autopsy, which I'll do as soon as she's brought to the mortuary. But I was here last night.'

Uckfield eyed her, surprised. The red Mini that Manley had mentioned, thought Horton. He knew that Gaye Clayton was a sailor like him but he hadn't known she was a member of the Tipner Sailing Club. No reason why he should know, they'd hardly discussed it. Corpses were more their usual topic of conversation.

Gaye added, 'I certainly didn't see her, although I was sailing in the harbour so I might have missed her arrival. But I didn't see a car parked that I didn't recognize when I left the sailing club just before ten.'

'Who else was here?' asked Uckfield sharply.

'Your chief constable, for one; Paul Meredew.'

Uckfield's craggy features registered surprise. Horton hadn't known Meredew was a sailor but then why should he; he'd barely spoken two words to the new chief on his recent tour of the troops. He'd only been in post five weeks.

Gaye added, 'Paul Meredew is a new member at the club. The commodore sponsored him; Councillor Dominic Levy.'

'Christ, it gets worse,' muttered Uckfield. 'The chair of the Police Committee *and* the Chief Constable. Anyone else I should know about at this club last night? The local MP? The Home Secretary?'

Gaye smiled. 'No, just Paul Meredew, Dominic Levy, Fiona Wright, who's a radiographer at the hospital, and me; and Richard Bolton, who owns Print Easy, he was behind the bar and he's also club secretary. There were a few more people in the club earlier having a drink but I don't know them. You'll need to check the times with Richard, or look in the log book. We all sign in, and sign out, so that should help, and Richard can give you their contact details.'

Horton said, 'Did you see anyone sailing around these waters?'

'There were several yachts and cruisers heading in and out of Horsea Marina to the north and some yachts further out towards Gosport and Fareham in the west. It was a beautiful evening although not much wind for sailing. Fiona and I were on dinghies.'

'Who was here when you left?' asked Horton.

'Councillor Levy, the Chief Constable and Richard.' Gaye glanced back at the body. 'It's a strange place for her to end up given her clothes, which on the surface of it look very expensive. Her jewellery also appears to be genuine. There's a hat pin, which looks as though it contains a diamond, and probably the reason why the hat stayed in position as she fell. She's also wearing two dress rings of sapphires and diamonds on her right hand, small diamond earrings and a gold necklace. No watch, though, and no mark where she might have worn one, which suggests she usually either took it off to sunbathe or she didn't bother wearing one.'

Horton was rapidly trying to recall if she had been wearing a watch in the video. He'd need to check. Uckfield's phone rang and he moved away to answer it.

'Is there anything else you can tell us, Dr Clayton?' asked Horton.

'Only that she's probably in her early to mid-forties and the sooner you can move her in this heat the better.'

Horton agreed and thanked her. He nodded Taylor and his team onto the wreck and stepped away from the scene. The silver undertaker's van had arrived and two police officers were standing

38

by with the awning to cover the area where the body lay and preserve it for further forensic examination. Horton didn't envy Taylor and his team working under it in this heat.

Uckfield returned with a face like thunder. 'That was Wonder Boy. He says Sawyer doesn't recognize the victim and she's not on file with the Intelligence Directorate as being an associate or girlfriend of Stapleton's but that doesn't mean she isn't connected with him. And Sawyer says, as she could be involved with Woodley's death, we're getting Eames.'

'*We're?*'

'You're back on the case. It's official. In fact you're going to have the pleasure of working with Eames.'

Horton had never heard of him. 'Who is he?'

'Europol.'

The law-enforcement agency for Europe. 'So Sawyer thinks Marty's connected with a European criminal gang.'

'Could be connected with King Kong for all they seem to know. You get Agent Eames from the Netherlands and I get DCI Bliss. Yeah, aren't I the lucky one,' Uckfield sniped cynically to Horton's surprised look. 'Dean wants her to re-examine the interview notes from the Woodley investigation and oversee the re-interviewing of Woodley's associates.'

There was no mistaking the sour note in Uckfield's voice, or guessing the unspoken comment which Dean must have voiced, 'in case you missed anything'. Asking a DCI to check the files of an investigation handled by a detective superintendent was like a kick in the balls. And knowing Uckfield of old, Horton didn't think he was going to take that lying down, or sitting even. Dean was playing a dangerous game if he thought he could intimidate the big man.

Uckfield continued, 'Return to the station and pick up Eames—'

'He's here already?' Horton asked puzzled and instantly suspicious.

'Just arrived.'

From where? Horton had heard of supersonic flight but no one got from the Netherlands that quickly. He could only surmise that Eames must have been working with Sawyer already.

Uckfield said, 'Check out the funeral party after Woodley's. If they don't know the victim then Marty Stapleton is right in the frame along with Reggie Thomas and the rest of Woodley's scumbag crew. Trueman's circulating pictures of the victim to all units asking for any sightings of her in and around the area where Woodley was attacked, and at the hospital and the marshes. He's also sent the video over to the video-enhancement unit for close-up shots of the victim. I've told him I want a frame-by-frame analysis of every toerag who attended Woodley's funeral. I want to know if one of them so much as glanced in the victim's direction. If a fly landed on Maureen Sholby's big tits yesterday I want to see it rubbing its legs and its eyes bulging with glee. Marsden's taking over here. He's on his way.'

Horton climbed on his Harley and headed back to the station, where no doubt Agent Eames would be waiting for him in the incident suite. Within ten minutes he had parked the Harley and was about to step inside the rear entrance when an attractive blonde woman in her early thirties hailed him.

'Inspector Horton?' she asked in an educated voice that Cantelli would have called posh.

'Yes,' he answered cagily while rapidly trying to place her. Swiftly he took in her navy blue trousers and striped blue and white blouse. She was carrying a short cream casual jacket. She didn't look like a social worker but she could be a lawyer, which was worse. No handbag or brief-case, though. Her fair hair was cut short and styled around a clear-skinned fair face with a hint of make-up. And her eyes were confident and a very deep blue.

'I'm Agent Eames. I've been assigned to assist in the investigation.'

Horton took the proffered hand not bothering to disguise his surprise. Uckfield was in for one too. Her grip was firm and her eye contact steady.

Crisply she continued. 'I've got the photo-graphs of the victim from Sergeant Trueman and the address of Amelia Willard's next of kin from DC Walters: Patricia and Gregory Harlow, 42 Bunyon Road.'

'Then what are we waiting for?'

She eyed the helmet in his hand and his leather Harley Davidson jacket with a slight frown.

'Do you have a car, Eames?'

'Yes, sir.'

'Pity,' he muttered, and catching her smile followed her towards it.

41

Three

'I don't remember seeing a woman of that description at my aunt's funeral,' Patricia Harlow announced brusquely, after Horton had made the introductions. They were standing in the scrupulously clean and methodically organized podiatry surgery in the front room of the 1930s bay and forecourt house. It smelt of disinfectant. The news of a brutal murder seemed to have had little effect on the squat, square-faced woman in front of Horton. Normally such news as he'd brought would have triggered a barrage of questions, or at least a muttering of concern and sympathy, but Patricia Harlow in the short white overall and dark trousers seemed more concerned about sweeping up her previous clients' nail clippings with the long-handled dustpan and brush. He had difficulty putting an age to her. The deep lines either side of her discontented mouth and the two smaller ones etched between her eyebrows made her appear more early fifties than late forties but he could be widely off the mark.

She'd kept them waiting for ten minutes, while attending to a client, and her next one, an elderly lady with softly curled grey hair and lively eyes, was waiting in the hallway outside, no doubt straining her ears for any gossip after she'd heard him announce who they were. A fan whirred gently in the far corner by the window but it did little to dispel the heat and only seemed to waft the disinfectant around.

At a nod from Horton, Eames pulled out the photograph Trueman had given her. 'Perhaps if you'd just take a look,' she said politely.

With an irritable sigh Patricia Harlow relinquished the dustpan and brush and snatched at the photograph. Horton watched her closely. Her face showed no emotion and her small dark eyes no recognition. She thrust the picture back at Eames. 'No. I've never see her before. Now if you—' She made towards the door but Eames stalled her.

'Could she have been a neighbour of Amelia's?'

'Her neighbours are over sixty and they were at the service.'

'A friend then?' persisted Eames.

'Amelia was seventy-three and that woman is clearly a lot younger.'

'It doesn't mean they couldn't have been friends.'

Pointedly consulting the clock on the wall above the client's chair, Patricia Harlow said, 'Amelia didn't have many friends and before you ask she didn't have any family either. Her son, Rawly, died in 2002 and Uncle Edgar died soon after. There is only me and my husband, Gregory.'

'And where can we find him?' asked Horton.

'I don't see why you need to bother him,' she said sharply, frowning.

'There's always the chance he caught sight of her.'

'He didn't.'

Horton said nothing and was pleased that

43

Eames kept silent too. After a moment Patricia Harlow was forced to add, 'He's event catering manager for Coastline Catering and he's on the Isle of Wight for the Festival.'

Where DI Dennings and most of the drugs squad were. But that was only a ten-minute trip across the Solent on the hovercraft or thirty-five minutes on the car ferry, less on the police launch. Removing a photograph of Daryl Woodley from his jacket pocket, he said, 'Do you recognize this man?'

She gave an exaggerated sigh and studied it briefly. Horton wondered if she might recognize it from the local newspapers. But she shook her head. 'No.'

'His name is Daryl Woodley.'

Clearly that meant nothing to her either. 'His funeral was the one held before your aunt's.'

'Then that woman must have been at that.' Her hand grasped the door handle. But Horton hadn't finished yet.

'We'll need a list of all those who attended your aunt's funeral with their contact details, please. How soon can you draw one up for us?'

'Is that really necessary?'

Horton held her exasperated glance and remained silent even though he felt like shouting, yes it bloody well is. Eventually she had to capitulate. Grudgingly she said, 'Call back after seven. I'll have it for you then.'

Horton would have liked it sooner and no doubt so would Uckfield, but Patricia Harlow was already showing in her elderly client.

'Charming woman,' Eames said sarcastically,

44

as they walked the short distance to the car. 'I wouldn't like to be one of her clients.'

'She could be sweetness and light to them.'

'It seems that the victim was there for Woodley's funeral.'

But Horton would reserve judgement on that for a while at least. He told her to head for the newspaper offices, giving her directions. 'Leanne Payne, the journalist who covered Woodley's funeral, and the press photographer, Cliff Wesley, might remember seeing the victim.'

'Won't that alert them?'

'They probably already know about it.' He thought of Ethan Crombie on his mobile phone. 'The newspaper won't be able to run anything until tomorrow anyway.' But that didn't stop the news appearing on the Internet or on television and radio, and for all he knew Crombie, or one of the others, might already have informed them. Perhaps uniform were keeping reporters and camera crew at bay at the crime scene right now and Marsden was making with the 'no comments'. The press were not Horton's favourite people but there were many times when they needed their assistance and this might be one of them.

He called Uckfield, who was not overly optimistic about that. So far no one from the media had been on to him. Horton relayed the interview with Patricia Harlow and added that he and Eames would also call in on the funeral directors to see if any of the pall-bearers or drivers remembered seeing the woman in the black hat. There was no point contacting Woodley's undertakers because they had left immediately after depositing the coffin in the chapel. There hadn't been any need for them to stay. Woodley had no relatives, and no one had booked or paid for a car to take anyone to a wake, if there had been one.

He rang off and addressed Eames. 'So what do Europol have on Marty Stapleton?' He'd not had time to discuss the case with her on the way to Patricia Harlow's because it had only taken them twelve minutes and most of that time had been taken up by Bliss's call. She'd rung for an update while Eames had used her satellite navigation to locate the Harlows' residence.

'Nothing that you don't already know, sir.'

Horton doubted that. 'Try me.'

She flashed him a glance and obviously caught his dubious expression. 'For the last two months I've been working on mapping and analysing major jewellery robberies that have taken place across Europe over the last fifteen years, liaising with officers across the Continent, trying to establish a connection between the robberies, apart from the jewellery that is, and if the proceeds are being used to fund criminal activity and if so what kind. Stapleton's series of robberies along the south coast of England, committed between 1997 and 1999, targeting jewellers and jewellery reps, were included. I'm sorry to say I haven't made any real progress. When DCS Sawyer reported that Daryl Woodley had been found dead and that he'd not only been in the same prison as Marty Stapleton but had attacked him, I was asked to fly over and liaise with the Intelligence Directorate to see if we could establish a new link or get further information. I only arrived yesterday. This morning I was with DCS Sawyer at police headquarters, when he took the call from ACC Dean about the dead woman. I was told to report to the ACC at the station and when I arrived I was given instructions to work with the Major Crime Team.'

So a desk Johnnie then and not operational, thought Horton. Eames might be better utilized working with Trueman in the incident suite rather than interviewing potential witnesses and suspects. He admitted she'd acquitted herself well with Patricia Harlow, but that had been basic stuff.

Eames was saying, 'I know from the file that Stapleton netted millions of pounds, which have never been recovered, and neither has he named his confederates, although one of them was caught with him; Billy Baldwin. He was sent down with Stapleton in 2000 and died in prison.'

'Of a massive blood clot on the brain, two months into his fifteen-year sentence.'

'Yes. Baldwin was in a prison in another part of the country from Stapleton and his death was not considered suspicious but he had shown signs of wanting to do a deal and get his sentence reduced.'

'And that would have been enough to bring Marty out in a rash and arrange to have Baldwin disposed of.'

'The autopsy confirmed natural causes.'

'It would.'

'You think it was rigged?'

Horton shrugged to disguise his true answer, you bet it was.

She continued, 'None of the stolen items have

resurfaced either in their original or in any other form. And we haven't been able to trace an account in Stapleton's name either here or abroad despite running a number of combinations of his name and his background through all the major banks and investment houses across Europe and in various international tax havens.'

'Right. No, I mean turn right here.'

'Oh.' She indicated and swung into the newspaper office car park.

He waited until she had silenced the engine before saying, 'Does the description of the victim match anyone you've come across while mapping and analysing?'

'No, not from memory, but I haven't run her profile through the computer. Someone in the Intelligence Directorate or one of my colleagues at Europol is probably doing that now.'

'Then let's hope they come up with something. Meanwhile let's see what the press remember about her.'

Cliff Wesley was out on a job but they were given directions to the newsroom on the third floor of the modern building, where they found Leanne Payne amongst a handful of reporters whose eyes were glued to their computer screens. Horton introduced Eames as a colleague without giving any reference to her working for Europol. That would have alerted Leanne Payne to the possibility of an international connection, which would have had her drooling with excitement. So far they had managed to keep any connection between Woodley's death and Stapleton quiet, but for how much longer Horton wasn't sure, especially as Leanne Payne had spoken to Reggie Thomas yesterday at the funeral.

Eyeing them both curiously she said, 'I don't expect you've come here voluntarily to give me a statement about Woodley's murder. And if you had managed to catch his killer, then Detective Superintendent Uckfield would be crowing about it to a packed press room.'

Ignoring her sarcasm, Horton said, 'What did you get from Woodley's mourners?'

She cocked her head on one side and gave a sardonic smile. 'That desperate, are we, Inspector? Hoping the local press will give you the lead you so badly need in this brutal murder?'

Horton didn't rise to the bait. She was trying to goad him, and he could well imagine the head-line, *Police dismiss murder because victim was a criminal.* Editorial would then pitch in and preach that no matter what the man had done he was still a human being and deserved the final dignity of his killer being found. Horton wanted that too even though Woodley had completely disregarded the dignity of his many victims, the last of whom had been a man in his eighties who Woodley had threatened with a knife, tied up and beaten, before stealing the small amount of cash the old man had. Woodley had got eleven years for that, double it wouldn't have been long enough as far as Horton, his colleagues and the man's relatives were concerned. The victim had died nine months after the attack, and in Horton's mind, Woodley had as good as killed him. The victim's daughter and her family had moved to New Zealand but no matter how far they went,

Horton reckoned the pain and trauma of the incident would never leave them.

Stiffly, he said, 'Withholding information is a serious offence, Miss Payne.'

She rolled her eyes. 'I got nothing out of them, which is what you'd expect. Oh, except that the police were corrupt and a bunch of wankers and worse.'

Horton said, 'We're used to such praise.'

She smiled, waved them into seats at the empty desk behind her and swivelled round to face them.

Horton said, 'Do you remember seeing a slender woman in a tightly fitting black dress, wearing a large black hat, at the crematorium?'

She eyed him keenly. Horton could see her journalistic antenna quivering like an aerial in a hurricane. 'High-heeled black court shoes, dark hair, nice sun tan. Yes, I noticed her. Is she connected with Daryl Woodley?'

He could see her fighting the urge to reach for her notepad and pen. His eyes scanned her desk but he couldn't see a Dictaphone.

'That's what we're trying to establish.'

'Who is she?'

'We don't know.'

For a moment she looked as though she didn't believe him then saw he was telling the truth. 'You're trying to trace her.'

Rather formally he said, 'A woman fitting that description was found dead at Tipner Quay this morning. We're treating her death as suspicious and trying to establish her identity.'

Her grey eyes widened. 'Can I use this?' She reached across her desk and grabbed her notepad.

50

Even if Horton said no he knew she'd ignore him. She was probably already calculating how soon she could sell the story to the nationals.

At a sign from Horton, Eames handed across the photograph. 'Have you ever seen her before, apart from at the crematorium yesterday?' she asked.

Leanne Payne studied it carefully then shook her head. 'No. Can I keep this?'

'No,' answered Horton.

Reluctantly she handed it back. 'Who discovered her? How did she die?'

Horton answered. 'Detective Superintendent Uckfield is in charge of the investigation, he'll be giving a press briefing in due course.' When, though, Horton had no idea.

Leanne Payne eyed him pleadingly. 'Can't you give me more than that?'

'It's too early in the investigation yet.'

'I've heard that one before.'

Eames said, 'When did you first notice the woman?'

'After Woodley's funeral when I was talking to Cliff. I thought she was there for the next funeral.'

Horton wondered if she'd call the crematorium to get the details of the funeral party following Woodley's to help her flesh out her story. Even if the crematorium staff wouldn't give her that information, she'd easily be able to get it from the name on the aisles where the flowers were laid out or possibly from the announcement of deaths in her employer's newspaper. From what he'd seen of Patricia Harlow he didn't think she'd be very pleased at being contacted by the press but he didn't doubt that she'd be able to handle it in her own imitable way.

He said, 'Did Cliff Wesley mention this woman to you?'

'No, but he might have taken pictures of her.' She leapt up. 'The picture editor will have them.' She set off at a pace, assuming they would follow. They did, along a short corridor to the next smaller room littered with photographs, news-papers, computer screens, keyboards and cables. Swiftly she explained the situation to a man in his mid-fifties with wild grey hair, who she intro-duced as Peter Kelvin. He called up the photo-graphs on his computer and Horton quickly scanned Woodley's mourners doing their best to look heartbroken both before and after the service. When pictures of him, Uckfield and Marsden came up on the screen he groaned inwardly. He had a feeling one of them was going to feature very large in tomorrow's newspaper along with a headline that contained the words 'police' and 'baffled'. There were no photographs of the woman in the black hat.

Disappointed, Leanne Payne said, 'Are you sure you can't let me have that picture of her? It might help speed up your inquiries.'

'Not at the moment,' Horton said firmly. He knew that she'd be on to Uckfield the moment they left. He asked the picture editor when Wesley might return.

'He's out on jobs for most of the day. You can have his mobile number, though.'

Eames took it down. Leanne Payne scurried

off to write her copy and make her phone calls. In the car Eames called Wesley but there was no answer. She left a message for him to call her urgently. Horton gave her directions to the undertakers who had handled Amelia Willard's funeral. They were fortunate to find the director in his office rather than conducting a funeral. His response to their questions was disappointing, though. After studying the photograph the large man with a thick greying walrus moustache said, 'I didn't see her either before or after the service. I'll ask the two drivers if they saw her.'

Horton left his number but he wasn't optimistic about gaining new information.

Heading back to the station, Eames said, 'He confirms what Patricia Harlow told us, which means the victim must have been there for Daryl Woodley's funeral.'

'Not necessarily.' Horton had been giving the matter consideration. 'She could have been there to visit a floral tribute left from a recent funeral, or a memorial written in the Book of Remembrance. She could have arranged to meet someone there, and was looking for them when Woodley's crowd emerged.'

'Wearing funeral clothes?' Eames said, making it clear she thought that unlikely.

'Why not? She might be in mourning herself, she might have worn them out of respect for her friend or the deceased, or perhaps she simply liked wearing black.'

Eames considered this but Horton could tell by her expression it was a theory she didn't much care for and Uckfield would probably be of the same opinion. He said, 'Have you seen the video?'

'No.'

'Then I suggest you review it when we get back. Let me know what you think.'

After fetching sandwiches from the canteen Horton headed for CID and an update from Walters on the garage proprietor who had sold the cars to Sholby and Hobbs.

'It's owned by a Craig Mellings, aged late thirties. No previous,' Walters reported.

Horton noted the empty burger container on Walters's desk and the smell of it lingering in the office, but at least this time Walters had had the sense to open a window.

'Sholby bought the Mercedes on the twenty-seventh of May and Hobbs the Audi on the first of June.'

Horton rapidly calculated. That was three days and eight days respectively after Woodley's body had been found. And the robbery at Mason's had been on the day after the attack on Woodley, which had taken place on Friday twentieth of May. He said, 'Dig deeper on Mellings and his business. Tell the local cops to keep a discreet eye and ear open but not to do anything. Any news on the metal thefts?'

Walters shook his head. Horton made for the incident suite with his sandwiches, noting on the way that Bliss was in her office with her engaged sign on the door, no doubt poring over the Woodley interview notes looking for a cock-up on Uckfield's part. Eames was sitting at a desk in the far corner viewing Clarke's video. Horton exchanged a brief word with Trueman before knocking and entering Uckfield's office. It was sweltering hot and Uckfield looked as though he was auditioning for a hog roast.

'Any sign of the victim on the crematorium CCTV?' Horton asked after reporting back and biting into his sandwich.

'The cameras cover the front of the chapel, the waiting room and the entrance gate and she only shows up outside the waiting room. There's no sign of her arriving by car, or any sign of her walking into the crematorium.'

Horton wondered if she'd entered the crematorium from the memorial gardens at the other end to the main entrance, where there were no CCTV cameras.

Uckfield continued. 'Trueman's got an officer checking out all the vehicle registrations we can get off the crematorium video in case one of the cars belongs to her, but there was no car left in the overflow car park outside the crematorium overnight. Dean's spoken to the Chief, who didn't see the victim at the boatyard, and the only cars he noted were the ones Dr Clayton told us about. He confirms he left the sailing club at ten fifteen with Dominic Levy and Dean's also spoken to him.'

'He has been busy,' muttered Horton.

'Yeah, busy annoying me by ringing me every five minutes to see if we've made any progress,' Uckfield snarled. 'Councillor Levy doesn't recall seeing a woman or a vehicle he didn't recognize and Dean emailed him her photograph. He claims not to recognize her. Trueman's contacted Richard Bolton on his mobile. He's in London. He says

55

the CCTV camera outside the sailing club hasn't been working for two weeks. He was going to raise it at the next committee meeting.'

Horton cursed.

'That's what I said. Bolton can give us a list of who was in the club last night, though. He'll be back about five thirty and says he'll go straight to the club and pick it up. He confirms he was the last to leave the sailing club, at ten twenty-five.' Uckfield gave an exasperated sigh. 'I've been through Clarke's video so many times my eyeballs ache. She glances at Woodley's mourners, in fact she more than glances, she stares at the buggers, but whether her expression is one of surprise, bewilderment or annoyance I can't make out. Maybe video enhancement will give us more.'

'Is she wearing a watch?'

'No, but as you said she is carrying a handbag. I've applied for a warrant to search Reggie Thomas's lousy bedsit in case the bastard's got it stashed away somewhere.' Uckfield hauled himself up. He turned to the window and pushed at it but it was already open as wide as it would go. 'Why doesn't someone fix this bloody air conditioning?' He turned back grumbling. 'All winter we freeze and when we damn well need it the bloody thing packs up.'

Horton was inclined to agree. His shirt and trousers were sticking to him and he could feel the sweat on his forehead.

Resuming his seat Uckfield continued. 'There are no reports of abandoned or burnt-out cars. Trueman's checked Hampshire and surrounding counties.'

They both knew that didn't mean the victim's car hadn't been abandoned or torched; just that no one had found it yet or had reported it. *If* she'd had a car. Horton thought of that sun tan. Was it possible she'd come from abroad? He suggested it to Uckfield, adding, 'She could have flown into Southampton Airport and caught a taxi to the crematorium.'

Uckfield's grey eyes narrowed as he considered this. Rising, he swiftly crossed to the door, threw it open and bellowed, 'Trueman.' A few seconds later the sergeant appeared.

'Get the victim's photograph circulated to Southampton Airport.'

Horton quickly added, 'And Bournemouth, Heathrow, Gatwick and Stansted.'

'Circulate her picture to all airports in the south,' commanded Uckfield. 'One of the aircrew might remember her, a good-looking woman like that can't have gone unnoticed.'

Horton refrained from saying that she could easily have been overlooked in such busy airport terminals.

Trueman nodded and disappeared as Eames appeared on the threshold. Horton saw Uckfield give her the once-over but this time there was no leer, and not even the hint of a lustful thought in his bloodshot eyes. Instead his glance was decidedly cool. Maybe his libido was suffering from the heat and overwork and his temper was certainly frayed. Usually the big man fancied anything in a skirt, or trousers come to that, if it was female, breathing and halfway passable. Although Uckfield had admitted to Horton that he drew the line at DCI Lorraine Bliss, adding with a sneer that she aimed her sights higher than a mere detective superintendent. But Horton dismissed Uckfield's claims that Bliss was having an affair with Dean. He just couldn't see it.

'Any thoughts on the video?' Horton asked Eames, hoping his own expression didn't betray any lustful thoughts. He had to admit Eames was very attractive.

'Not one of Woodley's mourners slips out of sight for a second,' she answered. 'The victim doesn't appear to acknowledge them and she certainly doesn't speak to them. Neither does she talk to anyone in the Willard funeral party. Could she have known you were filming her? Perhaps she saw the van with the darkened windows and she'd been warned about a possible police presence.' Clearly by Uckfield's frown he didn't like the sound of that. Detecting it, Eames quickly added, 'I called Cliff Wesley again but he's still not answering his mobile.'

Uckfield's phone rang. Eames slipped out but with a wave of his hand, Uckfield indicated for Horton to stay. Into the receiver Uckfield said, 'Sixty minutes. Yeah, in the conference room.' Replacing the phone he addressed Horton. 'I'm arranging a press briefing and if Cliff Wesley shows up I'll make sure he's asked if he remembers seeing the victim.' He consulted his watch. 'Get over to the mortuary and see what Dr Clayton's got. If she can give us something that will help identify the victim in the next hour tell her I'll buy her the most expensive drink on the bloody planet.'

Horton didn't think that would be much of an incentive. He'd reached the door before Uckfield called out, 'And take the blonde beauty with you.'

Four

'A few minutes earlier, Inspector, and you could have watched Tom sew her back together,' Dr Clayton greeted them cheerfully as they stepped into the chilly mortuary. Pulling off the unflattering but practical green plastic cap and running a hand through her spiky auburn hair, she eyed Eames curiously.

Horton swiftly made the introductions while trying to ignore the smell and his churning stomach. If he'd known he was going to come here he might have postponed eating the ham, salad and pickle sandwich in Uckfield's office. He saw Gaye's quizzical look when he mentioned where Eames had come from but he furnished no explanation and Gaye didn't ask for one. He thought how tiny she looked beside Eames, who had to be a good five feet eight inches while Gaye was barely five two. In the green loose mortuary garb she looked rather like a child wearing clothes that were too big for her, he thought, while Eames had a transparent plastic overall tied firmly around her slim waist over her trousers and shirt. She, like him, was also wearing the flat white mortuary wellington boots. And she looked as though she was born to wear them.

59

The 'blonde beauty' with notebook and pen in hand was coolly studying the corpse with its ugly great stitches down the chest and across the upper forehead as though it was a specimen in the laboratory, without any sign of revulsion.

'What's that?' she said, pointing to a mark just above the victim's right breast. 'A tattoo?'

'No, a birthmark in the shape of a butterfly I rather think,' Gaye answered. 'And it's the only distinguishing mark on her.'

Horton peered at it. He didn't think it was enough to make Uckfield happy.

Gaye continued, 'She has borne children, or *a* child certainly.'

So someone must miss her. Or had she also walked out on her child like his mother had walked out on him? He bet Eames had never experienced the pain of rejection. But this wasn't about him or Eames, he scolded himself. It was about a woman who had been brutally murdered. He put his full attention on what Dr Clayton was saying.

'She was very healthy: no deteriorating organs, no evidence of alcoholism or drugs, about forty-three give or take a couple of years and as I said at the scene, a woman who took good care of herself. She was well-groomed: eyebrows are beautifully shaped, fingernails and toenails are manicured and varnished.' Gaye pulled down the cover to the waist and lifted out the victim's right hand to show Horton the neatly shaped pink nails on the end of long slender fingers. 'She's certainly never done any manual work and I doubt she did much washing up, unless she wore rubber gloves, but I think household chores would be well down this lady's list of priorities. She looks to me to be a very high-maintenance woman.'

Eames said, 'Can I see her clothes?'

Dr Clayton pulled the trolley containing the evidence bags towards her and handed over the hat. Eames studied it for some moments. Horton caught Gaye's inquisitive glance. He shrugged a response.

'It's by Philip Treacy,' Eames announced, looking up. 'He's one of the top milliners in the country, and probably in the world, and it's a new creation, this season's or rather I should say part of the spring collection rather than the summer one.'

Gaye raised her eyebrows in surprise. But why wasn't he surprised? Somehow he expected Eames to know this kind of thing and he judged her knowledge wasn't gained from working at Europol on an investigation involving counterfeit designer wear. Her voice, bearing, manner and looks screamed class to him. He wondered how she'd ended up becoming a police officer.

'Expensive?' he asked.

'That depends on who you're asking,' she answered earnestly. 'About a thousand pounds new.'

'For a hat!' he exclaimed.

'A mere nothing, then,' tossed Gaye Clayton lightly.

Eames smiled. 'Even if she bought it second hand, which I doubt, it would have cost her about three hundred pounds.' She picked up the bag containing the shoe. 'This is a Jimmy Choo.'

'A what?' asked Horton.

61

By the way Eames eyed him he could see that she wasn't sure if he was taking the rise. He wasn't. Obviously seeing this she continued. 'Since Choo launched his label in 1996 he's built up a celebrity and wealthy client base. If we find the victim's bag, I expect it will also be a Jimmy Choo. The soles are showing a little wear but the heel has never been repaired. I don't think the victim would have gone to that much trouble.'

'Cost?'

'About four hundred, maybe five hundred pounds.'

'And the dress?'

Eames went through the same ritual, studying it intently before answering. 'Cotton blend with an exposed double-ended zip down the back, very provocative, and only someone with her kind of figure, shapely but slim and firm, would look good in it.'

Like you, thought Horton. He caught Gaye's glance and shifted a little uncomfortably seeing she'd easily read his thoughts. Eames hadn't, though. Still examining the dress she added, 'It's by Victoria Beckham, which means it cost somewhere in the region of two, maybe three thousand pounds.'

Horton eyed her disbelievingly.

'It might even have cost more,' Eames said. 'Everything I've seen so far is genuine and I would say bought new.'

'As I said,' Gaye chipped in, 'a high-maintenance lady.'

And clearly one who had money. Marty

62

Stapleton's money? he wondered. He could see that was what Eames was thinking. A thought occurred to him but it would keep.

Eames continued. 'Her underwear is silk, sexy and again very expensive. We might be able to trace her through the top fashion houses, designer shops or Internet sites that sell these kind of clothes but that would take considerable time.'

And resources, Horton thought, which they didn't have, unless Europol assisted. He looked at Gaye Clayton, hoping there might be a short cut.

Interpreting his silent plea she said, 'OK, so much for the entrée. Let's get down to the main course and see if that helps or hinders your investigations. There is no evidence that she was manhandled or subjected to any kind of physical abuse before being killed. She was also alive when she entered the water, but not for long. The stab wound is located on the right side of the back, twenty-one inches below the top of the head and five inches from the front of the body. The knife entered the skin, the subcutaneous tissue, and through the right seventh rib before penetrating the right pleural cavity. The estimated length of the total wound path is about four inches. A fatal wound causing perforation of the right lung and a haemothorax.'

'And the weapon?' asked Horton.

'A very sharp single-bladed pointed knife, difficult to say the exact size but approximately seven inches in length. There are no signs she put up a struggle. The knife was thrust upwards with some strength.'

'By a man?' enquired Eames, looking up from her notes.

'Not necessarily. A stab wound such as this can be made with minimal force. The important factor is the sharpness of the tip of the blade, and this one was very sharp. Once it has penetrated clothing and skin remarkably little force is required to follow through and create a deep knife wound. Also the faster the stabbing action, the easier it is to penetrate skin. However, the thrust of the knife was underhand, which suggests a man rather than a woman, who tend to favour overhand thrusts. She was killed some time between ten thirty and midnight.'

After everyone had left the sailing club, and by that time it was dark, thought Horton.

'Thirdly and most interesting is this.' Gaye pulled the cover further down until it reached the body's knees. 'As you can see from the pubic hair your victim was a natural blonde. The hair on her head was dyed black and her eyebrows and eyelashes were tinted black. And I discovered something else which is slightly unusual. She was wearing coloured contact lenses to make her eyes brown. Your victim was not naturally dark-haired and brown-eyed; she was a blue-eyed blonde, much like you, Agent Eames. Now why would she want to change her appearance?'

Why indeed? He glanced at Eames, whose brow puckered with thought as her posh pen hovered over her notebook.

Gaye added, 'I'll send her clothes for forensic examination unless you'd like to take them with you.'

Eames answered, 'No, but we'd like photographs of them please and of the birthmark.'

'Tom will email them to Sergeant Trueman. I've also sent fingerprints over to the fingerprint bureau and DNA for analysis. Oh, and two further things. She had sexual intercourse not long before death and it was consensual.'

With one of Woodley's mates! Unlikely, thought Horton. He frowned as his mind grappled with this new information.

Gaye said, 'She'd also eaten a meal five to six hours before she died, probably between five thirty and six thirty. Again there is no sign of her having been forcibly fed.'

'What kind of meal?' asked Horton.

'I'll let you know as soon as I can.'

Horton thanked her. He caught her quizzical glance before he left, which made him feel a little uncomfortable. Why, he didn't know, or perhaps he did. He wondered if Dr Clayton was a mind-reader as well as a pathologist. He hoped not because she might have sensed that Agent Eames disturbed him, and not just mentally either.

Outside he said, 'Does the fact she was really blonde strike any chords with you?'

'Not immediately but I'll circulate a revised description to Europol. I'll also issue a new photograph of the victim with her natural colouring once the photographic unit give us a computer-generated image.'

'It doesn't sound as though she was held somewhere against her will. And I can't see her having sex and eating a meal with any of Woodley's associates.'

Eames considered this. 'Perhaps she met someone before meeting her killer.'

That was entirely possible but why hadn't this person come forward? Perhaps whoever it was didn't know she'd been killed. He said, 'While we're here, let's see if we can have a word with Fiona Wright.'

They made their way to the radiography department in the hospital. Horton was mulling over Dr Clayton's revelations but he was still no nearer a conclusion by the time they located Fiona Wright. She'd finished with her patients for the day and waved them into seats in the small air-conditioned consulting room.

'I had been hoping to go sailing tonight,' she said, 'but obviously because of the police investigation, that's out of the question.' She pushed back her shoulder-length brown hair and gave them both a nervous smile. Horton guessed she was in her late thirties. There was no ring on her left hand or indeed on any of her fingers but that didn't mean she wasn't married or living with someone, she probably removed her jewellery for work.

She said, 'Gaye told me that you'd probably want to speak to me about that poor woman's death. Do you know who she is yet?'

'We're still trying to establish that.' He nodded at Eames, who took the photograph from her jacket pocket. As she handed it across to Fiona Wright, Horton wondered how much more different the victim would look blonde-haired and blue-eyed.

'Have you seen this woman before?' Eames asked.

After studying the picture carefully, Fiona Wright said, 'No. Gaye told me where her body had been found. I certainly didn't see her last night. I arrived at the club just after seven and left just before ten with Gaye. There was no one outside then.'

'Any cars parked that you didn't recognize?'

'Only a silver Range Rover.'

And Horton knew that belonged to the Chief Constable. 'Did you leave the club by the front entrance at any time while you were there?'

'No. There was no need. The dinghies are kept at the rear, near the club's slipway.'

Horton knew that. 'Did you see anyone on the quayside while you were sailing?'

'No.'

Horton asked if she'd seen any other craft heading towards the club or the quayside.

'Not that I can remember. There were several heading towards Horsea Marina, some large cruisers, a couple of yachts and a few motoring out into the harbour, but I didn't really take much notice of them.'

Horton had two questions left to ask and he wasn't hopeful that either would draw a positive response.

'Do you know a Daryl Woodall?'

'No.'

He showed her the photograph. 'Have you seen this man before?'

She glanced at the picture and then back at Horton. 'I've seen his photograph in the news-paper. He's the man who discharged himself from hospital and was found dead. I didn't come across

67

him while he was here. I'm sorry I can't help you, Inspector.'

Horton was too. He hadn't really expected anything. In the car he told Eames to head for Tipner Quay, drawing a curious look from her. He called Uckfield as she threaded her way through the rapidly building rush-hour traffic. Uckfield's phone was on voicemail. He must be in his press conference or with Dean. He rang Trueman and reported what they had discovered from Dr Clayton and requested him to get a revised photograph of the victim.

'We're on our way to the sailing club to get that list of members who were there last night and to interview Richard Bolton, the club secretary.' It was a good enough reason to call in at the quay but Horton had another one. There was something he wanted to check out.

Forty minutes later, Bolton, a large, round-faced, bald-headed man in his mid-fifties, had equipped him with a dinghy and a life jacket and Horton was sailing in the harbour. There wasn't much breeze, but enough. He wasn't skiving, although Bliss would claim he was, this was research. From here he could see the large brick and corrugated-iron-roofed boatshed. Could the victim have parked her car in front of it? If she had then no one would have seen it from the club or the road leading to the boatyard. The crane barge was still in place and the remains of the wrecked boat had the canvas awning stretched over where the body had lain. But that area had been clear before the wreck had been raised so it was possible that she'd arrived before dark and waited there.

Taylor and his SOCO team had finished working on the wreck and surrounding area, and the police diving operation was now in progress. Horton wondered if they'd find the victim's handbag, and the murder weapon. He'd asked Eames to relay a description of the latter to Marsden and the diving team.

He felt the little dinghy pick up speed as a sudden gust of wind filled the sails. It had been a long time since he'd sailed such a small vessel and, despite the seriousness of the occasion, he was enjoying it. He recalled the days spent on his former yacht, *Nutmeg*, with his daughter, Emma, with a tightening in his chest. He doubted he'd ever enjoy such moments again, and certainly not if Catherine had her way. He couldn't let her. He had to find time to contact his solicitor, Frances Greywell, for advice on how to gain greater access to Emma without resorting taking it to the children's court because he didn't believe he'd get a favourable hearing. Tomorrow he'd make that call.

That decided he concentrated on sailing. Sergeant Elkins in the police launch could have done this trip much easier and quicker, which was what Bliss would say and Uckfield might agree with her, but it had occurred to him that perhaps their killer had used a dinghy or small sailing boat last night, and slipped in to the quay, silently, catching their victim unawares before thrusting that knife into her back and pushing her into the water. He needed to see if it was possible. And there was also the possibility that the victim had arrived with her killer by boat either before or after Richard Bolton had left, which he'd claimed had been at ten twenty-five. Bolton hadn't seen the victim or her car.

But Horton was finding it difficult to navigate with precision on to the quay even in daylight, and in the dark it would have been extremely difficult, particularly as there hadn't been a full moon last night to light the way. He was rapidly concluding that the killer would need to be an extremely skilled sailor to have arrived by this method, and that, as far as he was aware, didn't fit the profile of any of Woodley's associates. It wasn't impossible, but as he saw Eames raise her hand to him, as he'd instructed, he thought it more probable that if the killer had come by sea he would have done so in a small motorized craft, such as a RIB, or a fishing boat equipped with lights. And that meant the victim would have been expecting it.

Steadily he brought the dinghy alongside the quay to the left of the diving operation.

Eames took up her role. 'I've been waiting ages for you. I didn't think you'd make it. We need to talk.'

'Get on board.'

Eames looked uneasy. 'I can't, not in these shoes.'

No. The victim certainly hadn't been dressed for sailing. 'OK. I'll come up.' He swung nimbly onto the quayside and tied up.

'What is it you want?' Eames said, turning away as though to look out to sea.

Horton came round behind her. 'You know.'

'I don't. I came here because you said it was urgent.'

Horton made as though he was carrying a knife. 'It is. As urgent as this.' And he thrust his hand into Eames's back, where Dr Clayton had indicated the position of the stab wound, with his arm wrapped around Eames's waist, trying not to think how nice she felt and smelt, and trying to ignore the stirring in his loins. He quickly released her. She staggered forward, then straightened up, with a slight smile.

'That's as far as I go, sir. Even I'm not keen enough to take a ducking in the line of duty.'

'Pity. Marsden looks as though he'd like to have given you the kiss of life.'

Marsden flushed. Eames looked amused. Horton quickly continued. 'She falls into the sea. The killer casts off and climbs back into the dinghy and sets off sailing again.'

Marsden said, 'Wouldn't it have taken him a while if he hasn't got an engine?'

'There was no one here and it's dark, but yes it would have taken an age with the small amount of sea breeze there was last night.' Even Gaye Clayton had commented on that. 'But if he had a boat with an outboard engine and had agreed to meet the victim after ten twenty-five, then there was no one here to hear him, and as Eames has just highlighted, if the victim had agreed to meet her killer here then she could hardly have walked far in her high heels.' Horton removed his life vest, adding, 'And that means she must have been brought here by a taxi, or she drove here, and if she drove then her killer couldn't have been alone, *if* he came by sea. There had to be two of them.'

71

Horton gazed out to sea, his mind working rapidly. He said, 'They could have arrived in a bigger boat with an engine and a cabin where the accomplice remained out of sight. After she's been killed the accomplice alights and drives the victim's car away to dump it while the other person takes the boat back to where it's usually moored, which could be anywhere along this stretch of water, or further afield even. But I can't see any of Woodley's crowd owning a boat.'

Eames said, 'They could have stolen one.'

He'd get Elkins to check. To Marsden he said, 'Make sure the dinghy gets back to the sailing club.'

'How?' Marsden asked surprised.

'You're a detective, figure it out. Did Marty Stapleton own a boat?' he asked Eames as they headed for the car.

'Not that we're aware of.'

'What about his associates?'

'There's no record or mention of boats, but it's possible one or more of them could have one.' She studied the area. 'It must have been very dark waiting here. There are no street lights or security lights. I suppose she could have left her car lights on, which could have guided the boat in.'

It was a good point. And there was no one in this isolated position to have seen that, therefore making it an ideal location for a rendezvous. 'She could have had a powerful torch, which she kept in her car, and that's in the sea along with her handbag.' If it was he hoped the divers would find it. After a moment he added, 'I wish we had a name for her.'

'I've been thinking about that. Salacia.'

'What?' He threw her a glance.

'It's the Roman name for the goddess of salt water.'

'Seems very apt.'

'Salacia was the wife and queen of Neptune, god of the sea. She was beautiful and crowned with seaweed.'

'Spot on,' Horton said, recalling the victim when alive and when her body had been lifted from the sea, covered with seaweed, dirt and sea creatures.

'She bore Neptune three children.'

Horton recalled what Dr Clayton had said, that Salacia had certainly borne one child, so where was that son or daughter? Why hadn't he or she reported their mother missing? Why hadn't anyone? He said as much as Eames started the car and headed towards the outer cordon.

'Perhaps the child has died, or she gave it up for adoption,' she answered. 'Or perhaps it's living abroad and not in regular contact with its mother. There's no record of Marty Stapleton having a child, legitimate or otherwise.'

'Doesn't mean to say he hasn't any, though. Have you traced all his girlfriends?'

'I doubt it. He was married once. She died in a car accident in 1996.'

'Convenient.'

'Yes.'

A car passed them heading for the boatyard. Horton recognized it instantly. 'Quick, turn round. That's Cliff Wesley.'

Eames expertly swung the vehicle around and

they drew up alongside Wesley at the outer cordon where PC Allen had stopped him. Through the open passenger window Horton addressed the dishevelled dark-haired man.

'We've been trying to get hold of you all day, Mr Wesley; is there something wrong with your phone?'

'Not my phone, my editor.' He looked hot and harassed. 'He's had me dashing about from job to job like a blue-arsed fly. If the newspaper put its hands deeper in its pockets and employed a couple more press photographers I might not have to re-do jobs that the so-called professional freelancers they engage cock up, which is why I've had to return here after all the fun is over,' he grumbled.

'I'd hardly call it that,' Horton said acerbically.

'Perhaps I could get a shot of the police divers.' Wesley jerked his head in the direction of the quay.

'Unlikely. A moment of your time, sir.' It wasn't a question. Horton climbed out and indicated he expected Wesley to do the same.

With a weary sigh he obliged. Eames followed suit.

'What do you know about this woman?' Horton nodded at Eames, who showed Wesley the photograph of Salacia.

'Leanne told me about her. She was at Woodley's funeral.'

'Did you see her talk to any of Woodley's mourners?'

'Not while I was photographing them. And I

didn't take any pictures of her either. My life might be a lot easier if I had done,' he complained, taking a packet of cigarettes from the top pocket of his short-sleeved white shirt. 'If I'd have known she was going to get herself killed I'd have ignored Woodley's sycophantic lot and concentrated on the poor cow.' He removed a cigarette and offered the packet to Horton, who shook his head. Eames did likewise.

'Did you see her arrive?'

'Not exactly.' He lit up and exhaled.

Horton wondered what the hell that meant. Before he could ask, Wesley continued. 'Superintendent Uckfield and his boy arrived and walked to the rear of the crem. I was in the car having a fag and checking the images I'd just shot which, judging by the expressions of the mourners, would make you think that Woodley was not only a blessed saint but had been loved as much as Mother Teresa. I thought I might get some more interesting shots after the funeral when Woodley's friends thought I'd gone.'

'Did you?' Horton recalled the photographs the picture editor had shown them.

'Only the one of you with the fat detective looking baffled.'

Yeah, thanks, thought Horton, knowing that was the real reason why Wesley had stayed on. He'd seen Uckfield arrive, thought he might get an interesting shot, and Horton wouldn't be surprised if he'd already sold the image to one of the tabloids. Tomorrow he, Uckfield and Marsden could be staring out of one of the national newspapers accompanied by indignant headlines that would make them look incompetent. It was par for the course but Dean was not going to be a happy man and Uckfield would go ballistic. Perhaps he'd better warn him.

Crisply he said, 'So *when* did you first notice her?'

'I'd checked the pictures, had a fag, and it was getting hot in the car so I got out and went to stand under the trees to watch for Woodley's mob. I didn't think they'd be long and they weren't. I'd only just got there when I heard them. So I walked back to the front and she was there. I thought nice-looking woman, good figure, smart. The mourners for the next funeral were arriving. I turned, took some more shots of Woodley's crowd and of you, then showed them to Leanne.'

Horton remembered seeing them in a huddle over the camera.

'I went back to the car, lit a fag and left.'

'And the woman?'

'I didn't see her again.'

Disappointing. Horton studied the careworn sharp-featured face and the slightly bloodshot eyes. There was no reason for Wesley to lie.

'Were the mourners for the next funeral still outside when you left?'

Wesley exhaled, and scratched his chin. 'I think they were going into the chapel. I don't remember noticing the woman with them, or I should say I don't recall seeing that hat. She could have taken it off I suppose but I think I would have noticed that dress and her figure in amongst a lot of older people. Any idea who she is?'

'Not yet.' Horton wasn't going to be drawn into

commenting any further. There didn't seem anything more Wesley could tell him but as a final shot he asked, 'Have you ever seen her before?'

Wesley again studied the photograph, Horton wondered if he should ask him to imagine her as a blonde rather than dark-haired but he'd hold back on that for now.

'No, can't say that I have.'

'We'll need a statement from you. Call into the station tomorrow,' he insisted, knowing that tomorrow Wesley's photograph of him, Uckfield and Marsden would be in the newspapers.

'If I can.'

'We'll send a car for you.'

'No need, I'll drop by,' Wesley said hastily and uneasily.

'See that you do.' And Horton thought the Super himself might want to personally take the photographer's statement. Horton wouldn't like to be in Wesley's shoes. Glancing at the clock on the dashboard he thought his own might be rather uncomfortable when he showed up in the incident suite. But before he did he told Eames to return to Patricia Harlow's house to collect that list of mourners who'd been at her aunt's funeral.

Five

'Bloody hell, it's the missing detective! I thought you had eloped with the posh tart,' exploded Uckfield, as Horton entered his office. Bliss was there and Horton could see that she was torn between disapproval of him for being so late and Uckfield for his politically incorrect comments.

'Where the hell have you been?' demanded Uckfield, nodding Horton into the seat beside Bliss.

'Sailing.'

'What?'

Horton hurried on before Uckfield burst a blood vessel and Bliss demanded his resignation for dereliction of duty, or for going against some regulation he'd never heard of. He explained his theory that the victim could have been taken to the boatyard by boat or that her killer could have arrived and left by sea after killing her. Uckfield looked far from convinced and Bliss was eyeing him as though he should be sectioned.

'I can't see any of Woodley's associates owning a boat,' she primly declared.

'They could have stolen one. I've got Sergeant Elkins checking.'

She didn't seem too pleased about the idea, probably because she hadn't thought of it herself. He added, 'And buying a small boat wouldn't cost much anyway, especially as Sholby and Hobbs are flush at the moment, or they were before they bought new cars for cash.'

Bliss eyed him sharply. He relayed what Walters had discovered. 'If it's a pay-off from Marty Stapleton for getting rid of Woodley then not only is the timing wrong for our victim being the paymaster but Woodley came very expensive and I can't see him being worth that amount of money when Reggie would probably have done it for a packet of fags. I think it's either money from the Mason robbery and this garage proprietor, Mellings, is involved—'

'Providing the van that was used,' Bliss interjected.

'Possibly, or Sholby, Hobbs and Mellings are involved in vehicle theft and fraud. Mellings could be fencing stolen cars and Sholby and Hobbs could be stealing them to order using Mellings as go-between to get rid of them. The cars Sholby and Hobbs are driving could be payment in kind, or stolen, re-sprayed and recycled, and I don't mean in the environmental sense. They're legitimately registered with new registration numbers but that might not be the vehicle registrations they started life with.'

Bliss addressed Uckfield. 'I'd like to pursue this with the Vehicle Fraud Unit. It might be something we can use to get more information out of Sholby and Hobbs on the Woodley investigation.'

For one awful moment Horton wondered if she was going to ask to have him pulled off the murder investigation to work on it but perhaps something in Uckfield's expression prevented her. Uckfield said, 'OK, but we bring Reggie Thomas in first thing tomorrow, before the bugger can wipe the sleepy dust from his bloodshot eyes, and you can interview him. The warrant's come through to search his mangy bedsit.'

'I'll keep you informed, sir,' Bliss said rising. No doubt, thought Horton, hurrying off to email the head of the Vehicle Fraud Unit, and to read through the case notes on the Mason's robbery.

A result on that would put a feather in her pony-tail and if it gave them new information on Woodley's murder it would put a ruddy great bow in it.

Once the door closed, Uckfield let out a breath. 'That should keep her amused and off my back for a while. So what else have we got?'

Horton swiftly relayed Eames's views on the victim's clothes and the possibility of enquiring at the top fashion houses.

'Got contacts there, has she?' Uckfield sneered.

'Probably.' But Horton registered Uckfield's note of sarcasm. He was curious to know why the big man had so taken against Eames. Perhaps he just didn't like her posh voice.

He then told Uckfield about Dr Clayton's findings ending with the fact the victim had disguised her appearance. Uckfield frowned as he considered this. Before he could speak though Horton continued, 'The reasons for this could be she's someone famous, such as an actress—'

'Unlikely!' scoffed Uckfield.

'She was known to someone in Woodley's crowd and didn't want to be recognized—'

'But she was and that someone killed her.'

'She was wanted by us, and hoped to go unnoticed.'

'In that dress! And wearing a ruddy great hat! Hardly a disguise if she was on the run.'

Horton agreed. She'd been wearing the right colour for a funeral but she could have dressed more conservatively.

'Or—'

'There's more!' Uckfield mocked.

'She was ordered to attend Woodley's funeral as the paymaster—'

'Yeah, we got that far—'

'Because Marty wanted *her* taken out.'

Uckfield frowned and opened his mouth to speak but Horton quickly resumed. He'd been chewing this idea over for a couple of hours and was keen to try it out. 'Let's say Marty wants shot of Salacia.'

'Who the hell is that?'

'It's Eames's name for the victim. Salacia was the Roman goddess of the sea.'

'Just shows what a good education can do for you; come up with poncy names.'

Ignoring Uckfield's jibe, Horton continued, 'Let's go back to the beginning. Marty arranges for Reggie Thomas to take Woodley out. Thomas tries to oblige but is disturbed attacking Woodley. Reggie gets one of his mates to pick Woodley up outside the hospital and take him to a remote place to die. Salacia shows up at the funeral as instructed by Marty. She gives Reggie the nod, which we all miss. Reggie agrees to meet her at Tipner Quay for the pay-off for dealing with Woodley. Salacia's been told by Marty, or via one of Marty's outside contacts, that Woodley has to die because of the attack on him in prison. Salacia believes it. Woodley is expendable, and perhaps Marty did want to get back at him. After giving Reggie the nod at the crematorium, Salacia returns to the car.'

'You mean her car?'

'No.' Eagerly Horton resumed, 'We've assumed from her sun tan that it's possible she lived abroad

81

and that she could have flown into the country. But perhaps she didn't come in on any scheduled flight. Perhaps she flew in by private plane. It's not so far-fetched, as you think, Steve,' he quickly added to Uckfield's incredulous stare. 'Marty's got millions stashed away. He could probably afford to hire a jet. A small light aeroplane could easily have flown into Southampton or any private airport around the region although I can't see her flying into the Isle of Wight, unless . . .'

'What? She swam across the Solent?' Uckfield said sarcastically.

'No, but she could have come from there by boat, and I mean a nice comfortable luxury motor-boat, like yours. It would only have taken twenty minutes, half an hour at the most to get across the Solent. On her arrival she caught a taxi, or had a hire car waiting or travelled with this person who had been paid to bring her into the country. He drove her to the crematorium for her prear-ranged rendezvous with Reggie. Dr Clayton says Salacia ate a meal and had sex before she was killed and it's unlikely she'd have done either with Reggie Thomas, or any of Woodley's asso-ciates. It's far more likely it was with whoever she came with.'

'Wouldn't this person have noticed she didn't come back?' Uckfield said dryly.

'Yes, and he's kept quiet because he's her killer. Reggie could have been told to stay away from the quay and keep his mouth shut.'

'Would Marty let Reggie Thomas live?'

'Not for long.'

In the brief pause that followed, Horton heard

the phones ringing in the incident suite. He continued. 'We need to check out all the private airfields and the marinas.'

Uckfield picked up his pen and began to play with it. 'Why would Marty want her killed?'

'For any number of reasons: he's discovered she's been cheating on him while he's been inside; she's been spending too much of his money; she's begun to blab; he's got bored with her; he just wants to show he's still boss, or could be for all of those reasons. And Stapleton's not going to tell us. He's kept quiet about her until now.'

Uckfield threw down his pen. 'OK, I'll buy it. Anything else?'

Horton reported the outcome of his brief interviews with Fiona Wright and Cliff Wesley, deciding to omit the bit about Wesley's photograph of them possibly being in the newspaper tomorrow. That certainly wouldn't improve the Super's mood. He'd find out about it soon enough and hopefully when Horton was some miles away. 'The funeral director called me while we were on our way to Patricia Harlow's to collect the list of mourners at her aunt's funeral. His drivers didn't see the victim while the service was being conducted and neither of them noticed her beforehand. They don't remember seeing her after the service either so unless she was with this unknown person in the crematorium gardens she must already have left, possibly with him. We've also got the list of the members who were drinking in the club last night. Aside from the Chief Constable and Councillor Levy there were only six people, two women and four men. Anything from SOCO?'

'There are tyre tracks in the boatyard, but they're too vague to be of any use. There's no forensic evidence where the body lay on the wreck but Taylor's sent the seaweed and fragments of wood from the boat for examination, for all the good it will do. Trueman's got teams checking the statements supplied by Manley and his divers, the boatman and the crane operative.'

'Any joy from your press briefing?'

'Nothing so far,' Uckfield answered gloomily. 'I've asked for anyone at the crematorium at the critical time to come forward but we'll probably get all the loonies and the usual nutters confessing to murder, including that mad woman from Gosport who claims to have killed everyone from the Duke of Buckingham in 1628 onwards.'

Horton gave a brief smile.

Uckfield rose and stretched his back.

Horton continued. 'Gregory Harlow is currently on the Isle of Wight at the festival. Despite what his wife says we need to make sure he doesn't recognize or know Salacia, so why don't I kill two birds with one stone tomorrow, interview Harlow, show him photographs of the victim dark-haired and fair-haired, and visit the prison. I can talk to the Head of Operations and see what I can flush out on Woodley, and the attack on Stapleton. I can also see what the Intelligence Directorate haven't told us.'

'Good idea,' Uckfield replied with enthusiasm.

'I'd also like to re-interview the landlord of the Lord Horatio and see if I can jog his memory. He might recall something new about Woodley's visit there before he was attacked. And I can get his reaction when I show him the photographs of Salacia. I'd like Eames with me.'

'I bet you would.' There was a tap on the door and Eames entered. 'Talk of the devil,' Uckfield muttered.

'I've checked the Marty Stapleton file and there's no record of Stapleton owning a boat or any reference to his known associates having one.'

'Doesn't mean they haven't got one now or hired one,' Uckfield replied then bellowed, 'What?' as another knock came at his office door.

Marsden entered flushed and excited. 'We've found her shoe, sir.'

'All right, no need to wave it about like a bloody trophy.'

'Sorry, sir. The divers are continuing the operation tomorrow morning.'

'Are they on a work to rule?' cried Uckfield with a pointed look at his watch.

'It'll be dark in less than an hour—'

'So? It's as dark as pitch down there anyway, what difference does the night make?'

'They need to take a break, sir, and er it will cost more if they have to work overtime.'

'They'll be having their own union next. I thought they were police officers like us.'

Eames, taking the evidence bag containing the shoe from Marsden, said, 'Where did they find it?'

'Lodged under some wood on the wreck below the one the victim was discovered on. The divers are searching the second wreck more thoroughly tomorrow for her handbag, and the murder weapon.'

Horton said, 'Ask them to look for a torch.'

'Yeah, to light their bloody way.'

Ignoring Uckfield's comment, Eames said, 'This matches the victim's. It's a Jimmy Choo.'

With heavy sarcasm, Uckfield said, 'Goody, now all we have to do is interview all of Jimmy Choo's customers who bought this shoe in a size six, ask them to show us their shoes and the woman who can't is our victim, just like bloody Cinderella, which about sums up this pantomime of a case.'

Horton wondered who the ugly sisters were.

To Marsden, Uckfield said, 'Tell Trueman I want a briefing tomorrow morning eight thirty sharp and I want everybody there. That includes you, Agent Eames.' He flicked her a glance. Horton couldn't interpret what was behind it but he thought he saw suspicion and resentment.

Dismissed, Eames and Marsden left. Uckfield's phone rang and Horton slipped away leaving him talking to his wife. He told Eames they were off to the Isle of Wight tomorrow after interviewing the landlord of the Lord Horatio pub, but he didn't relay his theory about Marty possibly having arranged Salacia's death. Time for that tomorrow.

In his office, he viewed his desk despairingly. At the rate his paperwork was piling up there'd soon be no rainforests left. He proceeded to push a few bits of the stuff around and replied to a couple of emails but his mind was elsewhere. He'd achieve nothing more by staying and twenty minutes later he was pulling into the marina. He caught sight of a large sleek motor cruiser on the waiting pontoon and the glimpse of a man in his early sixties on board before heading down the pontoon to his yacht. His eyes were scratching with the heat, dirt and fatigue. He felt in need of a long cool shower and an equally long cold drink but when he reached his yacht he drew up with a start; his body stiffened. Sitting in the cockpit was a tall, slim silver-haired man in an immaculate light grey suit: Detective Chief Superintendent Sawyer.

'Inspector, I wondered if I might have a word.'

It wasn't a question. 'If you've come to discuss the case, I'm off duty,' Horton answered tersely, climbing on board and unlocking the hatch, annoyed with himself for not spotting Sawyer's car in the marina car park. But perhaps Sawyer, or his driver, had parked further away so that he wouldn't see the car, wanting the element of surprise, and he'd certainly achieved that. How long had Sawyer been waiting? Not long, Horton guessed, but how had Sawyer known when he'd be arriving? Even if the man had been at the station and not headquarters some twenty miles away he couldn't see how Sawyer could have arrived before him.

'It's not about the case,' Sawyer answered.

No. Horton already knew that. There was only one reason why Sawyer was here and that was Jennifer Horton.

Six

'I have no idea what happened to my mother and I'm not interested,' Horton said, descending into the cabin.

'I don't think you mean that.'

Horton turned and held Sawyer's cool, penetrating stare. His dislike of the man was augmented by the fact that Sawyer knew more about his past than he cared for, but even without that Horton would have been suspicious of him. He considered Sawyer to be a man without conscience, practised in deception, emotionless and cold-hearted. And as if to prove his suppositions the bloody man wasn't even perspiring despite the heat. Sawyer should team up with the ice-maiden, Bliss, thought Horton feeling soiled and sweaty. He didn't offer him a seat.

Sawyer said, 'Have you found a copy of the missing photograph belonging to former PC Adrian Stanley?'

So that was it. He might have known. His stomach knotted with tension but he took pains not to show it or let it come through in his voice as he said, 'You mean the one of him receiving the Queen's Medal for Gallantry with his wife wearing a brooch. No, have you?'

'No.'

Horton believed him otherwise why else would Sawyer be here? And if Sawyer, with all his resources, couldn't locate a copy of that photograph then *he* certainly wouldn't be able to. But did Sawyer know where the brooch had come from? Had he or his team identified its origins? If so would he tell him? Only if he wanted something in exchange. The Sawyers of the world did nothing for nothing.

Making an effort to keep his tone conversational, Horton said, 'Adrian Stanley's son, Robin, doesn't remember his mother wearing the brooch, but then you know that.' Sawyer must have questioned him, as Horton had done.

'Do *you* remember it?' asked Sawyer

'No.' He wasn't sure if Sawyer believed him. That was his problem. Unable though to resist following this up, and unable this time to keep the bitterness from his voice, Horton added, 'And as all the photographs of me and my mother have been destroyed we won't be able to check.' And perhaps that was why their council flat had been emptied so quickly and so thoroughly after Jennifer's disappearance leaving Horton with only a few toy cars and clothes to take with him to the children's homes.

'Why is the brooch so significant?' he asked, curious despite his misgivings, wondering if Sawyer would tell him.

'Do you mind if I sit down?'

Horton did, very much, but it seemed it was the only way he was going to get more information out of the man. He nodded.

Sawyer slid onto the seat behind the table. Horton remained standing with his back to the galley. He heard the sound of a car pulling away and the engine of a small boat somewhere in the harbour.

Sawyer began. 'We believe it to be part of a private collection of historically significant and extremely valuable jewellery stolen from a house in north Hampshire in 1977, along with a collection of artefacts including Saxon jewellery. None of it has ever re-surfaced and the criminals have never been apprehended. Intelligence leads us to believe that the criminal gang behind that raid and many others over the years, including one of the biggest heists in London, netting jewellery worth forty million pounds two years ago, and across Europe, is transnational, responsible for more than a hundred and thirty robberies, with the value of stolen jewellery estimated at well over four hundred million pounds. We believe Zeus could head it up.'

The mastermind criminal that Sawyer and the Intelligence Directorate believed his mother had known and had possibly run off with. Horton recalled the conversation he'd had with Eames after they'd interviewed Patricia Harlow. Eames had said she'd been working on analysing major jewellery robberies across Europe, trying to establish if the proceeds of the robberies were being used to fund criminal activity.

'Are Marty Stapleton's robberies between 1997 and 1999 connected with Zeus?' he asked.

'Possibly.'

And was that the real reason why Sawyer had been so keen to pursue Woodley's murder? Sawyer thought it might lead him, via Stapleton, to a connection with Zeus. Did that mean Eames knew about his mother? If so, how much did she know? He turned away in case his anxiety registered on his expression. Opening the fridge he took out a Coke. He didn't offer Sawyer a drink.

Sawyer continued, 'We thought we might have caught one of the gang members in Stockholm four months ago but sadly he died before he could tell us more.'

'How?' Horton turned back.

'He was allergic to aspirin, something that wasn't discovered until after his death.'

'Suicide or murder?'

Sawyer lifted one elegant shoulder in answer.

'And that's the closest you've got to Zeus, one possible member of his gang apprehended in Stockholm?' Horton scoffed.

'He's a very clever man. And a ruthless one. His crimes don't start or stop at robberies.'

Horton didn't need Sawyer to spell it out for him; the robberies funded more criminal activity, such as trafficking drugs, people and art, blackmail, extortion, murder, you name it Zeus and his operatives probably did it. The timing of Eames's being put to work on the robberies obviously coincided with the death of this possible gang member in Stockholm, so Interpol and hence Europol must have got some new evidence as a result of it.

Abruptly he said, 'If Jennifer was Zeus's lover she must be dead.'

'You could agree to have your DNA run through the database.'

'And discover if she ended up in the morgue.' He'd already considered this many times.

91

'It would rule out one possibility.'

Horton felt a coldness strike him. He knew what the smooth- speaking bastard meant and it didn't have anything to do with his mother's death. Sawyer believed he was Zeus's son. And with his DNA on record they could match it against anyone they even remotely suspected of being Zeus. Horton said nothing.

'Do you remember Jennifer talking about any one man more than the others; or someone who called on her or she met or who took you out?'

I wouldn't tell you if I did. He shook his head, not trusting himself to speak.

'And you can't recall the brooch.'

'No.' He wanted Sawyer out of here and Sawyer could see it. 'Very well.' He rose but didn't make any attempt to leave. 'We believe that someone connected with Zeus will try to make contact with you.'

Horton's heart stalled. 'Who?'

'We don't know, but it must be obvious to you that your actions over the last few months have been noticed.'

Horton took a breath. He knew that. He also suspected that Sawyer had more intelligence than he was prepared to reveal. But whether that was to protect him or to expose him to Zeus, or one of his operatives, to see where it led he didn't know. Or perhaps he did. In Sawyer's terms he would be expendable if it got him Zeus. And Horton wondered if the real reason Eames was working with him was to see who made contact? But she couldn't be with him twenty-four hours a day, unless Sawyer had hoped he'd fancy her and ask her to stay with him. It was a good plan and it might have worked. He felt anger and regret.

Sawyer said, 'We don't believe you're in imminent danger because Zeus needs to know who you are and how much you know first.'

Horton heard the unspoken words: *in case you are his son. And if you're not then he will kill you.*

'I'm asking you once again to cooperate, Inspector. I can't order you to but it's vital that Zeus is traced and caught and as a police officer you will know that. The offer of acting DCI on secondment to the Intelligence Directorate is still open.'

'I'll think about it.'

'Don't take too long.' He didn't need to add, *or it might be too late.*

Horton watched him leave; his body was so taut it hurt. Sawyer turned into the car park above the marina where he halted and looked down at him, his expression inscrutable. Then he disappeared from sight, confirming to Horton that his car had been parked outside the marina.

He went below where he sank a glass of water in one go trying to release the knot of tension gripping his gut. The boat felt soiled as though his mother's presence and all the pain of his childhood had infected it. Sawyer had done that. It would never be the same again. He glared around the cabin that just over twelve hours ago he had been pleased with and now he hated it. He could smell the betrayal, the corruption. It seeped into his pores. It filled his mouth with bile. For years he had hated his mother for what she had done to him, now he hated her even more and along with her he hated that smug bastard Sawyer.

He couldn't stay here. He couldn't eat or rest.

Pulling on his running gear, he was soon pounding the promenade in the dark, running faster and harder than he usually did, yet he knew he could never eradicate the pain of her desertion. Finally he returned to the boat, physically and mentally exhausted. After a shower he lay on the bunk. He knew that Sawyer spoke the truth. He'd been left alone for years because he hadn't looked for his mother for years. But searching out former PC Adrian Stanley had changed all that. He tried to tell himself that that there was no threat to him from Zeus; he was probably not even of interest to Zeus. His mother was dead and that was it. But despite how many times he said it he knew it wasn't true.

He didn't expect to sleep but must have drifted off because the next thing he knew he felt the boat rock. Someone was onboard. He leapt up, his eyes desperately searching for a weapon. His fingers curled around a heavy torch. It wouldn't be enough to save him, not if his assailant came at him with a gun, but if he had a knife he might just be able to defend himself. He moved silently into the main cabin, his mind racing, his breath coming fast. There was a thump on the hatch. He frowned, why would his attacker warn him? Then someone was calling his name. Was it a trick?

'Andy, it's Ian, night security,' came the urgent softly spoken voice.

Horton let out a long slow breath. Swiftly he opened the hatch.

'Sorry to disturb you but there's been an attack.'

A cold sweat pricked him. Had Zeus's operative got the wrong boat? Or could this be a trick to get him out in the open or on board another boat where he'd be killed and Ian too? So what did he do, stay here and ask Ian to send for the police or go and investigate and take his chance?

'I'll put some clothes on.'

He threw on a pair of chinos and a T-shirt, feeling the rage course through him. Sawyer had made him feel fear. He could never forgive him for that or himself for allowing to be momentarily overwhelmed by it. And he was damned if he was going to let Zeus win. He'd lived with fear as a kid and he'd vowed then he would not let it get to him again and destroy him. The only way to deal with fear was to face it. He almost hoped it was bloody Zeus.

'What's happened?' he asked, stepping on deck and eyeing the anxious bulky man hovering on the pontoon.

'Mr Ballard, who came in late yesterday afternoon, has been attacked.'

'Badly?' Horton asked concerned, locking up.

'His head's bleeding but he insists it's just a surface wound and that he's OK. He won't let me call the ambulance or the police. I mentioned you but he didn't even want that until I said it was you or I call the police.'

While Ian had been speaking they'd made their

95

way up Horton's pontoon, past the marina office towards the waiting pontoon. Lights were showing below decks on the substantial and expensive motor cruiser, which Horton had seen earlier, before his encounter with Sawyer.

Ian called out softly, 'Mr Ballard, we're just coming on board.'

Horton climbed on deck, noting the luxurious and spotlessly clean cream leather interior, before making his way below where he found a man in shorts and a T-shirt in the main cabin bathing his forehead with a large piece of blood-soaked cloth and the first-aid box open in front of him on the table. He was slightly older than Horton had thought when he'd caught sight of him earlier, mid-sixties nudging late sixties probably, but with a body that told of a lifetime of fitness, and muscles that showed he had worked out for much of his adult life and still did. He looked up with an expression of wariness and frustration as Ian made the introductions.

'I'm OK,' he said hastily. 'I don't want a fuss.'

But Horton heard the slight tremor in the rich, well-educated voice.

To Ian, Horton said, 'Tea, strong and sweet.'

Ballard made to protest then changed his mind.

As Ian busied himself in the galley, Horton said, 'Let's take a look at that wound.' He eased away the cloth and saw a cut just above the right eyebrow, but it didn't look too serious.

'One of them struck me on the back of the head and I fell forward. I must have cut myself on the edge of the table,' Ballard explained.

Horton could see traces of blood on the corner

96

of the table. He turned his attention back to Ballard's forehead. 'It should have a couple of stitches in it.'

'I'm not going to hospital,' Ballard said determinedly.

Horton knew that tone. He wouldn't be shifted. This man was clearly used to giving commands and having them obeyed; ex-military, he conjectured.

'It's nothing. Just a cut. I'll be fine.' Ballard seemed to be recovering himself. He pressed the cloth back on the cut.

'I'll see if I can patch it up.' Horton entered a shower room, glimpsing the main cabin as he went, noting the ruffled double bed. Washing his hands he called out, 'What happened?'

'I was drifting in and out of sleep when I felt the boat rock a little. I knew it wasn't the tide or wind, different movement. Someone had come on board.'

Horton knew exactly what he meant. He returned and removed the bloody cloth from Ballard's forehead. Reaching for some antiseptic in the first-aid box he warned that it might sting.

'I got up quietly and grabbed the torch. I heard a voice. By the time I reached here there was a man over there by the galley.' Where Ian was standing, watching them while waiting for the kettle to boil. 'I shouted something, then got the blow on the head, must have spun round and fell, striking the corner of the table.'

'Can you give me a description of the one you saw?'

'He was wearing black trousers and a hoodie,

but that's all I caught a glimpse of, slim, young, I think, but I didn't see his face clearly. It all happened so quickly. I hadn't locked the hatch, bloody stupid of me I know but I simply thought it would be OK. I went down, the torch went out and that's all I remember until I came round and staggered up on deck and saw the security officer.'

Ian placed the mug in front of Ballard. Addressing him, Horton said, 'Did you see or hear anything?'

'Nothing. They'd gone by the time I got here and I didn't hear a motor. They must have rowed here or come by canoe. They could easily have come around by sea from the car park at the end of the road, or from a boat out in the harbour.'

'Have a word with the harbour master tomorrow, ask him if he heard or saw anything suspicious.' Horton fixed a large plaster to Ballard's cut saying, 'Has anything been stolen?'

'About two hundred pounds in my wallet, but my credit cards are still there. I've come away without a computer and mobile phone. I don't want to be contacted for a few days.'

Horton didn't ask why. It was none of his business and a man was entitled to his privacy. He finished dressing the wound. 'That should do for now, but you should see a doctor tomorrow morning.'

'I don't want a fuss.'

'Fuss or not, you could suffer concussion from that blow to the back of your head,' Horton said sternly.

Ballard frowned then winced as the gesture

tugged at the wound. 'I'm fine. I'll be off tomorrow.'

'Better make it the day after, give yourself a rest day,' Horton said firmly.

After a moment Ballard gave a weary smile.

'And perhaps it would be better if you came into the marina on a berth.'

Ian said, 'I'll find a suitable vacant berth and help you move the boat first thing in the morning, Mr Ballard.'

'Good. If you feel sick, Ian will call a doctor.'

Ballard smiled his thanks. 'I don't want to make a formal report, Inspector,' he added. 'It's only money. It could have been much worse.'

'It would help us to apprehend them, someone else might not be as lucky as you.'

'I'll feel fine in the morning.' Ballard sounded and looked determined. And judging by the steely gaze in his intelligent grey eyes in the suntanned, rugged face, Horton saw he had no option but to agree. For now. He might be able to persuade Ballard to change his mind tomorrow, but he doubted it. Ballard said he'd take some painkillers and lie down. Horton asked Ian to keep a very close eye on the boat for the rest of the night and check on him in the morning.

He returned to his yacht, made a coffee and took it up on deck. It was almost three and he was wide awake. The night was sticky, hot and silent. He stared around the marina. All was quiet. He turned his mind to the attack on Ballard. Were Ballard's assailants the same villains who had stolen that brass propeller from the boatyard in Fareham and from the compound at Northney

Marina just across Langstone Harbour? Did they approach the boatyards from the sea? Had they been looking to strip Ballard's boat of any brass on board? There was usually some on most boats. And had they gone to Tipner Quay on Tuesday night believing there might be metal there, and found Salacia instead? But that didn't fit with the theory he'd espoused to Uckfield. And after what Sawyer had said Horton thought he could discount the metal theft idea as far as Salacia was concerned. There clearly seemed a link with Stapleton.

He swallowed his coffee, went below and lay on his bunk. Light slowly crept into the sky. The seagulls started squealing. It was four fifty-five. In another hour he'd get up for work. He closed his eyes. When fatigue finally overcame him he dreamt of Salacia, who turned out to be his mother, and Ballard became his father.

Seven

Thursday

'X certainly doesn't mark the spot,' Horton said, looking at the pavement where Woodley had fallen. He'd asked Eames to park two streets away from the Lord Horatio pub where Woodley had been drinking before the attack. His head was aching from lack of sleep and too many thoughts swirling around it, which had been made worse by the heat in the crowded incident suite and Uckfield's bad-tempered briefing. The reason for the latter had been made clear as soon as Horton arrived, when Trueman had put in front of him the local newspaper and one of the nation's most popular daily tabloids. Uckfield was clearly no pin-up. Cliff Wesley had chosen a photograph that showed Uckfield at his fattest and his frowning worst.

'There's a better picture of him with you and Marsden in this one,' Trueman said, reaching for a third. 'But you only made page five.'

Horton winced. The article accompanying the photograph was written by Leanne Payne, who had obviously sold the story to the national newspapers, earning herself a by-line. It referred to two brutal murders with the headline screaming, 'Is there a serial killer on the loose in Portsmouth?' There was a quote from DC Marsden and more information about the dead woman than should have been released including the fact that her handbag was missing, and that her death could possibly be linked to Daryl Woodley's and have international implications. At least Marsden hadn't mentioned Marty Stapleton. That was little comfort, though. ACC Dean had hauled Uckfield in and the Super was beside himself with rage. Marsden had been only too pleased to take refuge at the quay, overseeing the commencement of the diving operation after Uckfield had threatened to cut off his, and anyone else's, private parts and boil them if anyone so much as breathed in front of a member of the press. They all got the message loud and clear. Bliss remained tight-lipped throughout the briefing but Horton thought he sensed her secret pleasure at seeing Uckfield in trouble. Reggie Thomas had been brought in protesting loudly and abusively about police harassment. Nothing had been discovered from the search of his bedsit except, Uckfield reported, dirty underpants, congealed food and fag ends.

Now, turning and surveying the litter-strewn road with low-rise council flats on one side and a boarded-up garage smothered with graffiti on the other, Horton said, 'OK, take me through it, Eames.' He knew the case by heart but a fresh eye over it might throw up something they'd overlooked.

With some notes in front of her from the case file, she said, 'The landlord of the Lord Horatio, Victor Wainstone, can't confirm what time Woodley left the pub and neither can anyone else who was interviewed and drinking there, but Wainstone says Woodley wasn't there when he was clearing away after last orders at eleven. The exact time of the attack on Woodley is not known, but he was found by a couple in their twenties, students from the University, returning home from a nightclub in Oyster Quays, at just after one in the morning.'

'There's student accommodation a couple of streets away from here; this would have been a short cut from the Hard,' Horton explained.

Eames nodded. 'They rang for an ambulance and the hospital called us.' She gazed around at the low-rise flats. 'Surely someone must have seen him or walked past him before one a.m.'

'If they did they would probably have stepped over him.'

102

Eames looked doubtful.

'It's a tough area.'

'But to leave him to possibly bleed to death.'

'They'd leave their grandmother haemorrhaging if it meant calling in the cops.'

She eyed him steadily and he was relieved when she shrugged and turned her attention back to the file. Last night he'd told himself she was off limits, but was she? Perhaps the way to discover how much she knew about Zeus and Jennifer was to get close to her. And that certainly wouldn't be a chore.

'This doesn't look like the sort of place Salacia would visit,' she said gazing around the street. 'She'd stand out a mile in her expensive clothes and jewellery. In fact she'd probably be the one to be attacked, not Woodley.'

'I don't think she was ever here.'

'Then why are we asking the landlord about her?' She flashed him a curious glance.

'Why not?' Horton replied, heading in the direction of the pub. He diverted his thoughts from Eames by considering again the attack on Ballard. Before the briefing he'd checked for any similar incidents and any reports of further metal thefts but nothing had been logged. He'd also asked Elkins to check with the Langstone harbour master for any boat movements in the early hours of the morning. Elkins had already reported back that no boats had been reported stolen on Tuesday night. He was going to see if he could find evidence of any of Woodley's associates owning a boat.

Eames was again consulting the notes as she marched beside him. 'Woodley didn't get a taxi here and none of the bus drivers questioned remembers seeing him. Nothing showed up on the CCTV cameras on the Hard. I suppose one of his associates could have brought him here. Or perhaps he walked.'

'Unlikely, knowing Woodley.'

'But if he was under instructions to do so and was paid for it.'

'Then he'd probably walk to John O'Groats.' Horton drew up outside the rundown pub. 'But if he was told to walk to prevent anyone being able to testify he was here then he'd hardly be drinking in a public place.'

'Perhaps he was thirsty and stupid.'

'He was certainly the latter,' Horton replied, banging his fist on the flaky and scratched brown paintwork. There was no answer. He tried again with the same result.

'Perhaps Mr Wainstone is out.'

'Or avoiding us.' Horton stepped back and hollered, 'Open up, Wainstone, or do you want everyone around here to know you're helping the police with their inquiries into the—'

A big bald head shot out of the first-floor window. 'For fuck's sake, shut up. I'm coming down.'

Horton turned to Eames. 'See, all we had to do was ask nicely.'

She smiled and his heart missed a beat. Damn.

The sound of bolts slamming back brought him back to the job in hand. It was followed by the door creaking open. A man with a prominent nose and bleary bloodshot eyes peered out. 'What the hell do you want now?' he hissed.

'A word.'

The bald landlord looked as though he was about to give them several and none of them very polite then changed his mind. He opened the door just wide enough to admit them. Walters would never have squeezed through but Eames had no trouble. He followed her, admiring her figure and the way she moved, not showily but with the grace of a dancer.

Wainstone slammed the door behind them. 'I've already told you everything I know about Daryl Woodley. I wish the bugger had never set foot in here.'

'I expect he does too.'

The smell of stale beer and dust hung about the shabby pub with its threadbare carpet, the original colour and pattern of which was a mystery to be solved only by the person who had laid it, if he was still alive, which Horton doubted. It looked as though it had been down since the pub had been built in the 1920s. This was the pub the brewery had clearly forgotten, which was probably a wise move on their part. Why spend money refurbishing something they hoped would be demolished by the council if the area was scheduled for some upmarket development? But the council knew that would mean re-housing hundreds of tenants and there was nowhere to put them in an island city that was fast becoming standing room only.

'I don't know why you're bothering me again. Haven't you got anything better to do?' He crossed splay-footed to the bar.

'Tell us about Daryl Woodley,' Horton said.

'For fuck's sake, I've already told you lot hundreds of bloody times.'

Eames stood poised with her notebook and posh-looking pen. Horton had no difficulty placing her in the Netherlands analysing data, but he did have difficulty with her being here. She looked too neat, too healthy, too attractive. Not that she showed any reaction to Wainstone's manner or language. On the contrary she looked as though this was an everyday occurrence for her.

'There's nothing to tell,' Wainstone snarled. He turned and poured a whisky from the optic behind the bar. Horton didn't bother looking pointedly at his watch; the gesture would have been wasted on the alcoholic landlord. Wainstone didn't offer either of them a drink and even if he had neither would have accepted. After swallowing a mouthful Wainstone gruffly continued, 'He came in about nine—'

'How do you know that?' Horton interjected sharply.

'Because I looked at the clock.'

'Why?'

'What do mean, why? I can look at the clock, can't I? I saw that it was about nine. He ordered a pint and took it to that seat over there.' Wainstone jerked his head at a table to the right of the door and not far from the gents' toilets. Horton knew this already. If he'd been hoping that Wainstone would deviate from his story it looked as though he would be disappointed.

Eames looked up. 'And he stayed there all night?'

'It was busy.' Wainstone tossed back his whisky

106

and wiped his mouth with the back of his tattooed hand. 'He might have gone out or to the toilet. I wasn't watching him every minute of the bleeding night.'

Horton eyed the landlord closely, there was something he wasn't telling them, but then that was nothing new. Nearly everyone they'd spoken to was keeping quiet about something. Was it drugs? Hans Olewbo of the drugs squad had claimed there was nothing going down here. Vice could throw no light on the matter either. That didn't mean though that it wasn't drugs, porn, prostitution or all three, just that they had no intelligence on it being that.

Wainstone was saying, 'He came in, ordered a drink and sat drinking it. I didn't see him talk to anyone and I didn't see him leave. He was still there when I called time at eleven so he must have left just afterwards and before I threw out the regulars.'

'Who were?'

'I've already told you. You've got a list of their names.'

Eames said brightly, 'Maybe there are a couple you forgot to mention, sir, easily done when you're busy. For example, this man.'

She thrust across a photograph of Reggie Thomas.

'No. He wasn't here.'

'Have you seen him before?'

'No.'

'Or any of these people?' Eames showed him a photograph of Woodley's mourners taken from Clarke's video.

'No.'

'If you could just take a closer look, sir, to make absolutely certain, then we won't ask the health and safety inspectorate to pay you a visit, or the vice or drugs squad, and neither will we alert the RSPCA or the endangered species crime team about the parrot you have in the back room.'

Wainstone looked alarmed. 'I've had Percy for years.'

'I'm sure you have, sir. And I'm sure that he is kept nowhere near food. Food and Hygiene Act, sir. It could affect the renewal of your licence.'

Horton was impressed.

Wainstone's eyes were shifting between them. Then he studied the photograph. 'I've never seen any of them before. OK?' He stormed around to their side of the bar, making sure to close the door that led into the back room and his living quarters and swiftly crossed the pub where he threw open the door. 'Now bugger off. I've got work to do before I open up.'

Horton stayed put for a while and watched Wainstone shift uncomfortably. Then crossing to the door he nodded at Eames, who retrieved the photographs of Salacia from the pocket of her jacket and put them in front of Wainstone's bleary eyes.

'Have you seen her before, sir?'

'No I bloody well haven't.'

'Or you might recognize her in this picture with fair hair.'

Wainstone dashed a glance at it. Angrily he said, 'I wouldn't recognize her if she was stark

108

bollock naked, because I've never seen her before.'

Horton said, 'Her body was found at Tipner Quay yesterday morning.'

'So? That's nothing to do with me.'

'I never said it was,' Horton answered smoothly. He held Wainstone's eye contact. Then said brightly, 'Do you have a menu?'

Wainstone started with surprise. 'Yeah, why? Want to book a table?' he sneered.

'If I wanted a colonic irrigation. Menu. I'd like a copy.' He held out his hand.

Wainstone gave an exaggerated sigh and whipped one from the table nearest him.

Horton took the greasy piece of laminated card. 'We might have to return to ask you further questions. This is a double murder investigation.'

'I've told you. I've never seen him or her.'

Horton looked him steadily in the eye. 'For once, Mr Wainstone, I'm inclined to believe you.' He turned on the threshold, unable to resist an exit line. 'After all, what would a nice woman like her be doing in a shit hole like this?'

Eight

'Burger and chips; sausage and chips; egg and chips; cod and chips. It's not exactly gourmet food,' said Eames, reading the menu Horton had handed her.

'And you'd know all about that,' he quipped.

'It was one of the subjects taught on my Higher Certificate in Finishing in Switzerland.'

He threw her a surprised look. Was she joking? Maybe not. 'Didn't think there were any finishing schools left in these emancipated times.'

'Oh, yes, and places are in great demand, more so than ever. But I am partial to cod and chips.'

Perhaps she expected him to buy her some. 'I'll send Walters next time. It's his kind of food but it doesn't sound like the type of last meal Salacia would have eaten.' They were still waiting on the analysis of stomach contents from Dr Clayton. 'What was all that about parrots and endangered species?'

'The tattoo on his hand extending up his arm was of a parrot and I saw the cage through the open door. Last year I worked on a case on trafficking in endangered species. We managed to identify and apprehend a group of criminals illicitly trading exotic birds from South America. It might not sound much but there's big money to be made and sadly it's a growing area with the involvement of organized crime groups. Many of the routes used for smuggling illegal immigrants and drug trafficking are also used for smuggling rare animals, corals and valuable plants. Maybe Victor Wainstone does more than keep a parrot for himself, and it's always good to throw in the line about endangered species, gets them nervous.'

'I'll remember that.' It was a good piece of observation but he had no need to tell her that. 'I think he's telling the truth when he says he's never seen Salacia or any of Woodley's chums. I want a quick look around the area before we return to the car.'

They crossed the road and instead of turning right into a tree-lined road of council flats that would bring them back onto the main road where the car was parked they headed south in the direction of the Hard and the waterfront. After about twenty yards the road curved left, east-wards, the flats giving way to the rear gardens of those in an adjoining street and a small park on the opposite side of the road. Horton stopped at the bend and looked back at the Lord Horatio. Then he crossed the road, with Eames following. He wondered what she was thinking. Clearly this wasn't what she had been raised to. But this area had been home for him for three years in a chil-dren's home and then with a couple of foster parents he'd rather forget, until his last and loving foster parents, Bernard and Eileen Lichfield, had moved from here after he'd been with them a while, he couldn't remember how long, to a better area on the eastern edge of the city, not far from where Cantelli lived. There he'd changed schools for the third and final time since the age of eleven. He'd still had his rebellious moments but Bernard and Eileen had been patient and loving and had understood. And he wished he could thank them for that.

He drew a breath, pushing aside the memories that seemed determined to haunt and torment him, and stopped under the shelter of the trees bordering a small space of green and a play area where two young women wearing hijabs were pushing toddlers on swings. There were shrubs to his right and two elderly men eyed them from their viewpoint of a park bench. He could see the entrance to the Lord Horatio. Woodley's assailant could have waited here until Woodley left and then followed him. But he could also have waited outside the pub. If it was Reggie Thomas he couldn't have been inside the pub because Woodley would have seen him, unless they had left together with Woodley completely unsuspecting that Reggie would try to kill him. But that would mean not only was the landlord lying, but so too were those they had managed to find and question who had been drinking in the pub that night. Still, that wouldn't be surprising. Lying was a way of life for Wainstone and most of his regulars.

He gazed around; there were no security cameras. One of the occupants in the flats opposite might have seen someone lingering but if they had they'd not said during the house-to-house. But as he'd said to Eames, silence was the common currency in these parts. Most viewed the police as vermin.

He continued walking. Eames fell into step beside him. The road once again swung south past a derelict boarded-up building displaying graffiti. After another twenty yards they came out onto the busy main road. The pavement opposite was packed with young people in their twenties spilling out of coaches, and from the nearby railway station, many wearing brightly coloured Wellington boots even though the day was hot and sunny, and nearly all of them carrying heavy rucksacks or bags.

'I know where they're headed,' Eames said.

It didn't need great detective powers to work out it was the same place as they were going and where half the local police seemed to be, including DI Dennings: the Isle of Wight Festival.

Turning to Eames, he said, 'Take the car to the ferry. I'll meet you there.'

He caught a glimpse of curiosity before she turned and headed back to the car. Horton stood and surveyed the area. Across the road were the public toilets and then a cafe in front of which was a taxi rank. Then came the road which led to the railway and bus station, where Woodley could have alighted. Next was a coffee stall doing a brisk trade with tourists and festival-goers, and on the Hard was the Net Fishermen's Association hut and the small tourism office in front of the iron-clad historic ship HMS *Warrior* and the entrance to the Historic Dockyard and visitor attractions, where hordes of foreign students and more tourists were congregated. Recalling what Sawyer had said last night about Zeus sending someone to suss him out, Horton scanned the crowds. There didn't appear to be anyone following him and neither had he spotted anyone at the marina earlier that morning. No car had followed them from the station. But that didn't mean there wasn't someone.

He crossed the road and headed east towards the entrance to the waterfront shopping centre, sparing time to cast a glance at the church which had recently been robbed of its brass plaques. That investigation looked like going nowhere at the moment unless the Environment Agency had something to report on illegal scrap-metal merchants or uniform came up with some new intelligence. But he noted that all the thefts on land at least had taken place in this area, which to his mind meant someone living locally. Not that that got him much further forward. It was densely populated and close-mouthed, as he'd already indicated to Eames.

He dived into the crowded malls, registering who was behind, ahead and beside him. No one looked remotely interested in what he was doing. Last night he had vowed he wouldn't live in fear, and now he told himself that neither would he live his life looking over his shoulder for pursuers. He'd deal with it *when* it happened because he knew it wasn't a case of *if* it happened.

He thought about the robbery in north Hampshire in 1977 that Sawyer had told him about. He was curious to know more about it and decided to look up the case notes when he had time. Perhaps there would be a description of the jewellery stolen. He wasn't sure where that would get him but it was worth a try.

He came out onto the bustling waterfront and paused at the railings to stare across the narrow stretch of water to the marina and the tower blocks of Gosport opposite. Several yachts and small craft were making their way into the harbour and out to the Solent. If he decided to pitch in with Sawyer, Bliss would probably put the flags out and declare a public holiday. He'd miss working with Cantelli, but that needn't stop him seeing the sergeant and confiding in him. Cantelli knew more about his past than anyone else, including Catherine, and Steve Uckfield, who had once been a close friend until ambition had got in the way. But he was reluctant to burden the sergeant with his personal problems. Cantelli had a large family to look after, and Horton certainly didn't want to put him at risk.

He watched the Wightlink ferry begin to ease its way into its restricted berth to his left. To say he didn't care for Sawyer was a massive understatement, but should he shelve his personal feelings for the sake of discovering the truth? And he *would* be helping to flush out a notorious criminal. Should he accept Sawyer's offer?

He turned and headed for the car-ferry terminal. There would be time to consider it later. For now he had a ferry to catch and a blonde waiting for him and even across the distance of the busy car park, and up against some stiff competition from many of the young and pretty festival-goers, Eames shone out like a beacon on a dark night, attracting lustful and wishful glances from the men and admiring and resentful ones from the women, though clearly she wasn't aware of it. She smiled at him as he headed towards the car. Again he wondered what on earth had made her join the police when she looked as though she ought to be running some posh art gallery in Mayfair.

Twenty minutes later they were sailing out of port and he'd fetched a coffee for himself and a bottle of water for Eames, thinking how Cantelli would have hated this. He got sick just looking at the sea, a decided drawback to living in a seaside city. She didn't ask him where he'd been or what he'd been doing. That notched up a point in her favour.

'I'll call in,' he said heading for the deck.

'I'll come with you. It's too nice a day to waste sitting inside.'

He was tempted to retort that he didn't need minding before telling himself he was being too touchy. That was Sawyer's doing. On deck though he walked away from her without giving an explanation and found a quiet spot. He turned back to see her leaning on the rail, looking out to sea, the breeze ruffling her blonde hair. She lifted a hand to brush a few stray strands off her face. He couldn't see her eyes because of the sunglasses but there was no denying she made a striking figure. He turned away.

It took a while for Trueman to answer.

'Anything new?' asked Horton, hopefully.

'I got a PC to take Cliff Wesley's statement without Uckfield knowing that he'd come in. I didn't fancy mopping up the blood. The Super gave another media appeal after the briefing. It was the ACC's suggestion.'

More like a command, thought Horton.

'That, and the national newspaper coverage, means the phones haven't stopped ringing. Walters has been roped in to answer them. DCI Bliss is interviewing Reggie Thomas.'

Lucky old Reggie. 'Anything useful from the appeals?'

'Salacia's been seen in Milton Keynes, Market Harborough and all points west of Plymouth but nowhere within a twenty-mile radius of Portsmouth.'

Horton wasn't surprised. Public appeals always resulted in speculative sightings and a great deal of wasted time. But sometimes, just occasionally, they got a result.

'And Mrs Harlow's been on the telephone to make a formal complaint about the press hounding her because we gave her name to them.'

'We?' There was a slight pause that told Horton that was not what Patricia Harlow had said. She'd obviously named him.

'I've passed her over to Communications and I've told Marsden to stay at Tipner Quay until he finds something belonging to the victim, even if it's a broken fingernail, otherwise he might have to apply for a transfer. I'm thinking of putting in for one myself.'

And that wasn't like Trueman. He rarely got fazed by pressure. His exasperation was explained by his next words.

'The ACC's been in the incident suite and Uckfield's office more times in the last two hours than in the last two years, demanding an update, asking if anything new has come in, poking about on my desk and tut-tutting at the crime board. I think there might be another murder by the end of the day and we'll have to lock up the Super. Pity you didn't take him to the Isle of Wight with you.'

And Uckfield was probably wishing he had come. Horton reported back on the interview with Victor Wainstone then asked if they had the results of stomach contents for Salacia.

'Lobster.'

Not the Lord Horatio cuisine, then. 'And that's it?'

117

'Except for traces of vegetables; mangetout and asparagus.'

'No doubt washed down with champagne.'

'Best with a Pouilly-Fuissé, preferably one about five years old.'

'And I had you down for a beer man,' Horton said surprised.

'Only when the Super's buying and I don't think he'll be doing that for some time unless we get a quick result.'

'Better stick to water, then.'

'We're doing a check on all the restaurants in the area which served lobster on Tuesday, as well as asking around at the supermarkets, fishmongers and delicatessens.'

'Check the fish market at the Camber. Either Salacia or the man she was with could have bought a lobster there.' It was too much to hope that someone might have seen and recognized her. He rang off promising to update Trueman the moment he had anything worth reporting and told him not to hold his breath. Then he rang the marina and enquired after Ballard.

'He says he's feeling fine and he looks OK. We've been checking on him every couple of hours. He's getting fed up with us,' Eddie answered.

'Better that than finding him unconscious. I'll look in on him when I get back but I've no idea when that will be.'

'You on that murder case,' Eddie asked with relish, 'the woman found in that old wreck? I read about it in the paper this morning and that boss of yours has been on the telly.'

Horton said he was on the case and rang off before Eddie could ask any more questions. Not that Horton would have answered them. He joined Eames, who was eyeing the wooded coastline of the Isle of Wight as it came closer. He thought she looked troubled.

'My family have a house on the Island. It's over there, behind those trees and around the point from Wootton. We use it in the summer and at Christmas, or rather my family use it.'

She looked solemn and sad for a moment and Horton wondered if she was regretting her decision to join the force, or perhaps her family disapproved of her choice of career. They had to be wealthy to own a holiday home but he'd never doubted that. Despite his earlier promise not to take an interest in her background he found himself saying, 'Why did you join the police?'

She eyed him closely for a moment, causing his pulse to beat a little quicker. Then she smiled and said brightly, 'To find myself a nice husband, of course.'

Her reply took him aback for a moment before he returned her smile. It was clearly a subject she didn't want to discuss. He understood that completely. He relayed what Trueman had said about the lobster and wine.

'Good choice, but I'd probably go for a Chablis, Grand Cru 1997.'

'I'll pass your tip on to Trueman.'

'It's not the kind of meal any of Woodley's associates would buy,' she said.

'No, even given Sholby and Hobbs' sudden rise in income. But it could be the type of meal the man who brought her into the country would buy.'

'*If* she lived abroad.'

'OK, then, the man who drove her to the crematorium and away again.' But Horton was convinced Salacia had been living abroad.

The announcement for passengers to return to their cars came over the loudspeaker and twenty-five minutes later Horton was showing his warrant card to the security officers at the backstage entrance to Seaclose Park. The festival kicked off tonight and the fields away from the main performance areas were packed with tents and people. He asked where they could find Gregory Harlow, the event-catering manager for Coastline.

'The blue and white tent,' came the answer. 'It's the one that's kitted out like a beach cafe with deckchairs, sand and surfboards.'

Following directions, and leaving the car inside the gates, as instructed, they threaded their way through the hordes of workers and security officers across the bone-hard field towards a giant blue-and-white-striped tent emblazoned with the words, 'Coastline Cool'. It was one of many they passed, along with several coffee stalls, ice-cream kiosks and fast-food outlets. The hot midday air resounded with the sounds of shouting, drilling, banging and a blast of music loud enough to be heard on the mainland six miles across the Solent.

'I'm glad I don't live round here,' Horton said, with feeling, spotting the bulky figure of DI Dennings talking to a lean fair-haired man in his mid-to-late forties outside the Coastline Cool tent. Dennings was wearing the navy polo shirt and dark trousers of the official festival security officers.

'Most of the residents move out for the festival,' Eames said.

'Can't say I blame them.'

Dennings glanced across at them but gave no indication of recognition or hint of surprise, but Horton glimpsed the anger behind his eyes as they drew level. He guessed Dennings was thinking they were there to muscle in on his operation, or spoil it.

'We're looking for Mr Gregory Harlow,' he said, politely.

'You've just found him,' answered the man beside Dennings.

Horton showed his ID and introduced Eames as a colleague. He caught Dennings' baffled look as he obviously tried to place her.

'We'd like a word, Mr Harlow.'

'Can't you see I'm busy?'

'This won't take long. There are a few questions we'd like to ask you in connection with the death of a woman.'

His expression showed no surprise, only extreme agitation and fatigue. Horton thought he might be a few years younger than his wife.

'Do you have to ask them *now*? We're way behind. The first bands are due to play in less than six hours.'

'Is there somewhere we can talk in private, sir?' Eames said politely, ignoring his plea and eyeing Dennings pointedly. She didn't know him.

'I'll leave you to it, Greg. Thanks for the coffee,' Dennings said pleasantly enough but

Horton could tell he was bursting with curiosity.

'You'd better come inside,' Harlow said grudgingly, leaving them to follow him through the tent. Horton cast an eye over it. It was decorated with fishermen's nets, lobster pots, sand and shells. Several people were putting out metal folding chairs and tables, while soul music blared out. At the bar, workers were busily stocking the shelves.

'In here.' Harlow led them to a tented extension behind the bar which was clearly a storeroom and rest room. Turning to them he made no attempt to conceal his irritation. 'I haven't a clue who this woman is, my wife told me you'd been asking questions about her, and I didn't speak to her at the funeral.'

'You remember seeing her, then?'

Harlow ran a hand across his perspiring forehead and wiped it down the front of his T-shirt which was emblazoned with the company logo and 'Coastline Cool'.

'No.'

'Can you take us through the events leading up to your aunt's funeral, sir, when the hearse turned into the crematorium?' asked Horton.

'I've already told you I didn't see her,' Harlow snapped.

Horton held his hostile eye contact and said nothing. Eames remained silent. Eventually Harlow was forced to continue. In clipped tones, he said, 'Pat and I were in the car behind the hearse; we arrived just before the service. We got out. I nodded at a couple of people, neighbours of Amelia's. We followed the coffin into the chapel. That's it. Now if you've—'

'What the hell's going on here?'

Horton swung round to find a slender man with keen features about mid-fifties glowering at them. He was dressed casually and expensively in beige trousers and a short-sleeved pale blue cotton shirt open at the neck. Harlow's fair face flushed and he shifted uneasily. 'It's the police, Ross. It's OK, it's got nothing to do with the festival,' he hastily added before addressing Horton. 'This is my boss, Ross Skelton, he owns Coastline Catering.'

Skelton barely glanced at Horton. Levelling his still irate gaze on his employee he said, 'If it's nothing to do the festival then sort it out in your own time and not mine.'

With deliberate politeness Horton said, 'We won't keep Mr Harlow from his work for very long, sir.'

Skelton frowned before stomping off. Horton heard him shouting at someone in the main tent.

Harlow quickly addressed Horton, 'I've told you I can't help you. I have no idea who she is.'

He turned away but Eames, taking two photographs from her trouser pocket, said, 'This is the victim at the funeral and another picture taken of her with her natural colouring. Do you recognize her?'

'No.'

'If you'd take a closer look, Mr Harlow.'

Reluctantly Harlow stared at the photographs. Watching him carefully, Horton thought he detected a ghost of a reaction but whether it was of recognition it was difficult to say.

123

Thrusting the photographs back at Eames, Harlow said, 'I've never seen her before.'

'How about this man?' Eames passed across a photograph of Daryl Woodley.

'Look, I've no idea who they are. Now I've got work to do.'

Horton let him go.

'Very tetchy,' said Eames when they were heading back towards the security entrance.

'He's clearly under pressure.' Horton nodded towards Harlow's bad-tempered boss, Skelton, who was now having a go at his staff at one of his coffee stalls. Horton could see Dennings waiting for him by the car. Despatching Eames to buy some sandwiches and a couple of bottles of water, Horton made for him.

'What the hell are you doing here?' Dennings hissed.

'It's too long and too complicated to explain.'

'Not if it has something to do with my operation.'

'Don't you mean the Border Agency's operation?'

'I'm not having you mess things up, Horton.'

Horton swiftly told him about the murder at Tipner Quay and that the dead woman had been seen at the crematorium the same time as Patricia and Gregory Harlow, who had been there for their aunt's funeral. 'What are your views on Gregory Harlow?'

'Seems OK.'

'When did he arrive here?'

'No idea.'

'He must have logged in.'

124

Dennings entered the temporary security office. Horton followed.

'His van was checked in Wednesday morning at seven thirty-five.'

So Harlow must have been at home the night of his aunt's funeral. That didn't mean he stayed home. He could have gone out to meet Salacia. But would he have eaten lobster and had sex with her? There was no evidence to suggest that Salacia had any connection with Gregory and Patricia Harlow and no evidence to say Gregory Harlow could have killed her. The Harlows' reaction to Salacia's deaths weren't what he would call normal but in this line of work he'd long since learnt that there was no 'normal'.

Another blast of ear-deafening music filled the air. This time it didn't seem to want to stop. By the time it did Horton could see Eames heading for the car. He made a point of politely thanking Dennings for his help adding, 'Enjoy the festival.'

Horton climbed in. 'Just checking Harlow's movements,' he explained, taking his sandwich from her. He wasn't going to tell her who Dennings was. It didn't concern her or their investigation.

'I did the same with Gregory Harlow's boss. He said he hoped we weren't going to come around bothering them every five minutes. And he wasn't too happy that Gregory Harlow had taken Tuesday afternoon off to attend his aunt's funeral. Skelton expected him back Tuesday night; the senior staff sleep on site in a caravan during the festival, but Harlow called in to say he wouldn't be back until Wednesday morning.'

So why did Harlow change his plans? Or perhaps he hadn't intended to return on Tuesday night but had just told Skelton that to pacify him. On the other hand he could have been emotionally drained after the funeral and didn't feel up to returning to work. Or perhaps Patricia Harlow was upset and her husband had stayed home that night to comfort her.

A prolonged blast of music followed them into the town of Newport. With feeling, Horton said, 'I never thought I'd be glad to visit the relative peace and quiet of a prison.'

'Then let's hope there's not a riot on, sir.'

Nine

Geoff Kirby, Head of Operations, rose from behind a modern desk in the small office and stretched out a large, strong hand. Horton hadn't met him before. His first impressions were of authority and intelligence. He wondered what Kirby's were of him. He hoped his claustrophobia didn't show. He tried to shut out the sounds of the prison, which had followed him into Kirby's office in the central administration block. There was no slamming of doors or rattling of keys here, they were all in Horton's mind along with the smell of men and disinfectant that reminded him too much of his days spent in children's homes.

Eames had been despatched to talk to the officers

who had worked on Woodley's wing, and to enquire about Reggie Thomas. She'd already caused quite a stir at the reception area and on their way through the prison both from prisoners and officers. She showed no sign of being aware of it but he knew that she was and that it didn't affect her in the slightest. Another lesson they must have taught her at that Swiss finishing school, he thought.

'I'd like to talk to you about Woodley's attack on Marty Stapleton,' Horton said after Kirby gestured him into the seat opposite.

'I gave a full report to Detective Chief Superintendent Sawyer and to Detective Superintendent Uckfield,' Kirby answered a tad tetchily, his brown eyes studying Horton warily.

'I know but we're following up some new information.' Horton didn't say what that was and Kirby didn't ask although he looked as though he wanted to; perhaps something in Horton's expression prevented him. He would tell him about Salacia but first he wanted to hear about Woodley in case it triggered some new thoughts.

'He was a slippery sod, a shirker, always feigning illness, trying to get out of his duties, although he rarely did.'

So nothing new there. 'Was he close to Reggie Thomas while he was in here?'

'Not particularly, no,' Kirby answered somewhat cautiously. 'Thomas wasn't here very long. He came from Wormwood Scrubs a year before his release, which was three months ago. He was released a week after Woodley.'

'But they were on the same wing.'

Kirby nodded. 'For six months, yes.'

127

'Why was Thomas transferred from Wormwood?'

'Same reason as Marty Stapleton was transferred out of here, violence. Thomas was attacked in Wormwood, more than once. It was thought best to remove him and as he was serving the last year of his sentence he was sent here, closer to home.'

'Was there any trouble with him?'

'No. Too eager to get out to dirty his nose. The same went for Woodley in the end.'

'After the attack on Stapleton?'

'Yes. He never did a thing wrong after that, or before it come to that.'

And Horton found that interesting. The attack had occurred last September. Woodley had been released in March. He said, 'Why did Woodley attack Marty Stapleton?'

'Probably didn't like the colour of his eyes.' Horton gave a small smile. Kirby continued, 'Stapleton probably said or did something to get up Woodley's nose, you know what it can be like in here, just being in the wrong shower at the wrong time is enough.'

'Is that what happened?'

Kirby shrugged but Horton was rapidly reading between the lines, there was a great deal more to this attack than he'd read in the report. And perhaps Sawyer knew that. Horton also got the impression that Kirby was reluctant to elaborate on it, and the reason for that could be because it reflected badly either on him or on the prison, or both. His silence forced Kirby to add rather reluctantly and testily, 'Stapleton was

128

transferred after the attack and he's still inside, so he can't be Woodley's assailant.'

'No, but Stapleton could have organized it from the inside for revenge. Why transfer Stapleton and not Woodley?'

'Stapleton was a bully. It was believed he provoked the attack. There were quite a few inmates and prison officers glad to see him go.'

Horton thought he smelt an undercurrent here. 'Are we talking gangs?' He saw immediately that he'd hit a raw spot.

Defensively Kirby said, 'We have an active and highly successful violence-reduction strategy. The Woodley incident was a one-off.'

'But it highlighted weaknesses inside the prison and with your strategy.'

Kirby narrowed his eyes and his lips tightened.

'Look, Geoff, I'm not here to blame, or criticize, I just need to understand if what happened with Stapleton could lead us to discovering who killed Woodley and why. And before you answer you should know that there's been another murder, a woman. Her body was found in the sea at Tipner Quay on Wednesday. We don't have an ID yet and we're not certain she is connected with Woodley, or Marty Stapleton, but she was last seen at Woodley's funeral.' Or rather, he added to himself, at the crematorium. There had been that small reaction from Gregory Harlow that made Horton wonder if they'd got the wrong funeral. If so he was wasting his time.

Kirby sat back with a heavy sigh. 'We knew that Stapleton was head of a notoriously powerful gang on the outside and that he was building up his power base here. We could control it, move people around, that was until Victor Riley arrived and he challenged the status quo. What we didn't know was that Stapleton and Riley were actually rival gang masters in London and that was the real reason why Stapleton was moved, not because of Woodley's attack, although it gave us the perfect excuse. We needed to break up the gangs. We never let that come out officially, or on the inside, but I'm sure most of the inmates read the situation perfectly.'

And discounting what he might or might not have seen in Gregory Harlow's reaction a new thought occurred to Horton. Salacia could have been connected with Victor Riley's gang. Could Woodley also have been associated with this other gang? He said, 'Did Woodley attack Stapleton under Riley's orders?'

'Not that we could prove. When Riley arrived three years ago he joined forces with two smaller gangs in order to build his power base, Woodley was in one of those. After the attack Riley's and Stapleton's gangs were broken up but as you know gangs can re-form, it's a constantly fluid situation.'

'Where were Stapleton's minders at the time of the attack?'

Kirby shrugged.

'They were told by Riley to vanish?'

'Possibly. I don't know. Riley had influence. He could be very persuasive.'

Horton noticed the past tense. 'He's also been moved?'

'Yeah, to the great prison in the sky, or in hell hopefully. Died three weeks after the attack on Stapleton and before you go looking for suspicious circumstances there aren't any. He had a massive heart attack during recreation in front of several witnesses including prison staff, and there was a thorough post-mortem, which confirmed it. After Stapleton was transferred, Woodley went back to being his usual snivelling slippery self but with a respect surrounding him that made me want to puke every time I witnessed it. But like I said he kept his nose clean.'

Horton's mind was racing with thoughts. Victor Riley couldn't have ordered Salacia or Woodley to be killed, then, unless he'd left instructions. But he couldn't have known he was going to keel over from a massive heart attack. But if Salacia was connected with Riley then it made some kind of warped sense that Marty Stapleton might want her taken out as some kind of revenge, or as a warning to Riley's mob on the outside that he was top dog and not to mess with him, and the same for Woodley.

Removing the photograph of Salacia with dark hair, Horton handed it to Kirby. 'Do you recognize her?' He didn't expect a positive response unless Stapleton or Riley had had a picture of her in their belongings but that seemed too big a break to hope for. But Kirby hesitated and Horton felt a prick of excitement. Was it possible they were correct? Were they going to get the break they so desperately needed?

Kirby studied it for some time. Horton waited. He hardly dared to hope.

131

'There's something familiar about her.'

Horton handed across the computer-enhanced photograph of the victim with fair hair. 'Does this help.' He saw instantly that it did. Kirby recognized her. 'You know who she is?' Horton asked eagerly.

'No. But I've seen her picture before.'

Horton's first thoughts were that Salacia must have been an actress, like he'd posed almost as a joke to Uckfield, and they'd all failed to recognize her, but the worried expression on Kirby's face quickly scotched that idea.

'Where?' he asked keenly.

'Here. I remember her because I was surprised he should have her photograph. And now I come to mention it the timing was rather odd too.'

'Who had it?' Horton's mind raced. 'Reggie Thomas? Marty Stapleton? Victor Riley?' he fired off.

'No. Daryl Woodley.'

So it was possible that Woodley had known her and that she'd been at the crematorium for his funeral. Harlow's reaction, if there had been one, and Horton now doubted that, had nothing to do with the victim.

'She was younger than here, though,' Kirby was saying. 'About ten years I'd say at a rough guess. And in the photograph I saw she was wearing a strapless summer dress standing on the deck of an expensive-looking boat, gazing out to sea with a frown on her face as though puzzled by something in the distance just like she is in this picture. She looked classy, not at all Woodley's type, which was one reason why I remember her.'

132

By using a suitable graphics package on the computer Horton knew they could get the photograph altered to show her younger, but perhaps they didn't need to go to that much trouble for an identification to be made. Kirby had said she'd been wearing a strapless summer dress.

'Is there anything else you remember about her, any distinctive marks?' He held his breath waiting for the answer.

Kirby looked surprised then nodded. 'Yes, a birthmark or a tattoo; I couldn't see which exactly, just above her breast, the right one I think. I thought it was a tattoo because it was in the shape of a butterfly and very attractive, drawing your eye to her tits, and they looked like nice tits.'

Not so nice now, Horton thought, recalling with a suppressed shudder the mutilated body on the cold mortuary slab. The birthmark clinched it. Then he recalled what else Kirby had said. Leaning forward he said excitedly, 'You mentioned the timing being odd and not looking Woodley's type being one reason why you remember seeing the photograph, what's the other reason?' He had already guessed what was coming but he'd let Geoff Kirby tell him.

'We were searching Woodley's cell immediately after the attack on Stapleton, and that's when we came across the photograph.'

'And you'd never seen it before?'

'No. And neither had the officer who searched Woodley's cell with me, Rob Bridewell, but another officer might have come across it at some stage though Woodley never mentioned a woman and no woman came to visit him, certainly not her.' He stabbed a finger at the photograph. 'We would have remembered a good-looking woman like that.'

'What did you do with the photograph?'

'Put it back where we found it. It had nothing to do with the attack on Stapleton. We were looking to see if Woodley had been paid for his services but we didn't find anything that works as currency in here stashed away.'

'Was it in Woodley's possessions when he was released?'

Kirby was already tapping into his computer. After a moment he said, 'No.'

'Was he searched?'

'Of course but not with the aid of a rubber glove if that's what you're thinking.'

Horton smiled briefly before adding, 'How about Reggie Thomas?'

Again Kirby consulted his computer. 'No photographs. I'll check Stapleton's file.'

'And Riley's.'

While he waited Horton tried to work out the significance of the photograph and the timing of its discovery. Several ideas sprang to mind but he didn't have the luxury of time to pursue them to any conclusion. He would once outside.

Kirby said, 'No photographs on either Stapleton or Riley. And I never saw this photograph in their possession.' But again Kirby confirmed they hadn't been strip-searched. 'I don't remember Woodley, Thomas, Stapleton or Riley talking about any woman but I'll question the staff. I'll also make enquires about the photograph.'

Horton reached for his card. 'Call me if you discover anything about her or the photograph, no matter how insignificant. I'll leave these pictures with you.' He could get others.

He thanked Kirby for his cooperation and found Eames waiting for him in reception. They headed for the exit. She confirmed that Woodley had never uttered a word about any woman, except the ones he found in porno magazines and saw on the telly. Horton relayed what he'd discovered from Kirby.

'So the photograph was planted while Woodley carried out the attack on Marty Stapleton,' she said after they had checked out and were heading to the car.

Horton's thoughts exactly. 'The attack was used as a diversion because whoever planted it couldn't be seen doing so, he'd be traced back to the main man.'

'Victor Riley?'

'Or Stapleton. Reggie Thomas could have planted it. He was on that wing then.' And Uckfield would like that.

Eames zapped open the car. Climbing in and letting down the window, she said, 'Perhaps Salacia grassed up Victor Riley and he wanted Woodley to get revenge when he got outside.'

'If he did then someone else has carried out his instructions.'

'It could be someone who was released just before or after Woodley who was connected with Riley's gang inside the prison.'

Horton was annoyed he'd missed that. He should have asked Kirby for a list of names. He'd call him and request one to be sent over to Trueman. 'Do Europol have anything on Victor Riley?'

'I didn't come across his name when I was cross-referencing and analysing the robberies. I'll check.' She reached for her phone.

Horton forestalled her. 'On the ferry.' He stretched the seat belt around him. He'd ask Trueman to pull Riley's record and Uckfield could ask the Intelligence Directorate if they had anything on him.

Eames pulled away. 'But that doesn't explain why Woodley was attacked and left for dead before he had the opportunity to kill Salacia.'

'It does if once outside Woodley decided he wasn't going to play ball. Stapleton or Riley, whichever of them has ordered Salacia's death, gets to hear that Woodley's chickened out and orders someone to take him out and then kill Salacia.' Eames frowned in thought. Before she could speak though Horton quickly added, 'I know, why bother with Woodley at all when this other killer could have carried out instructions.'

While waiting to board the ferry, Horton rang Uckfield to be told by Trueman that the Super was with Dean.

'DCI Bliss has got nothing out of Reggie Thomas. She's letting him stew while she has a go at Maureen Sholby to see if she can break her alibi for the time of the attack on Woodley.'

And probably trying to see what she could get Maureen to tell her about her husband's other criminal activity, which could relate to that new car of theirs.

136

Trueman said, 'We've got Wayne Sholby in another interview room shouting his mouth off about unfair arrest and demanding a lawyer. We've told him he is not under arrest only helping us with our enquiries into the death of his close friend in light of new evidence, and that he's free to go at any time, but he won't leave while Maureen's here.'

'No, he's too scared she's going to open her big mouth and drop him right in it. And Darren Hobbs?'

'Can't be found at the moment.'

'Convenient. Anything turn up from the interviews of Amelia Willard's mourners?' He hoped that at least one of them might have seen Salacia exchange a word or glance with someone.

'No. And we've run them through the computer, they're all clean, not so much as a driving conviction amongst them. And the six sailing-club members who were in the club the night Salacia was killed don't remember seeing her or a car.'

Horton relayed what had happened at the prison and asked Trueman to pull everything they had on Victor Riley and to tell Uckfield that he'd need to check with the Intelligence Directorate.

On the ferry, Eames went up on deck to call her boss at Europol. Horton took the opportunity to call his solicitor but his fingers froze over the phone as Sawyer's warning flashed through his mind: *We don't believe you're in imminent danger because Zeus needs to know who you are and how much you know first.* Would Zeus use Emma to find out how much he knew? His blood turned to ice and he shuddered despite the heat. With

137

sick bastards like Zeus was reputed to be, threatening to hurt someone you loved was a way of getting you to cooperate. And perhaps Zeus would want a tame copper in his pay. Rigid with fear for Emma and furious with Sawyer for letting his words influence him Horton made to ram the phone back in his pocket when it rang.

'What?' he bellowed at it.

'You all right, Andy?' came Trueman's surprised voice.

'Yeah, fine, what is it?' Horton grunted, trying to control his fear and anger.

'Can you get over to Tipner Quay. Marsden says the divers have found something and I'd like you to check it out before we tell the Super.'

'Salacia's handbag?' asked Horton, eagerly. Or it could be the murder weapon.

'No, a bracelet, and it's still attached to what's left of an arm.'

'Shit! Whose arm?'

'No idea. But it isn't Salacia's, both were accounted for,' Trueman said somewhat facetiously.

Horton rang off after saying they'd be there in about twenty minutes. He gave Eames the news. She looked surprised and then thoughtful, and as they sailed past the ancient walls of Old Portsmouth he knew she was thinking the same as him. How on earth did this link with Woodley and Marty Stapleton?

Ten

The divers had recovered a humerus, a femur, a pelvic bone and a skull. Clarke had been and gone and Horton, using his mobile phone, had taken a photograph of the bracelet before despatching it in an evidence bag to Joliffe for forensic examination. He showed the picture to a very hot and troubled Uckfield, who had arrived a few minutes ago. 'It looks like an identity bracelet.'

'Worn by a Second World War serviceman?' Uckfield asked hopefully.

Hardly, thought Horton, but he knew why Uckfield had suggested it. He was thinking of the munitions barge and if the item and the bones were those of someone from the war it meant they could put this investigation on a slow burner and concentrate on the current one.

'Sorry to disappoint you, Steve, it's modern, and the kind a woman would wear. As you can see it's small, chain-linked with an oblong flat surface in the middle. Once Joliffe's examined it we might get more.' He didn't dare say such as a name, because he didn't want to push their luck. He hadn't seen anything inscribed on it, but it had been filthy and he hadn't wanted to tamper with it and destroy any evidence they might possibly get from it, which after being immersed for so long he guessed was unlikely.

'It could have been washed up near the bones and have nothing to do with them,' Uckfield suggested hopefully.

'It was found entangled around the radius and ulna at the lower end, the wrist.' Horton indicated one of the bones laid out on a black plastic sheet in front of them on the quay. 'The bones weren't displaced from the munitions barge either. They were on the second wreck.'

'Doesn't mean this is homicide, though.' Uckfield was clearly determined to stick to his viewpoint. 'Whoever it was could have been killed accidentally or committed suicide.'

'But that still begs the question, why there are two deaths in this boatyard?'

'All right, no need to rub it in and hang a bloody great neon sign on it.' Uckfield exhaled and ran a hand through his short dark hair. 'Is this linked with Marty Stapleton?'

It was a question Horton had discussed with Eames when they'd seen the first of the remains brought up by the divers. They were still diving for further bones.

'Eames says there's nothing on file that Stapleton was ever in Portsmouth or used this route to get his stolen goods out of the country but the Intelligence Directorate and Europol might not have discovered that.'

'The rate we're carrying on we might as well blame Marty for the sinking of the *Mary Rose*.'

Horton permitted himself a smile. 'I don't think he was around in Henry VIII's day.'

'Have you checked? Probably some scumbag relative of his opened the portholes or whatever

140

they had in Tudor warships. You think Harry Foxbury, the previous boatyard owner, might have something to do with this?'

'I can't see why Foxbury would want to kill Salacia here and draw attention to another body unless he's some kind of nut,' and that was possible, although Horton had never heard of any trouble with Foxbury. Trueman had confirmed he was clean when he'd run Foxbury through the computer. 'But he must know something about the wrecks. Eames is trying to contact Foxbury now.' Horton glanced in her direction across the boatyard. She seemed to be having some success because she was speaking into her phone. Marsden stood a discreet distance away from them obviously still wary of Uckfield's wrath, talking to the officer-in-charge of the diving operation.

Horton added, 'Foxbury might be able to tell us how long the wreck has been submerged, which might give us some idea of when this person died, and Dr Clayton's going to examine the remains in the morning. The divers will recover what they can tonight. We've got about two hours of daylight left. But the wreck won't be raised until tomorrow.' He'd instructed photographs and a video recording to be made using specialist underwater cameras and the position of the remainder of the bones to be mapped before being recovered. Tomorrow a forensic archaeologist from the university would examine the video footage for an in-depth analysis of the wreck.

Uckfield turned away. 'How on earth did Manley and his crew miss it?'

'They wouldn't have been using the same

141

equipment as us to explore the wrecks for evidence, and there was no need for them to search the middle wreck. They were more concerned with getting the live ammunition off the barge.' Horton saw Eames come off the phone and cross to Marsden.

'They seem to have missed a bloody lot,' grumbled Uckfield. 'One of them could be involved. Kevin Manley doesn't have an alibi for the time of Salacia's death and neither does Ethan Crombie. Either of them could have arranged to meet Salacia here and kill her.'

'Were either at the crematorium?'

'No. They were both here,' Uckfield replied gloomily. Then he brightened up. 'But they could have met her on a different day and elsewhere. There's no evidence she flew into the country on Tuesday, either on a scheduled flight or a private plane. She could have been living locally, or anywhere in the UK for that matter. We've assumed an awful lot from that suntan. She might have been to Majorca, or the Isle of Wight, on holiday. I'm going to Swansea tomorrow to see if I can jog Stapleton's memory about Salacia, and I'll ask him about that photograph. Can Geoff Kirby be trusted? He's not making it up, is he?'

'I don't see why he should.'

Uckfield began walking to his car, which was parked just inside the cordon. 'DCS Sawyer's coming with me and if Stapleton runs true to form we'll get nothing out of our trip except a blast of wet Welsh air, it's bound to be raining, always is in Wales. Bliss couldn't break Maureen

Sholby's alibi but she's convinced Maureen's hiding something.'

'When isn't she?'

'I've had to release Reggie Thomas. We've got nothing on him. Even the threat that Marty Stapleton might send one of his bad boys after him didn't make him wet his pants and plead for witness protection. So either he's developed nerves of steel, which is unlikely, or he has an even more powerful protector than Stapleton, or he has sod all to do with it.'

Which wouldn't please Sawyer. It didn't look as though it pleased Uckfield either. They drew level with Eames and Marsden.

Eames said, 'Harry Foxbury lives in Langstone, that's about five miles out of Portsmouth to the east.'

'We know where it is, Agent Eames. We work here,' Uckfield replied frostily.

'Yes, sir,' she replied unfazed, adding, 'I've spoken to his wife, who told me that he's on his boat at Horsea Marina—'

'And we also know where that is.'

'Sir. Debbie Foxbury read about the body being found and asked her husband whether he should contact the police but he said, "The yard has nothing to do with me any more." I didn't mention the fact that human remains had been recovered. I asked for the name of the boat, and said could Mr Foxbury call us when he returned home.'

Uckfield zapped open his car. To Horton he said, 'See what you can get out of him. I'll brief DCS Sawyer about this.'

Half an hour later Eames was keying the

143

security number the marina office had given them into the keypad at the bridgehead. Horton realized that Foxbury's boat was on the same pontoon as his father-in-law's yacht. He only hoped Toby Kempton wasn't on board. He didn't relish an angry exchange in front of Eames, although Toby was more likely to give him the cold shoulder. With relief Horton saw that Toby's yacht wasn't in its berth. Foxbury's gleaming motor cruiser was, though. It was far bigger and newer than Horton had anticipated and he estimated must have set Foxbury back at least a cool six hundred thousand pounds.

'That old boatyard must have been worth a lot of money,' he said quietly. And he'd like to know how much.

Eames hailed Foxbury and a few seconds later a bulky man in his mid-sixties appeared on deck wearing beige shorts and an oversized brightly patterned floral shirt open at the neck to reveal grey hair matching that on his round, suntanned and heavily lined face. Eames made the introductions and asked if they could speak to him.

'Come on board.' Foxbury eyed Eames licentiously as she nimbly climbed on deck.

Horton followed suit, quickly surveying the boat and noting the tender on the rear with two powerful Suzuki outboard engines. 'Nice craft, Mr Foxbury,' he said admiringly, though it wasn't to his taste. 'How long have you had it?'

'Bought it at the Southampton Boat Show September before last. I used to sail but the wife doesn't like it. She doesn't mind this, though, doesn't mess her hair up.' He smiled at Eames.

She returned it with what seemed like genuine warmth tinged with a dash of coquettishness. Surely she couldn't fancy the old devil? No, she'd quickly got the measure of Foxbury and was just softening him up. Perhaps there was a side to Eames he hadn't noticed. Perhaps she was a better cop than he'd given her credit for. And perhaps she hadn't been seconded to work with him to get close to him as he'd suspected after Sawyer's visit because she'd not even given a hint that she fancied him. Probably didn't.

Foxbury continued, 'With a cruiser you can shoot across to France or the Channel Islands without it taking all day, although I've only been to the Hamble today. This is about the body you found at my old boatyard, I take it?' Foxbury led them below deck. 'Drink?' They both refused. He poured himself a glass of white wine from a bottle that was half full before waving them into seats behind the table in the spacious cabin that smelt strongly of alcohol and perfume. He slid onto the seat nearest Eames and at right angles to her. Horton surmised by his heightened colour and slightly clumsy manner that it wasn't his first bottle of the day. Horton hoped he wasn't driving home.

'So who is she?' Foxbury asked.

Horton felt like asking the same question but his thoughts were on the owner of the perfume, because it wasn't Mrs Foxbury; Eames had said Debbie Foxbury had been shopping all day and was now at home.

'That's what we're trying to establish, sir.' Eames reached for the photographs from the

145

jacket resting on her lap and handed across two pictures, one of Salacia with dark hair taken at the crematorium and the other the computer-altered image showing Salacia with fair hair. Foxbury placed his wine glass on the table and took them from her making sure to touch her fingers. Eames didn't recoil or react in any way. Foxbury sniffed and with a slight frown of concentration studied the photographs. Horton could hear a boat making its way into the marina. 'Do you recognize her?' Eames prompted after several seconds had passed.

'Can't say I do.'

He placed them on the table. Horton watched him closely. A lie or the truth? He couldn't tell.

'How about this man?' She placed the photograph of Woodley on the table beside the pictures of Salacia.

'I saw him in the newspapers and on the telly. He's the one they found dead at the marshes.' He eyed them curiously. Horton could see him trying to fathom out the connection, or perhaps trying to work out how much they knew.

'Have you ever seen him before that?' asked Eames.

'No.'

Foxbury's gaze was steady. Horton hadn't expected him to say anything different. He said, 'What about Marty Stapleton?'

'What about him?'

'You know him?' Eames asked barely disguising her surprise.

'Never heard of him. Should I have done?'

Horton swiftly continued, noting that Foxbury

was enjoying playing with them. 'What can you tell us about the three wrecks that are being salvaged?'

Foxbury picked up his glass and took a swallow before answering. 'One is a Second World War ammunition barge. The navy paid my dad to take several off their hands after the war but that one sunk before he could tow it out into the Solent and he left it there because it would have cost too much to raise. That must have been about 1948.'

Foxbury paused to top up his wine glass. Horton wondered if the gesture was designed to give himself time to think of a lie before continuing. But he had no reason to suspect Foxbury of anything, except that two bodies had turned up in his old boatyard and that was too compelling a coincidence to overlook, especially if they took Woodley out of the equation. But there was no reason to do that. And, as Horton had said to Uckfield, he didn't think Kirby was lying about the photograph found in Woodley's cell. The boatyard was also close to Woodley's home ground and that of his fellow mourners. He left the thought hanging and concentrated on what Foxbury was saying.

'The wreck on top of the munitions barge was recovered from the harbour. I remember its engine failed and it was towed in. There was an old man on board. I expected him to come back for it but he never did. It was left just off the quayside, slowly rotting, and it broke its mooring in a storm and sank over the barge.'

'When?' asked Eames.

Foxbury shrugged. 'Late eighties, early nineties.'

And was the elderly man their bones? If so then perhaps the bracelet they'd found had no connection with the human remains after all. Horton said, 'Weren't you curious why he didn't return? Didn't you contact him and ask him to move the yacht?'

Foxbury eyed him as though he were mad. 'Why should I? I dealt in old boats, and wrecked boats. It didn't bother me it being there. It was just one of many. If the owner wanted it he had only to return and take it away.'

And had he returned and accidentally drowned while trying to recover it? Or had he been killed because he'd returned and witnessed something illegal? And could that be linked to Stapleton or Foxbury? Foxbury didn't look uneasy, though.

'Do you have his contact details, sir?' asked Eames.

Foxbury eyed her as though she'd just asked him to explain quantum theory. 'You must be kidding, love.'

'What was the boat called?'

'No idea and before you ask we didn't keep records, or rather we did but only those for the tax man,' he added somewhat hastily, throwing a glance at Horton.

Yeah, I bet. 'And the other wreck on top of that?'

'That was towed around for scrap in 2002. We took off anything that we could sell and we were going to break up the hull when the next morning we found she'd sunk, so we just left her there.

And don't ask me who owned that either because I don't remember. And I haven't got any paperwork.'

'You said "we", who worked with you?' asked Eames, her pen poised.

'They came and went, love. I can't remember their names.'

Convenient. 'Didn't you keep records of employees?' Horton asked.

'When I needed to but I wouldn't have them from back then.'

The law didn't require anyone to keep records beyond six years. And Horton was guessing that Foxbury employed casual labour and much of that was cash in hand avoiding paying tax and national insurance and all the hassle that went with employing staff. There didn't seem much more they could learn from Foxbury, but Horton wasn't ruling him out of the investigation yet. He slid along the seat so that he could stand at the opposite end of the table to where Foxbury was sitting. Eames could slide along after him. He decided not to mention the bones. They'd save that for another time. Taking the hint, Eames put away her notebook and followed suit.

'Is that it?' Foxbury asked, somewhat surprised. Horton wondered what he had expected.

'If you remember the name of the yachts or the people who owned them would you let me know?' Horton stretched out a business card. Foxbury took it.

'We'll find our own way off.'

Foxbury shrugged but at the bottom of the steps up to the deck Horton paused. 'Can you tell us where you were on Tuesday night, Mr Foxbury, just a formality,' he added smoothly at Foxbury's frown.

'Here.'

'All night?'

'No. I came back from the Isle of Wight late Tuesday evening.'

'With your wife?'

There was a moment's hesitation and an avoidance of eye contact before he answered. 'No. Alone.'

'So no one can confirm this,' Horton asked lightly.

'Do they have to?' Foxbury's expression hardened.

'What time did you get into the marina?'

'What's this got to do with that woman's death?' he replied brusquely.

'You might have seen something at the boatyard.'

'Well I didn't. It was dark. I got in about nine thirty and got home around eleven thirty.'

Horton thanked him. As he stepped off the boat he caught sight of a sleek yacht heading towards the pontoon. On it was the lean figure of his father-in-law. That had been a close thing.

Eames said, 'There was a woman with him on that boat on Tuesday. It could have been Salacia.'

'Not if it was the same woman who's been on the boat with him today.'

'You mean the perfume. He could have broken a bottle of Salacia's perfume while trying to get rid of her things, which he could have thrown overboard while out on the boat today. Perhaps he took it out hoping to get rid of the smell before his wife goes on board.'

That was possible.

'And he's drinking white wine,' Eames added. 'A Grand Cru Chablis, I noticed.'

'Hardly conclusive evidence.'

But Eames was not to be put off. 'He met Salacia at the airport, took her to the crematorium where she arranged a meeting with Reggie Thomas, or another of Woodley's mourners, for later. Then he took her back to his boat, where they were for the remainder of the afternoon and evening and where she left her things. He could easily have deposited Salacia at the quayside for her meeting, or alighted with her, stabbed her and tossed her into the sea, before returning here, and without anyone from the sailing club seeing or hearing him. He might be lying about the time he returned here.'

'He probably is.' And Horton had another variation on Eames's theory, which tied in with what he'd said to Uckfield yesterday, that Salacia could have flown into a private airfield on the Isle of Wight, where Foxbury had met her and brought her across on his boat in time for the funeral, or rather in time to meet her contact after it. But theories weren't hard facts. And he still wasn't happy with the idea of Foxbury using his former boatyard to dispose of Salacia.

He said, 'There's a lot of money sloshing around him and that bothers me. Find out how much he was paid for that land and see what else you can dig up on him. Tax and employment records, associates, property, cars . . .' His words tailed off as a car he recognized pulled up two rows behind theirs.

'Anything wrong, sir?'

Only my estranged wife's arrival. Horton said, 'Find out if the lockmaster knows what time Foxbury left the marina on Tuesday morning and when he returned. Take the car. I'll wait here.'

With a slight rise of those perfectly shaped eyebrows Eames did as she was told. Horton saw Catherine's enquiring and slightly hostile gaze follow her before she headed for him.

'What are you doing here?' she said waspishly.

'How is Emma?' He didn't see why he should explain anything to her.

'She's fine. I—'

'When is the parents' evening?'

'What?'

'At the school.'

She flicked back a strand of blonde hair. 'I don't know.'

Horton laughed lightly and without mirth. 'You used to be better at lying than that, Catherine. I'll call the school.'

'It doesn't concern you,' Catherine snarled.

She was referring to the fact that he didn't pay Emma's school fees, because her father had insisted on doing so, most probably to cut him out of the family. That would have to be sorted. If anyone was paying for Emma's education it was going to be him. But he knew what Catherine was doing. It had taken him a while but he'd finally got the measure of her. She was deliberately goading him so that he would lose his temper, and then she'd use that against him, to try and prevent him from seeing his daughter. He'd fallen for it before, he wasn't going to again. And an idea had occurred to him about how he could get to see more of Emma, without putting her in too much danger from Zeus, or one of his henchmen. It wouldn't be foolproof and he would need to be vigilant but if he attended the parents' evenings and other activities his daughter was involved in where parents and guardians were admitted, then he'd at least get to see her.

He said, 'I'll see you at the parents' evening.' He marched towards the road before Catherine could reply. Only when there did he look back. Catherine was halfway down the pontoon. As though aware of his gaze she halted and turned round. Their eyes connected for a moment before he turned away and began walking towards the marina office to wait for Eames.

Eleven

The daytime lockmaster remembered Foxbury's boat leaving the marina about mid-morning on Tuesday but he couldn't be specific about the time or when it had returned. He also claimed he hadn't seen a woman on board but Horton knew she could have been in the cabin below and well out of sight until they were through the lock.

In the incident suite, Eames called the night

lockmaster at his home, while Horton updated a weary, hot and cross Uckfield, who was pacing the floor.

'Anything from Joliffe?' Horton asked hopefully, glancing at the photographs of the bracelet on the crime board, though judging by Uckfield's grim expression he already knew the answer would be negative.

Trueman shook his head.

Uckfield said, 'And the bugger's gone home.'

Trueman rubbed a hand over his chin as if to say, Think we should too, but he said, 'We've got some information on Victor Riley. He was convicted of armed robbery on a bank in London in 1994. A clerk was shot and paralysed. Riley got twenty years. The Met and the Serious Organised Crime Agency had been after him for years for extortion, robbery, violent assault but he'd been too well protected, until the bank job. He wasn't on it but he was the organizer. One man grassed on him and gave the Met everything they needed to put him away.'

'Bet he was popular,' Horton replied.

'He went under the witness protection scheme, and there's no record of who he was and where he is now, or if there is they're not telling us.'

Eames came off the phone. 'The night lockmaster didn't see Foxbury's boat leave the marina or return. He says the lock was on free flow from between three forty-four a.m. and four thirty-four a.m. so any boat could have gone out or come in during that time without being noticed, but the timing's wrong for Salacia's death.'

'Everything's wrong in this investigation,'

grumbled Uckfield. He addressed Horton. 'The divers have recovered all the remains, so see what Dr Clayton can give us tomorrow while I swan off to Swansea, and I won't be singing in the valleys unless Stapleton decides to join the choir, which is about as likely as Wales winning the World Cup.'

Dismissed, Eames went home and Horton did the same after dropping by his office to find an email from Bliss saying that Walters would be working with her on the possible vehicle fraud operation and the Mason's Electricals robbery, which she believed Sholby and Hobbs were responsible for. As if he hadn't told her! There was no mention of the metal thefts, which clearly Bliss had shelved at the scent of a new and more high-profile investigation. If she could get some vital information out of Sholby and Hobbs that could assist in an arrest in the Woodley investigation she'd be ACC Dean's pet and the Chief's blue-eyed girl, despite her eyes being green. And that would really hack Uckfield off.

Horton turned to his voicemail, where he found a message from Sergeant Elkins.

'There's no sign of any of Woodley's known associates owning a boat. They still might though because that lot would rather risk a fine if they were caught in the harbour than bother to register it. Nothing new to report on assaults on boat owners or anyone acting suspiciously in Langstone Harbour and no new metal thefts.'

Tomorrow, Horton would ask Elkins to see if he could find any sightings of Foxbury's boat at any of the marinas on the Isle of Wight for Tuesday.

There was, thankfully, no sign of Sawyer or his car in the marina when Horton reached it, or any unexpected visitor sitting in the cockpit of his yacht, but he'd only been on board a couple of minutes when someone hailed him and he looked out to find Edward Ballard on the pontoon.

'I wanted to thank you for your help last night,' Ballard said.

Was that only last night? It seemed like ages ago. Ballard was sporting a clean plaster on his forehead and seemed to have fully recovered from his ordeal. He looked tanned and relaxed in shorts and a polo shirt, and Horton again noted the tautness of his muscles.

'Think nothing of it. Would you like a drink?' he asked surprising himself. He rarely went in for company and although he was tired, he suddenly thought that talking to Ballard might free his mind from thoughts of Zeus, the case and Catherine. He didn't expect Ballard to accept, but he did with alacrity.

'I won't stop long, though,' Ballard added, climbing on board. 'It's late and you must be tired. I saw on the news about the murder of that woman at the boatyard and Eddie in the marina office said you were working on the investigation.'

Ballard's words brought him up sharply. Ballard, like Foxbury, had a powerful motor cruiser, with a tender on it. Where had Ballard sprung from last night? Did he know Salacia? Had he really come here to thank him or was it to pump him for information? But if he was involved then why hang around after killing Salacia, and if he had come into this marina to pump him for information then how had he known that he was on the case and where he lived? No, he was way off beam with that one. He was beginning to feel the effects of the long day and the heat. His brain felt ragged. He, like Uckfield, was simply desperate for some answers and he'd seized on this poor man as hopefully being able to give them a lead on the case. Next he'd be suspecting every passing yachtsman of murder.

Horton offered him a choice of drinks and handed over a Coke before grabbing one himself. He found himself saying, 'What we don't understand is why she was at the old boatyard at Tipner. Do you know it?'

'No. I've seen it on the charts though when sailing into the harbour. Do you know why she was killed?'

Horton gave his stock policeman's answer, 'We're following up a couple of possible lines of inquiry.' He gestured Ballard into a seat and sank down heavily opposite, across the table.

'On the news that police officer said you're trying to establish her identity. You'd think someone would have missed her, a mother, husband, lover, father?'

'Perhaps there isn't anyone.'

'Not even children? A daughter or son?'

There had been one according to Dr Clayton, but as Eames had suggested the child could have been given up for adoption, or died. 'Perhaps they don't know that she's missing.'

Ballard looked thoughtful. 'I guess she could have told them she was going to be away for a few days.'

'Or perhaps they're not a close family and only keep in touch infrequently. Once a year at Christmas is sometimes all some families manage, if that, and, as you say, if she had friends then she might have told them she was going away on business or on holiday.'

'She appeared to be a nice-looking woman. Her picture was on the news.'

'Have you ever seen her before?'

Ballard's head came up with surprise. 'Me? No. Why do you ask?'

'I've asked so many people it's become a kind of habit,' Horton joked, wearily.

Ballard gave a smile. 'And here's me making you talk about it when that's the last thing you probably want to do. I came to say thank you and to tell you that I'm heading off early tomorrow morning.'

'Where are you going?'

'France, I think, for a while.' He took a pull at his drink and surveyed the cabin. 'Do you live on board?'

'Most of the time,' Horton replied, not wanting to be drawn.

'It's nice.'

'Bit smaller than yours, and not as fast,' Horton answered, taking a swallow of his drink and adding, 'How long have you had your boat?'

'Not long.'

'Been around much in it?'

'The Channel Islands, Spain, France, here.'

'Wish I had the time. Are you retired?'

'Sort of. I have some investments. I dabble a bit here and there.'

Evasive thought Horton but then there was no reason why Ballard should tell him his life story, just as he wouldn't relay his.

Ballard rose and consulted his watch. A Rolex, Horton noted, and genuine. 'I'd better be going. Thanks again for your help.' He had hardly touched his drink. He stretched out a hand and Horton took it noting the firm dry grip and the steady confident eye contact. He thought he detected something behind the eyes in that brief glimpse but he couldn't define what exactly.

Ballard turned away and climbed on deck. Horton followed him.

'I've asked for any further incidents like the one that happened to you last night to be reported to me. I'll let you know if we catch whoever attacked you. How do I get in contact?'

'Forget it. I don't want any fuss,' Ballard said, smoothly and pleasantly.

'It would help us to secure a conviction if you'd press charges.'

'Sorry, but I'd rather not.'

Horton let him go. He watched him strike out down the pontoon. Before he reached the security gate Ballard turned and raised his hand. There was something in the gesture that tugged at the back of Horton's mind. It had the smack of a farewell in it. And why shouldn't it? Horton was hardly likely to see Ballard again.

He stayed on deck long after Ballard had disappeared from view, scouring the marina and the car park. There was no one about and he recognized all the cars in the car park. Why wouldn't Ballard give him his contact details? OK, so the

159

man was entitled to his privacy but Horton wasn't just anyone. He replayed their conversation, mentally dissecting it. Had he missed something? Had Ballard merely been thanking him for being a Good Samaritan and making chit-chat about the murder case, or had there been something more to his visit? He recalled that brief eye contact. What had he seen? There was something, he was sure of it but what, he couldn't define.

He thought back to what he had seen on Ballard's boat. One cabin door had been ajar but there had been nothing on the ruffled double bed. He hadn't seen into the other cabin. In the shower room, where he had washed his hands before attending to Ballard's cut, there had been men's toiletries: toothpaste, toothbrush, electric razor, aftershave, expensive brand. No women's toiletries but then Ballard would have cleared them out if they had belonged to Salacia. Could he be involved? Could he be her killer? But why not clear out after her death? Why come into Southsea Marina? Had he wanted to tell him something but couldn't bring himself to? No, he must be wrong. Then what was it that bothered him so much about Edward Ballard? It was there, at the back of his mind, nagging at him, tormenting him.

He returned to the cabin, and stood just inside it. First Sawyer had shown up here and then Ballard, but had they arrived at the marina in that order? Had Sawyer got here before Ballard? He'd certainly arrived before Horton, which he'd already considered surprising. Had Sawyer known that Ballard was here? Was that why Sawyer had been at the marina? Ballard was connected with Sawyer.

Or could he be connected with one of Sawyer's investigations. And was that investigation to do with Marty Stapleton and Salacia? Or . . . Horton stiffened. Was Ballard connected with Zeus? Was that why Sawyer had been here and had warned him?

His eyes swept the cabin. Ballard's can of Coke was on the table. Reaching into his jacket pocket Horton pulled out a pair of latex gloves, stretched his fingers inside them, and poured the almost full can of drink down the sink. Then taking out an evidence bag he dropped the can inside it, sealed the bag and labelled it: Assault, Edward Ballard, and wrote the date, estimated time and place. Tomorrow morning he'd allocate a crime number and send the can for fingerprints and DNA. It was highly irregular because he hadn't obtained Ballard's permission, and whatever he discovered wouldn't be admissible, but he didn't think Ballard was connected with Salacia anyway. No, unless he was very much mistaken Ballard was connected with DCS Sawyer and that meant Zeus. And he suspected that when he ran Ballard through the computer tomorrow morning he would find precisely nothing.

Twelve

Friday

'There's not a lot I can tell you about her,' Dr Clayton announced when Horton arrived at the mortuary early the next morning. He'd already been into work, entered the assault on Edward Ballard on the computer and sent the can off for fingerprints and DNA testing. He'd also spoken to Simon, the marina manager, and discovered that Ballard had paid for his mooring by cash and hadn't given an address or left a telephone number. There was nothing wrong in that but Horton gave instructions that he was to be informed when Ballard left the marina.

'Anything wrong, Andy?' Simon had asked, concerned. Horton had told him he just wanted to make sure that Ballard didn't suffer any after-effects from the attack. He wasn't sure if Simon had swallowed it but he'd asked no further questions. Simon had called him on his mobile at eight twenty-five, as he'd been leaving for the mortuary, to say that Ballard had left the marina. Horton had then rung Elkins and asked him to contact the Border Agency to track Ballard's boat but not to stop it, and to find out if it had been berthed at Horsea Marina on Tuesday night. As he'd predicted, Ballard hadn't shown up on the computer.

There was nothing more he could do on that

162

score but there was plenty on the matter of the bones laid out in front of him, and he brought his full attention back to them and Dr Clayton. She'd said the remains were those of a woman, which ruled out Foxbury's elderly man, but the fact that it was a woman made it even more likely there was a link with Salacia's death. He hesitated to even silently frame the words 'serial killer' which the newspapers had emblazoned across their pages. But this serial killer, if it was one, had left a long gap before killing again and the divers had said there were no further bodies lying in the deep.

'The sacrum is short and wide, not long and narrow as it would be with a male,' Gaye Clayton was explaining, 'and amongst other indicators the sacroiliac joint is small not large. She's also Caucasian, and from the measurements of the femur and humerus, and consulting the tables we use to determine height, she was five foot one inches. The pattern of fusion of bone ends to bone shaft, plus the general condition of the bones, indicates she was in her early twenties.'

It was a start but he needed more. 'Any idea when she died?' Foxbury had said the wreck she'd been found on had been there from the late 1980s and the one above it from 2002, but Horton wasn't sure he could rely on his evidence.

'No, sorry. We need to conduct further laboratory tests to determine that, but if blood pigments are present in the bones then it will be less than ten years. We should be able to get DNA from the teeth, which are in good condition.'

But whether it would match with anyone they had on the DNA database was another matter.

Reading his mind Gaye said, 'I know, you want more. But there's not much I can tell you. We can compare the degradation rate of DNA extracted from the recovered rib bones to determine the time interval since the death of the victim. And if you don't get a DNA match from the database we can do a three-dimensional facial reconstruction to give you an idea of what the victim looked like based on the size and shape of the skull.'

All that was helpful but it would also take time and Horton, like Uckfield, was impatient for a speedier result. 'What about cause of death?' he asked hopefully while preparing himself for disappointment. But Dr Clayton surprised him there.

She picked up the skull and swivelled it round. Horton found himself staring at a gaping hole. 'I don't think such extensive damage was done by it washing up against an underwater obstruction. Of course,' she added, replacing the skull on the slab, 'that might not have been the actual cause of death but it does indicate she was struck violently on the back of the head.'

'Could she have fallen?'

'Accidental death, you mean?'

Horton nodded.

'If she did accidentally strike her head against something on land, someone then pushed her body into the sea instead of calling for help. And if she accidentally fell into the sea and landed on that wreck then she would have struck her forehead not the back of her head. I can't be a hundred per cent certain, of course, it is possible she could have stumbled and slipped over the quay backwards, but the size and type of wound doesn't look consistent with that. It looks to me as though you've got yourself another homicide, Inspector.'

And that wouldn't please Uckfield or the ACC. He wasn't too happy about it himself, and the newspapers would go to town on it. He thanked Dr Clayton and headed for the station, mulling over what she had said. Was it linked with Salacia's death?

At the station, he called Uckfield on his mobile and relayed Dr Clayton's findings. As predicted they didn't improve the Super's mood. Horton had no idea what Sawyer's reaction was as the two men headed for Wales. Uckfield's phone was on speaker but Sawyer made no comment.

Horton rang off feeling irritated and frustrated and wondering where the hell they went next with this inquiry. He hoped that Uckfield might get something from Stapleton and that Eames, who was working away at one of the computer terminals in the incident suite, might dig up something on Foxbury that would throw a light into the dark corner of this investigation. They had a body and bones, both without an ID, and no idea why either woman had been killed or by whom, or even if they were connected. It couldn't get much worse. Or could it?

Trueman hailed him. Holding out the phone he said, 'It's Joliffe.'

Horton took the receiver expecting the worst. Joliffe's Scottish tones reverberated down the line. 'There are three letters engraved on the bracelet, Inspector. The initial E followed by the letter L then a gap and then the last letter, E.'

'How many letters altogether?' asked Horton. It wasn't much but it was better than nothing.

'Six at the most, probably five.'

'Anything else?'

'It's silver and it fits a small wrist.'

Horton thanked him and quickly relayed the information to Trueman, adding, 'OK, a girl's name beginning with EL, five letters, ending in E, any ideas?' Horton thought of Cantelli's daughter Ellen but that didn't end with E.

Trueman quickly logged on to the Internet and a web site of girls' names. 'Could be Elaine.'

'Any with five letters?'

'Elise. Ellie. No others but it could be a pet name, a surname or even a foreign name.'

'Let's hope not. Start with those three.'

Trueman called up the missing-persons database while Horton crossed to the crime board hardly daring to hope they might strike lucky. They needed something. His eyes caught Eames's as she glanced up. She gave him a brief smile but he saw nothing more than general friendliness in it. He told himself he was relieved. *Who was he kidding?*

He crossed to her. 'Anything?'

'Harry Foxbury was investigated by the tax office in 1998. No irregularities were discovered. He's got two spent convictions for driving offences; one for driving without due care and attention in 1995 and the other for speeding in 2004. He sold the boatyard for re-development to the council and a private investment firm four years ago for two million pounds.'

166

Very nice, thought Horton but before he could answer Trueman cried out.

'Andy, we've got a match.'

Horton spun round surprised. 'That was quick.'

'Came up almost immediately. Nothing under Elaine or Elise but there's an Ellie Loman from Portsmouth, reported missing July 2001.'

He didn't recall the name but in 2001 he'd been seconded to Basingstoke. He flashed Eames a glance. She said, 'According to Foxbury the second wreck was there but not the one on top of it where Salacia was found.'

Horton's pulse quickened. 'The timing sounds right. Go on,' he said eagerly to Trueman.

'Ellie Loman, aged twenty-one, auburn haired, five foot one inches, slim. Lived in Portsmouth with her parents. Hold on, there's more. I'll print off her picture while I access the file.'

It fitted with Dr Clayton's original findings. They had to be on the right track. With rising excitement he collected the photograph from the printer and studied the small oval face, the green eyes looking shyly into camera and the long shiny auburn hair. She'd certainly been an attractive young woman, feminine and delicate. He tried not to think of her as the collection of rotting bones on Dr Clayton's mortuary slab. There was still a chance that they weren't Ellie Loman's and the bracelet had been lost or discarded, but Horton knew in his gut it was her. But was her death connected with Salacia's?

Trueman continued. 'Right, here we are.' Horton returned and stood hovering by Trueman's side, while Eames rose and moved close to him.

167

Reading from the screen Trueman said, 'Ellie Loman was last seen on Sunday 1 July 2001 or rather she was heard that morning by her father, Kenneth Loman. She called up to his bedroom to say goodbye at seven twenty-five. Loman knew the exact time because he looked at the clock, surprised that she was up and out of the house so early on a Sunday. He didn't become concerned about his daughter until later that night. He called us at twelve ten p.m. The call was logged but Loman was told she'd probably decided to stay with friends overnight and had forgotten to get in touch. She wasn't underage or vulnerable. There was no reason to call out the guards.'

'Did Loman know where his daughter had gone?' asked Horton.

'He assumed out with friends. Loman was told that if he didn't hear from her, or she didn't show, by the morning, to let us know. He called again on Monday at eight seventeen a.m. and a unit was despatched at ten fifteen.'

'Had she ever done anything like this before?'

'No. She had never been in any trouble and her parents claimed she always told them where she was going.'

'Not this time she didn't,' Horton said quietly, his brain whirling with possibilities.

Trueman followed his line of thought. 'Initially her disappearance was put down to a young woman simply leaving home, wanting a bit of fun or running off with a man.'

His words were like barbed wire in Horton's brain. It was what they said about Jennifer.

'And it might have stayed that way but according

to this, or rather reading between the lines, it seems her father insisted her disappearance be fully investigated and he took it to the Assistant Chief Constable. They were probably in the same Lodge.'

And Jennifer had had no such influential connections, or if she did have then they certainly didn't create a fuss. Perhaps because they wanted it kept quiet.

Trueman gave a soft whistle. 'The ACC passed it down to CID. The investigating officer was Dean, who was then the Detective Chief Superintendent in charge of CID. He and Mike Danby, who was the DI, worked on the case.'

Danby, who now ran a private security company protecting the rich and famous. Jennifer Horton got a PC while Ellie Loman had the full weight of the CID. 'Do you remember the case?' he asked Trueman, pushing aside his bitterness.

'No. I was working in Gosport CID then.'

Twelve miles' drive around the harbour and four miles if crossing by ferry. And even if Cantelli were here Horton didn't think he'd be able to help because if his memory served him correctly Cantelli had been working in Vice.

Trueman continued reading from the computer screen. 'Kenneth Loman said he was recovering from a hangover and stayed in all that day. His drinking chums verified that he'd drunk heavily the night before.'

Eames said, 'I'm surprised he remembers her calling out goodbye to him, and the time.'

'He's still living at the same address.' Trueman looked up. His expression rarely registered emotion but Horton could see the glint of triumph in the sergeant's dark eyes. 'There's a connection between Ellie Loman and Salacia.'

Yes! This was it at last, the breakthrough. He sensed Eames's excitement beside him.

'The main suspect in the disappearance and possible murder of Ellie Loman was the man she was believed to have been meeting that day: Rawly Willard.'

And there was only one Rawly Willard that Horton had come across recently, or rather heard of. He swiftly recalled what Patricia Harlow had told him; with disappointment he said, 'If he's the late Amelia Willard's son then he can't be Salacia's killer because he's dead. According to Patricia Harlow he died in 2002.' But he had seen a flicker of something register on Gregory Harlow's face when Eames had shown him the photograph of Salacia.

'Check that Rawly Willard really is dead and how he died. And get everything on the Ellie Loman case,' Horton commanded, picking up the phone. 'Eames, you help Trueman.' Horton punched in Uckfield's number.

He quickly relayed the news to Uckfield, who confirmed he didn't remember the case. He'd been working in the rape unit then. Horton said, 'This means Salacia could have been at the crematorium for Amelia Willard's funeral and not Woodley's.'

'But that doesn't explain why Woodley had her photograph.'

It didn't explain a great many things but Horton didn't say that. Woodley and Reggie Thomas

170

were both in prison in 2001 and so were Stapleton and Victor Riley.

Uckfield said, 'I'll call Dean and see what he remembers from the case.' And Horton wondered if he heard a smug note in Uckfield's voice at the thought that Dean might have cocked up, and that he might solve a case that Dean had failed to. But it was early days yet.

Horton said, 'I'd like to re-interview Gregory Harlow. I'll also talk to the Lomans.' It wasn't a job he relished but he was eager to learn as much as he could about their daughter, and probe the link between her death, Rawly Willard and his cousins Patricia and Gregory Harlow.

He tossed up whether to take Eames with him and because he wanted to and for the wrong reasons he decided to leave her assisting Trueman. He didn't stay long enough to see whether or not she was disappointed. He doubted it. He asked Trueman to request a unit to meet him outside the Lomans' house. He knew that it was going to be harrowing for the Lomans but better to know what had happened to your daughter than live in limbo for even more years than they had already, imagining, hoping, praying and speculating, trying to put it to the back of their mind and get on with their life while it ate away at them, turning them sour, bitter, disappointed, angry and bewildered. Or was he thinking of himself?

He pulled up outside the stone bay and forecourt terraced house, noting that it was only a few streets away from where Patricia Harlow lived. He hoped the Lomans were at home. There was

171

a car outside but that didn't necessarily belong to them.

The police car drew up behind it. PC Kate Somerfield climbed out.

'Has Sergeant Trueman briefed you?' he asked.

'Yes.'

He could see that she was mentally preparing herself for what lay ahead. Having been the bearer of bad news several times she knew the drill, although she, like him, could never predict the reaction. He knew that she was keen to get into CID. She was also slightly wary of him because she'd been one of many female officers who had actually believed that ridiculous rape charge before he'd been exonerated.

He caught sight of a woman in the downstairs window. Mrs Loman? Probably. He hoped she wasn't alone. No, there was a man with her. But that could be anyone, a friend, relative or new husband, though Trueman had said the Lomans still lived here, or rather Kenneth Loman did. He caught the man's eyes and watched his casual glance swivel to the uniformed Somerfield. Within a second Horton registered surprise, dread and finally a sadness that drained the blood from the man's face and seemed to suck the very life out of him. It stabbed at Horton's heart before he mentally pulled himself up. He saw that there was no need to tell Kenneth Loman why they were here. He already knew.

Thirteen

'You've found her,' Loman said in a voice so heavy with sorrow that it made Horton's heart ache. He felt Somerfield's tension beside him.

Gently he replied, 'We've found some remains that we believe might be Ellie's.'

'Remains? Yes, yes I see. It would be after all this time.'

But Horton knew Loman didn't see. How could he when the last mental image he had of his daughter was a living, laughing, feeling human being and a voice calling up a cheerful goodbye to her hungover dad? They were standing in the narrow passageway. Before Horton could reply a woman's voice rang out.

'Who is it, Ken?'

Loman drew in a breath and pulled his sagging body up with an effort. He gestured them into the small front room where a smartly dressed, extremely thin woman was sitting in the bay window with a table in front of her frowning over a large puzzle. She looked up and smiled as they entered.

'My wife, Marie,' Loman introduced. He was holding himself together but Horton could see the strain of it etched in every pore of his face and every muscle of his lean and slightly hunched body. How old was he? Fifties? Sixties? He looked more like eighty.

173

'This is Detective Inspector Horton and Police Constable Somerfield. They've come to talk to me about some robberies that have been happening near by.'

Somerfield looked confused. Horton didn't blame her, he was too. He swiftly took in the photographs of the Lomans' pretty daughter scattered around the room before his glance once again fell on Marie Loman.

'How awful,' she said. 'I hope you catch whoever is doing them.'

Hastily, Loman said, 'I'll take them into the kitchen for a coffee, would you like one, dear?' Loman's voice resounded with false jollity, and to Horton's ears of desperation, to both of which Marie Loman seemed oblivious. Loman was near breaking point. It wouldn't take much to push him over the edge.

'Please.'

Loman shuffled down the passage into a room at the rear of the house. 'You must excuse Marie,' he said once they were in the small modern kitchen. He made no attempt to put the kettle on. Horton thought he'd aged another five years in the last five minutes. 'Shortly after Ellie disappeared Marie contracted a rare inflammatory brain disease. It's left her memory disjointed. She can only remember faces, names and events from before Ellie disappeared, nothing since. She has an extremely short memory.'

Horton studied Loman as he tried to comprehend what that meant.

'You get used to it,' Loman said, but clearly he hadn't. 'If you go back into the room now she won't remember you or what you said. She's done that puzzle a million times but each time she comes back to it it's fresh to her.'

Horton couldn't even begin to imagine how exhausting life must be for Kenneth Loman. Marie Loman's condition meant she would always believe Ellie was alive and about to walk through the door meaning Kenneth Loman would not only have to bear his grief alone, but also relive it again and again and again. No wonder the man looked worn out. Who wouldn't? Horton didn't say he was sorry because there was no point. Being sorry didn't help Marie and Kenneth Loman.

He said, 'Shall we sit down?' Loman nodded and perched on the edge of a hard chair at the table. Horton took the seat opposite while Somerfield stood close by. 'We won't know for certain if the remains we've found are Ellie's until further tests are carried out but we have strong indications that it is your daughter. We also found this.' He placed on the table in front of Loman a photograph of the bracelet. 'It contains the letters E, L and E and was silver.'

Loman picked up the photograph. 'Ellie used to wear it every day. It was a Christmas present from us when she was . . .' He took a sharp breath which turned into a gulp and then a sob. Somerfield swiftly crossed to the sink and poured him a glass of water.

Horton waited while Loman buried his face in his hands and sobbed. It came from deep within his chest and wrenched at Horton's heart. Somerfield blinked rapidly and took several deep breaths before she placed the glass in front of Loman. Touching him lightly on the shoulder, she said, 'Drink this, sir. It will help.'

No it won't, thought Horton, with anger, nothing will ever help.

With a supreme effort Loman pulled himself together and took a gulp of water. He dashed a hand across his eyes, then rose and splashed his face with cold water before scrubbing it vigorously with a towel. It was as if he hoped to scrub away the pain, thought Horton.

'Where did you find Ellie?' Loman asked, returning to the table. He took the glass of water in his bony, trembling hands but he didn't drink.

'The old boatyard at Tipner.'

His head came up. 'My God! I used to take her there when she was young.'

So a favourite place then and somewhere perhaps *she* had suggested as a meeting place with her killer. Or her killer knew she was familiar with it and suggested it.

'How young?' asked Horton.

'When she was a little girl, right up to when she was about fifteen. I don't mean the old boatyard exactly but to the shore by the sailing club. I used to keep a small day boat on the trots there and we'd go out into the Solent, fishing. Ellie loved fishing.'

'What happened to your boat?'

'I sold it not long after Ellie disappeared. I didn't have the same enthusiasm for fishing any more.'

But he'd had the boat when Ellie had gone missing. Kenneth Loman had been questioned, but how extensively, wondered Horton, given that his buddy was the then Assistant Chief Constable? Had he seen his daughter return from being out with a man and in a fury had killed her? If he had though surely living with his wife's condition would have been enough to make him confess. Even prison might be better than the life he'd been living. Unless he saw it as his punishment, said the small voice inside Horton.

He said, 'Do you know Harry Foxbury, the boatyard owner?'

'I saw him once or twice and nodded a greeting, but that's all.'

And had Ellie been with her father then? Could Foxbury have tried it on with Ellie and ended up killing her when she threatened to tell some years later? He'd leave that line of questioning for later, when they had more information. 'Did Ellie mention any boyfriends or special friends? Was she close to anyone?'

'She didn't talk about anyone except the people she worked with in the visitor centre at the Historic Dockyard. There was one man though who was sweet on her, Rawly Willard. He was a tour guide there but he claimed he was out walking on the day Ellie disappeared. He had a bit of a crush on Ellie, she was a beautiful girl . . .' His voice faltered. Horton remained silent, letting him compose himself. After a few moments Loman continued. 'Ellie told two of her work colleagues on the Friday before she disappeared that she was seeing this Rawly Willard on Sunday but she never mentioned it to us, and when the police searched her room there was no mention of him or the meeting either. Ellie didn't keep a diary and there was nothing on her computer about him. The police questioned him but they couldn't get anything out of him, though you know that. He killed himself. They thought it might be guilt over . . . over Ellie, do you still think that, Inspector?' He looked hopeful.

Horton hadn't known about Willard's suicide though Trueman had probably discovered that by now. He resorted to his stock answer. 'It's too early to say. Anything you can tell us could be helpful. If you feel up to it.' Loman nodded. Horton continued. 'Did Ellie take anything with her when she left?'

'I was in bed. I didn't see. She just called out to me but Marie checked her things for the police and said that Ellie must have been wearing her dark blue trousers, a white crop top and a denim jacket, and she took two bikinis. One was white, the other striped blue and red and new. Ellie bought it on the Wednesday before she disappeared.'

And that suggested she was going somewhere she could sunbathe or swim.

'Did she take a towel?' Horton asked.

Loman looked bewildered by the question. 'I don't know.'

Horton wondered if that had been asked first time around. Judging by Loman's reaction it hadn't, but then perhaps Loman had forgotten that. He would check the file.

He said, 'Do you still have any of Ellie's belongings?'

'Her room is exactly as it was the day she

disappeared. It would have confused and upset Marie if I'd changed it. Besides I always hoped Ellie would come home, but as the years went by I knew it was unlikely. I thought she might have run off with someone that she thought we'd disapprove of although she never hinted at being involved with anyone.' Loman ran a hand through his thin grey hair. His eyes looked harrowed.

'Would you mind if we took a look around it?'

'I'll show you where it is.' He hauled himself up, his movements like that of a very old man. Horton's heart went out to him as they followed him up the stairs to a large room at the front of the house overlooking the street and similar houses opposite.

Loman surveyed the room as though, Horton thought, he was memorizing it for the last time. 'Ellie was very tidy. She was no trouble, not as a baby or a teenager, a lovely girl. I'm sorry.'

They let him go. Some moments later they heard him being sick in the bathroom. Somerfield made to go to him but Horton prevented her. 'Leave him.'

'Poor man.'

Horton agreed and he'd very much like to catch the bastard who had put him through such heartache. Briskly he said, 'I'll take the books; you look through her clothes and jewellery.'

The bedroom was tidy and spotlessly clean. It was decorated in pale lemon with several photographs scattered about the surfaces: on the old-fashioned mantelpiece above an empty grate, on the dressing table and chest of drawers and some on the bookshelves. They were of Ellie as a child

179

with her parents, as a young woman and with girl friends. Perhaps the two friends she had worked with in the Historic Dockyard. And there were some of her with her father fishing, on his boat. Horton picked up the coloured frame on the bookshelf and stared at a small fishing boat with a cuddy. He couldn't see the name of the boat but he'd get that from Loman before they left and the details of whom he'd sold it to and when. Horton didn't think it would be relevant to the inquiry, or that Loman had killed his daughter, but it was best to check.

He replaced the photograph and scanned the spines of the books. Ellie's taste had been for romance novels and clearly she'd been a great fan of Mills & Boon. There were stacks of the thin paperbacks, which were well thumbed. He picked a few at random and fanned them, hoping but not expecting to find a note. A thorough search would have been made first time round. He wondered if someone had led her on romantically with the purpose of killing her. He thought of their other victim, Salacia, and what the two women might have had in common. He didn't see Salacia as a reader of this kind of material, though there was no reason why she shouldn't have been. He checked for inscriptions on the inside pages but there was nothing.

After a moment, Somerfield said, 'Her clothes are fashionable for 2001; chain-store stuff: skirts and dresses, a couple of pairs of trousers and jeans. Her jewellery is cheap. No sign of birth pills or condoms.'

Was that mentioned in the case file? It was a

good point and Somerfield had done well to think of it. He said as much. She looked pleased at the praise. He'd check with Trueman.

As Horton had expected their search yielded nothing, but it gave him more of a feel of who Ellie Loman had been. They found her father waiting for them in the kitchen with a blank expression on his haggard face. He tried to pull himself up when they entered but it was too much of an effort so he stayed seated.

Horton again sat opposite him. He'd leave him be in a moment. He said, 'Can you remember exactly what your daughter said when she called up that morning?'

'I've been over it again and again trying to see if there was anything in her words that could help find her but there wasn't she just said, "I'm off now, Dad. Not sure when I'll be home but don't wait up for me." '

'So she expected to be out all day and into the night.'

'I don't know. I've thought since that she might have said it jokingly. But it was why I didn't call the police until it was just after midnight. She wouldn't stay out that late without telling us. Oh, I know she was a woman and not a teenager, she didn't have to clock in, but she never liked us to worry. Ellie was very considerate. She wasn't one for night clubs. She went to a couple of parties when she was a teenager, friends from school and then college, but she wasn't interested once she started work.'

'Did she go to work in the Historic Dockyard straight from college?'

'Yes. She loved the job. Marie and I were surprised, because Ellie was quite shy and there she was dealing with the public. She did a course in tourism at college and she loved helping people. She liked history so the dockyard appealed to her. She started working there when she was nineteen.'

'Did she have a weekend job while at college?' He wondered if she could have met somewhere she'd known from there.

'No.'

'How did she sound that last day?'

'Bright, cheerful. She had a laugh in her voice.' Loman faltered. He swallowed hard before continuing. 'She was always like that, though, she was rarely down.'

'What used to get her down?'

'Someone being cruel.'

'To her?'

'No, to anyone, people, animals. If she read about it or heard it on the news she'd get upset. She couldn't believe that people could be like that. She always saw the good in people. I guess that must have been her downfall.' A spark of anger lit his tormented eyes. 'Some bastard spun her a yarn and she fell for it. Perhaps this Willard pestered her so much and when she finally said no he killed her and then hanged himself because he couldn't live with what he'd done. May he rot in hell if there is one, which I doubt.'

There was a moment's silence before Horton said, 'Do you know if Ellie was on the Pill, or took any other contraceptive measures?'

'I've no idea and I'd rather you didn't ask

Marie. It might upset her. She won't understand why you want to know.'

'That's fine but if you could give us permission to access her medical records that would help.'

'You have it. Do whatever you need to if it will help to catch the bastard who killed her. Do you know how she was killed?'

'We're still waiting test results, but from the initial examination it looks as though it was a blow to the head. There is a possibility that it was an accident and she fell into the sea but we're treating her death as suspicious until we have evidence to say otherwise.'

Loman nodded.

'We'll also need to take a DNA sample from you.' Horton guessed there might be one on file taken at the time of Ellie's disappearance from something belonging to her but he'd get Somerfield to take one from Loman before she left. It might save time. 'We'll be able to confirm if the remains are Ellie's by matching the DNA against yours. Just a few more questions, Mr Loman. What was her mood like before that Sunday?'

'Same as usual,' Loman answered wearily.

'Exactly the same,' pressed Horton. He didn't want Loman to fabricate something but to really consider if there had been any change in his daughter.

Loman's face creased with thought as he tried to remember. 'She just seemed very happy. She was out quite a lot I remember the couple of weeks before she . . . before then.'

'In the evenings?'

'Yes, but not very late. She came home from

work later than normal, about nine o'clock or thereabouts. She said she'd been for a drink and a meal with friends, but she didn't say who.'

And had anyone confirmed that, wondered Horton. 'What about the weekends?'

'When she wasn't working she went shopping, spent time in her room, nothing different.'

Loman looked in danger of collapse.

Horton wasn't sure how Loman was going to take the next question but he had to ask it. 'Can you give us the date when you sold your boat and the buyer's contact details?'

But Loman was prevented from answering by the appearance of his wife in the doorway. 'Oh, we've got company. Why are the police here, dear?'

'We're just going,' Horton said hastily, forcing a smile. He felt like a heel running away.

Loman pulled himself together with a quick glance at his wife he said, 'I'll just show Inspector Horton out.' He left his wife to PC Somerfield.

At the door Horton said, 'Would you like Somerfield to stay with you for a while? She can call someone to help you. Your doctor perhaps?'

'No. I'd rather you use all the resources you have to make sure that it is Ellie you've found and to discover why she died and who killed her.'

'We'll allocate a police liaison officer to keep you fully informed, Mr Loman, and to help protect you from the press. Sooner or later they'll get on to it, I'm afraid. Meanwhile if you could give Somerfield the details about your boat that would be helpful.'

Loman didn't ask why he wanted it. Horton

quickly pressed on, 'If there is anything you recall, anything that was different about Ellie or her movements before that Sunday, call me, any time.'

Loman took Horton's card. 'Don't you think I've been doing that every minute of every day for all these years?'

Yes, he knew. For years he'd pushed all thoughts of his mother's disappearance to the back of his mind, but in the last eleven months he'd been trying to recall her mood, movements and visitors before that November day when she disappeared. It never went away. Suddenly a distant and vague memory, like an out of focus image, played at the ragged edges of his mind. He tried to identify it but couldn't.

Irritated he pushed it away, called Trueman and relayed the gist of the interview with Loman. 'Find out if anyone asked her doctor at the time if she was taking any form of contraceptive. Loman's given his consent for us to access his daughter's medical records. I'd also like to know if anyone asked the Lomans if Ellie took a towel with her that Sunday. Two bikinis and no towel suggests she was going somewhere where they were supplied and not to the beach or a swimming pool, at least not a public one. She might have been going to a private house with a pool or out on a boat for the day, which could have returned to Foxbury's yard. There could have been a violent quarrel and the boat owner killed her and threw her body in the sea. Or perhaps someone was waiting for her return on the quayside or he saw her unexpectedly, they quarrelled and he killed her, or she slipped and struck her head and he pushed her body into the sea. Whoever she was going out with though she kept secret from her parents, which means they wouldn't have approved of him.'

'Probably married.'

'We'll need to check the members at the sailing club in 2001. Get the list from Richard Bolton. Ask Eames to get the names of any of Foxbury's employees for 2001, though I suspect they weren't on the official payroll. Foxbury told us he used to own a sailing yacht so see if she can find out if he had a boat in 2001 and what kind, also if he had a house with a swimming pool. Get Eames to re-interview him and to tell him about Ellie Loman. I'd like to know his reaction. Somerfield is getting details of the boat owned by Kenneth Loman at the time of his daughter's disappearance. I don't think he killed his daughter but find out just how thoroughly he was questioned. He could have discovered she'd gone out with one of his fishing chums, a work colleague or friend, a married man he disapproved of. Where did he work?'

'Ran his own business, a small engineering company.'

'Find out what happened to it. What have you got on Rawly Willard?'

'He claimed he was out walking on the day Ellie disappeared, on the coastal path around Chichester Harbour. He didn't own a car so he caught the train to Chichester and walked along the canal path to the marina and on to Itchenor, but he didn't have a train ticket to verify that and

186

nobody at Portsmouth Station where he caught the train remembered seeing him. His clothes, including those he was wearing that day, were sent to forensic but there was nothing found on them to connect him to Ellie Loman. His room was also searched. He lived with his parents, Amelia and Edgar Willard, in Southsea. He was questioned twice but stuck to his story. He committed suicide on 6 January 2002. His body was found hanging from a tree in Stansted Forest.'

'That probably explains Patricia Harlow's hostility towards us.' Horton recalled her frosty manner.

'But not why she and her husband didn't tell you about Ellie Loman.'

'Why should they? We weren't investigating that and neither of them could have known where Ellie's body was.'

'Unless they were involved in her death.'

'And we've nothing to say they were, or have we?'

'No.'

'And the only connection between them is the appearance of Salacia at the crematorium the same time as their aunt's funeral.' And that tiny reaction from Gregory Harlow, he thought. He consulted his watch. With a bit of luck he might make the twelve thirty sailing. 'I'm going over to the Island to question Harlow. Apply for a search warrant for the late Amelia Willard's house; I don't think Patricia Harlow will let us in without one. It's probably too late to find anything that links back to Rawly Willard and Ellie Loman but you never know. And see if you can trace any of Ellie's former work colleagues.'

He rang off and made his way to the Isle of Wight ferry, keen to see what Gregory Harlow's reaction would be to the news they'd found Ellie Loman.

Fourteen

'He's not here. I haven't seen him since last night,' Ross Skelton, Harlow's boss, bellowed above the music. The festival was in full swing. The noise was giving Horton a headache, which made him feel old. Maybe he was getting old, or perhaps it was lack of sleep and too much thinking and he'd done a considerable amount of the latter on the ferry crossing without getting any further forward with the case. Now he was annoyed to discover that Harlow was missing, something he hadn't expected, and Skelton was clearly livid. 'He's left me short-handed which is why I'm here, sorting out his mess, and not where I should be, which is running my business. It's a bloody nightmare. I've got contracts to fulfil. If he shows up now he's fired.'

They were in the small tented area at the back of the main Coastline Cool tent, which was packed. In addition to the music coming from a stage in one of the fields soul music was booming in Horton's ears from the tent.

'Is his van here?' bellowed Horton.

'No, and he's not answering his phone either,' roared Skelton.

'When did you last see him?'

'When he was talking to you and that good-looking copper. But my staff say he was here last night until about ten thirty and then he disappeared just when it started getting busy. No one's seen him since, including my staff at my three coffee stalls here.'

Did Patricia Harlow know that her husband wasn't where he was supposed to be?

Skelton continued, 'I've been to Harlow's caravan, he sleeps, eats and shits on site at a big gig like this, but the bastard isn't there and he doesn't look as though he slept there last night either, which Haseen confirms.'

'Haseen?'

'His caravan-mate, assistant event-catering manager.'

Several thoughts were running through Horton's mind. Had Harlow killed Salacia? Had he taken fright after their questioning and gone on the run? Did he know that Ellie Loman's remains were at the boatyard and think it only a matter of time before they discovered them? But how did that fit with Woodley having a photograph of Salacia in his cell? Then an idea occurred to him. There was a way.

He shouted, 'Does your company have any dealings with the prison here?'

'What's that got to do with Greg?' Skelton yelled back, surprised. Horton said nothing, forcing Skelton to add, 'Yeah, we deal with the prison. We deliver catering supplies to them. I've got three divisions: Coastline Coffee Stalls, Coastline Outside Catering and Coastline Catering Supplies.'

'And has Gregory Harlow delivered to the prison?'

'He was working on the supplies side of the business until I promoted him to event-catering manager nine months ago, wish I bloody hadn't now.'

This was sounding more promising by the minute. 'How long has he worked for you?'

'Ten years. And he's been a damn good employee, until now.'

Until they were getting close to the truth about what happened on the first of July 2001. 'I'd like to talk to Haseen.'

'He's working.'

'It's important.'

Skelton rolled his eyes and threw up his hands. 'Might as well lose more money. I'll fetch him.'

Horton followed Skelton into the crowded, overheated and noisy main tent and surveyed the scantily clad women in flimsy summer dresses or shorts that barely covered their arses and tops that certainly didn't cover all of their tits. The men of all ages were just as meagrely clothed, most wearing shorts and without shirts. The tent was dimly lit and stank of sweat, perfume and beer. Skelton's staff were behind a long counter serving drinks, mainly alcoholic judging by the mood in the tent, although Horton did see some of the occupants, squatting on the floor, which had been covered with imported sand, with soft drinks. He saw Skelton shouting something in

190

the ear of a dusky-skinned good-looking man in his mid-twenties before his eyes fell on a muscular bulky man on the far side; DI Dennings, looking every inch the cop rather than a security officer, he thought. He didn't acknowledge Dennings and vice versa, but Dennings had seen him all right.

His phone rang. Seeing it was Trueman, Horton stepped back into the small tent and through it to the outside but it made little difference to the noise level. Answering it he put a finger in his other ear. 'You'll have to speak up,' he bawled above the music.

'Ellie Loman's medical file has been archived but we should have access to it tomorrow. Her GP can't remember if Ellie was on the Pill and I can't find the question having been asked during the original investigation or the fact noted that she didn't take a towel with her. We should also have access to Rawly Willard's health records tomorrow and Loman sold his business a year after his daughter disappeared.'

Horton quickly told Trueman that Harlow was missing and that he was following it up along with a possible connection with the prison. Seeing Haseen approaching, Horton hollered down his phone, 'I'll call you back.'

'You wanted to see me?' Haseen shouted. His eyes were bloodshot and he looked as though he hadn't slept for a couple of days but there was nothing fatigued about his restless manner. Horton guessed that was caused by something entirely different to overwork.

Horton asked him when he last saw Gregory

Harlow. Any more conversations at this level he'd end up losing his voice as well as his patience.

'About ten o'clock last night. It was manic. I don't remember the exact time. He didn't sleep in the caravan.'

Something about the way Haseen said this alerted Horton. 'Did you?'

Haseen smiled and then shrugged. 'I thought Greg had probably got off with some tart, there's plenty to choose from.'

And that was obviously what Haseen had done. 'He was known to do that?'

'*Everyone* does that here, even the hired help like me.' He looked smug, and at the same time contemptuous. Horton didn't care for his arrogance but there was no law against that.

'What time did you get to the caravan last night or should I say this morning?'

Haseen grinned. Horton wanted to wipe it from his face.

'About eight o'clock. Would have been sooner but I couldn't get away from her. Nice little goer, off her head on something.'

And Horton wondered if it was 'something' that Haseen had given her.

'Did any of your work colleagues see Gregory Harlow after ten thirty last night?'

'You'll have to ask them but none of us left the tent; except for a pee. We were rushed off our feet.'

Horton told him he could go, located Ross Skelton and got the registration number of the van Harlow was driving. He said he'd notify

192

Skelton when they found Harlow and took his mobile number.

Weaving his way through the crowds he tried not to look like a cop but he felt conspicuous in his short-sleeved pale blue cotton shirt and chinos. He looked too neat, too clean and he felt too old even though there were many men older than him. He'd almost reached the backstage entrance when a black Range Rover pulled in. A voice hailed him with a hint of amusement. 'Are you here for the festival or have you changed your mind about that job I offered you?'

Mike Danby. Horton might have known he'd be here, given his clientele. He crossed to the car and shouted, 'If they chuck me out you'll be the first person I'll call.'

'Why would they do that?' Danby said surprised.

'I've got a DCI who thinks I'm the lousiest copper on the planet and she's itching to get shot of me.'

'I'm sure you can handle her.'

Horton sometimes wondered, especially if her new-found friend was ACC Dean as he was rumoured to be, although Horton wouldn't go so far as Uckfield's claim that they were having an affair. 'Are you handling the festival security?' Horton shouted.

'Only for the acts. I'm on my way to pick up Tammy Freiding. She's singing now,' he added to Horton's baffled look.

'Have you got a minute to talk?' asked Horton, though 'talk' was hardly the right word for a conversation conducted at this level. 'It won't take long.'

'Hop in, it's quieter and cooler.'

Gratefully, Horton climbed into the car. The air was decidedly chillier but the noise followed him.

Danby said, 'I'll drop you back to the entrance. It'll be a bit quieter there.'

Horton thought he'd have to take him midway to the Solent to escape this din, but the row lessened as one of the acts finished, and Horton swiftly told him they'd found human remains at the old Tipner boatyard which they believed were Ellie Loman's. Danby looked surprised and then sorrowful.

'After all this time, when was it? Hold on, July 2001. It was bloody hot like this. She went missing. Are her parents still alive?'

'Yes.' Horton didn't explain about Marie Loman, it would take too long and wasn't necessary. 'What do you remember about the case?'

'We initially believed that she'd run off with a man but her father insisted she hadn't. He called in the big guns and when we started asking questions we discovered that she had arranged to meet this guy.'

'Rawly Willard.'

'Yes, that's him, quiet sort of chap, fair, slight, intelligent, bit of a loner. Only he claimed he wasn't her boyfriend although he'd like to have been. He denied that he was meeting her that day, but she'd told her work colleagues he was. We couldn't break him and there was no forensic on him, in his house, or his car. But Dean will tell you all this. He was in charge of the case.'

'Did you check out Kenneth Loman?' Horton saw by Danby's surprised look that they hadn't.

'We had no reason to.'

'Or his boat?'

'Didn't know he had one.'

'A small one, he kept it on the moorings near the sailing club at Tipner.'

'Ah.' After a moment Danby added, 'We had no reason to suspect that she'd gone sailing with anyone, let alone her father. We didn't even know he went sailing.'

'Fishing.'

'So he could have been lying about her leaving the house alone. Took her out, killed and dumped her body.'

'It's one theory.' Danby hadn't mentioned the significance of the bikinis and no towel. Horton said, 'Anything unusual or different about the case stick out in your mind?'

'No. Except that there seemed no motive for her disappearance and we couldn't match it with the disappearance of any women about her age in the area or in the country. Her parents claimed they hadn't argued with her, and that she was a model daughter and her boss and work colleagues agreed that Ellie Loman was sweetness and light, not an evil thought or bone in her body. She was well liked by everyone.'

'Not everyone, it seems.'

'No.'

'Did you check her medical records?'

'Probably. I don't remember anything about her being on drugs or pregnant.'

He pulled up by the security office and silenced the engine. The music was still playing but it wasn't so ear-splitting. Horton said, 'We've got another death in the same location. A woman, about mid-forties. She was last seen alive at the crematorium at the time of Daryl Woodley's funeral. Do you remember him?'

'Vaguely. I read about his funeral in the local newspaper. Nice picture of you and Uckfield. Bet he loved that.'

'Not a lot. Woodley had a photograph of the victim in his cell. This is her. Do you recognize her?' Horton showed him the photograph of Salacia with fair hair.

Danby shook his head.

'This is what she looked like when last seen.' Horton handed across the picture taken at the funeral.

'No. Who is she?'

'That's what we're trying to establish. The funeral after Woodley's was of Amelia Willard, last surviving member of the Willard family. It was organized by her niece, Patricia Harlow, and her husband, Gregory.'

Danby's eyebrows went up. 'I see. But Woodley didn't come into the frame for Ellie Loman's disappearance, probably inside at the time.'

'He was.'

'So how does he figure in it now?'

'No idea, but I'm working on it. Do you remember interviewing Gregory and Patricia Harlow about their cousin's disappearance?'

'No. Should we have done?' Danby said surprised.

'Maybe. Gregory Harlow, who works for Coastline Catering, in their tent here, seems to have gone walkabout.'

'I didn't think you'd come all this way just to talk to me. So he could be involved in both deaths.'

'It's beginning to look that way. What do you remember about Harry Foxbury?'

'The boatyard owner. Fox by name and fox by nature. We suspected him of using the yard for smuggling at one time but couldn't catch him or prove it.'

That was interesting. 'When would this have been?'

Danby thought for a moment. 'It wasn't long before Ellie disappeared, 1999, no 2000. Let me know how it pans out and if you need any more help. I'm here all weekend.'

'In a tent?'

'Ha bloody ha. No, I'm staying at a place along the coast not far from Osborne Bay, it belongs to Richard Eames, or rather Lord Eames.'

'*Lord!* As in the House of Lords?' Horton cried, surprised. Could he possibly have any connection with Agent Eames from Europol? No, that was too fantastic, she must come from another branch of the Eames family, but she had been to a Swiss finishing school and she had mentioned that the family owned a place along the coast.

'That's the one. Why, do you know him?' Danby answered amused and surprised.

'Never heard of him.'

Danby eyed him disbelievingly and then smiled, amused. 'But you've heard he's got a daughter in the police. She works for Europol and she's a looker.'

That clinched it. No wonder she talked posh.

She'd not said that she knew Danby when his name had come up in connection with the Ellie Loman case. Did Uckfield know of her background? Was that why he hadn't made a pass at her?

Curious, Horton said, 'What do you do for his lordship?'

'Carry out security checks; act as personal bodyguard and supply security officers as and when he needs them.'

'For what?'

'Receptions, business trips abroad, his horses. He's got land dotted all over the world, and a nice little property in London.'

And Horton knew that Danby's 'little' meant the opposite, and was probably worth millions.

'I'm impressed by the exalted circles you move in.' Horton opened the car door.

'Drop by for a drink if you get the chance, though Richard won't be there. Or his daughter, more's the pity.

Did Danby know she was here, working with him? It appeared not but then Danby was adept at hiding his real thoughts. He said, 'Don't think I'll have time, but thanks anyway.'

He watched Danby's car glide away towards the back of one of the giant stages. Eames had said nothing about her family house being loaned to pop stars or Mike Danby for the duration of the festival. But then why should she? It had nothing to do with the investigation, but he recalled that slightly troubled look on her face when they'd been sailing into Fishbourne on the car ferry. Perhaps she'd had a falling-out with daddy, which could have been over her decision to become a cop. Lord Eames had probably had other ideas for his daughter. He recalled her quip about joining the police in order to find a husband, and her smile as she'd said it, knowing that she had used humour to disguise her true emotions and to deflect any further questions. It had worked. And it was none of his business. From now on she was definitely off-limits, which was a shame, but he couldn't see what he could possibly have in common with a girl like Eames, except the job. And he scrapped all ideas that Sawyer would use her to find out if and when someone from Zeus might make contact. He considered that too wide off the mark. And that brought him back to Edward Ballard. He'd heard nothing about Ballard's movements from Elkins yet.

He pushed thoughts of Eames and Ballard aside and asked security if anyone had seen Harlow's van leave. No one remembered it but the log showed it had been checked out at 22:35 the previous evening and it hadn't been checked in again. He found a uniformed police officer and showed his ID. He asked to speak to the officer in charge of the drugs operation. He couldn't request to speak to DS Olewbo from the Portsmouth drugs squad because he knew that Hans was undercover. He told the uniformed inspector that they might like to check out Skelton's staff in the Coastline Cool tent and in particular Haseen Nader. No, he had no intelligence; just something Nader had said when he was interviewing him in connection with another matter.

He called in, couldn't get hold of Trueman and got Marsden instead who said the diving operation at the quayside had finished with no sign of Salacia's handbag or a torch. The wreck that Ellie Loman's remains had been found on was being raised by Manley and his team, and the press had picked up on the story. He'd left PC Seaton in charge. Horton told Marsden to check with the Wightlink and Red Funnel ferries to see if Harlow had left the Island. Then he made for the prison.

Fifteen

Geoff Kirby was surprised to see him back so soon and was clearly a little irritated, if his expression was anything to go by. But after Horton had explained about the discovery of the human remains and the fact that Harlow seemed to have gone missing, he relaxed slightly and called up the computer files. Fifty minutes later Horton was heading back to Portsmouth on the ferry with some of the information he needed. It wasn't conclusive but there was a link, as he explained to Trueman on the phone.

'Coastline Catering Supplies deliver fish and frozen food to the prison. They have a branch on the Island and another in Portsmouth. Although Gregory Harlow used to deliver from the Portsmouth office, I called Skelton and he says that Harlow did occasionally work for the Island branch when they were short staffed. Kirby is sending over a list of all the delivery drivers for the period three months before the attack on Stapleton. It's possible either Gregory Harlow or one of his work colleagues, under Harlow's instructions, got that photograph of Salacia to an inmate who then made sure it got to Woodley. But I'm not sure how Stapleton fits in with the Harlows and Ellie Loman.'

'There's no record of Harlow's van having been booked on any of the car ferries.'

That didn't mean that Harlow hadn't crossed to the mainland, he could have abandoned the van close to the ferry terminals, or elsewhere on the Island, and returned as a foot passenger. But where would he have gone after that? Horton asked Trueman to put out a call for Harlow and his van both on the Island and the mainland.

'Has the search warrant come through for Amelia Willard's house?'

'Yes. It's a different address to the one on the Ellie Loman case file. Amelia Willard moved to the new address in 2004, two years after Rawly died and a year after her husband's death.'

'Which means there's probably nothing left of her son's belongings.'

'And if there had been then the Harlows could already have cleared it out following their aunt's death.'

'Apply for a search warrant for the Harlows' house, Dave,' Horton instructed. He didn't expect any revelations but they needed to be certain, especially in the light of Harlow's vanishing act. 'I'll go straight to Amelia Willard's house.'

Trueman relayed the address. Horton said, 'Has Eames returned from her interview with Foxbury?'

'On her way back now.'

'Ask her to collect Patricia Harlow and take her to Amelia Willard's house, but to say nothing about Gregory Harlow being missing. I'll meet them and a unit outside in an hour.'

Horton grabbed some food and had just taken a bite into his sandwich when Elkins rang.

'Edward Ballard's making for Guernsey,' Elkins reported.

Not France then as he'd said. But a man had the right to change his mind.

'I've asked the Port to alert me when he arrives. His boat's not registered at any of the marinas there. I've checked.'

That was good thinking and Horton said so. 'Any joy with Horsea Marina?'

'Yes. Ballard arrived there on Monday and paid cash for two nights' berthing. He left late on Wednesday evening.'

Which coincided with his arrival at Southsea Marina.

Elkins continued. 'The lock master says he doesn't remember *Lazy Days* going out of the marina during that time but it is possible that a small dinghy or RIB could easily have slipped in and out alongside or behind a larger boat in the dark.'

And the same could be said for Foxbury's tender, which Horton had seen on his motor cruiser. But Gregory Harlow's disappearance made it look increasingly unlikely that either Foxbury or Ballard were involved in Salacia's death.

202

He rang off after asking Elkins to notify him when Ballard reached Guernsey. He spent the remainder of the ferry crossing speculating on the reaction he'd get from the abrasive Patricia Harlow. Did she know her husband had gone walkabout? Maybe? Did she know why? Had she lied about not knowing Salacia? It seemed that her husband had, and if Salacia hadn't been at the crematorium for Woodley's funeral then perhaps she had been there to see Gregory Harlow. Could Harlow have been the man Ellie Loman had spent her last day with and Salacia, whoever she was, had discovered this and had threatened to tell? But why wait all these years? Had she only just found out? If so how? Had Harlow confessed it to her in a post-coital daze after drinking wine and eating lobster, then realizing what he'd done he'd killed her?

As Trueman had said they'd get little, if anything, from the search of Amelia Willard's house but it would be interesting to see Patricia Harlow's reaction when he told her about Ellie Loman. According to Danby this would be the first time she'd been questioned about her.

When he arrived outside the house, not far from Southsea Common, some thirty minutes later, he was surprised to find it much smaller and shabbier than he'd expected. The tiny terraced house fronted straight onto the pavement in a road of similar houses sporting satellite dishes on the front elevation on one side of the road and wheelie bins on both. A patrol unit was parked outside number fourteen and Eames was waiting for him in her hired car with a cross-looking Patricia Harlow.

203

'I've got better things to do than watch you tear my aunt's house to pieces,' Patricia Harlow snapped, as she unlocked the door and they entered the musty smelling narrow passageway. Horton nodded at the two uniformed officers to begin their search. 'I've had to cancel several appointments,' she continued. 'This is most inconvenient for me and my clients. I shall be making a formal complaint to your Chief Constable regarding this harassment over the death of a woman I know nothing about. And I shall demand financial compensation for loss of earnings.'

'Of course,' Eames answered politely but wearily. By her tone, Horton guessed she'd already heard this several times on the journey here. With a slight nod he gestured Eames towards the rear of the house and remained in the hall with Patricia Harlow. From the glimpse into the small front room Horton didn't think there was much to 'tear to pieces'. She'd said nothing about her husband being missing, so Horton surmised Ross Skelton hadn't called her to ask her if she'd seen him, probably too busy at the Festival.

'I don't know what you expect to find,' Patricia Harlow added, her expression stern as the sound of drawers opening came from upstairs.

Nothing significant clearly, Horton thought. 'Shall we go into the kitchen.' It wasn't a question but a command. He stood back and gestured her forward. After a moment she marched towards it, annoyance in every short step.

It was larger than the Lomans' kitchen but not much. It was also dated, with cupboards in a shiny sickly grey and a worn dark grey Formica worktop. Eames, who had been searching it, gave a slight shake of her head. She'd left the cupboards open and Horton could see they were empty. There was also a gap where the fridge must have been and another where a washing machine had once stood. It was spotlessly clean, though. Through the window, devoid of curtains or blinds, Horton could see a small concrete-covered yard with a rotary washing line, and beyond that a high wall, which backed on to the houses in the next street.

'Let's sit down.' He waited for Patricia Harlow to sit, which she did primly on the edge of one of three wooden chairs at a small table pushed up against the wall, before sitting himself. Eames took up position next to him and opposite Patricia Harlow, who sat tight-lipped and frowning.

Eames removed her notebook from her jacket pocket. Danby's words flashed through Horton's head. This tiny kitchen in this tiny house was probably smaller than one of Eames's daddy's horse boxes. The sound of PC Allen searching the front room brought his thoughts back to the job in hand. He could hear Johnson clomping about upstairs. Despite the heat outside the house was cold.

'Tell me about your aunt?' Horton began.

'There's nothing to tell. I don't know why you're here. She was old and ill and she died.'

'Of cancer you said, what kind?'

'Is that relevant?' she replied tartly.

'Anything could be in a murder inquiry.'

'Murder? Oh, you mean that woman at the

crematorium. You must be mad if you think my aunt—'

'Another body's been found. We believe it to be that of Ellie Loman.'

Clearly that was a surprise. For a moment she was speechless then her eyes widened as she made the connection and scornfully she said, 'So that's what this is all about, you're still persecuting Rawly after all these years, even though the poor man is dead, driven to his death, may I add, by the police harassing him. He never met her. He never saw her the day she disappeared and he never dated her. And if you think there's anything left of my aunt's belongings that will incriminate him then you are completely insane, not to mention the fact that you are wasting taxpayers' money, and my time.'

Evenly Horton said, 'Is that what he told you, that he had never dated her?'

'He worked with her, he liked her, but he never asked her out.'

Eames looked up. 'Why not?'

Patricia Harlow eyed Eames with something that bordered on contempt. Unaffected by it, Eames added, 'Ellie Loman was an attractive young woman.'

'That doesn't mean Rawly went out with her.'

'But he'd like to have done,' insisted Horton.

Patricia Harlow's eyes swivelled to Horton. 'Rawly was a quiet man, sensitive. He didn't have a great deal of confidence or experience when it came to women.'

And did that mean that when he finally plucked up the courage to ask her out he'd been rejected

206

and hurt enough to kill her? Or perhaps he'd seen her with another man and in a jealous rage had killed her and pushed her body in the sea? But there had been no evidence to corroborate that. Could he have obliterated it so completely? And whatever the circumstances, Rawly Willard certainly hadn't killed Salacia.

'Your aunt's cancer? What kind was it? We can find out from her medical records but it would be quicker if you told us.'

'I don't see why you want to know.'

'And I don't see why you are being so evasive,' retorted Horton, sharply. He knew it wasn't relevant to the inquiry but he wasn't going to let her get away without answering. And her carping was beginning to get on his nerves.

'Rectal cancer,' she grouchily replied.

'Thank you.'

'There's no need—'

'Did you know Ellie Loman?'

'No.'

It was said too quickly and her eye contact was evasive. 'Let me rephrase the question, Mrs Harlow. Did you ever meet Ellie Loman?'

'No.'

Another lie.

'Did your husband?'

'No.'

Horton left a few seconds silence before saying, 'What were your aunt and uncle like?' She looked disconcerted by the sudden change of conversation, as Horton had intended.

'They were decent law-abiding people. My uncle was a very principled man.'

'Harsh?' asked Eames.

'No. Fair. Upright. He tended to see things in black and white. He worked for the Inland Revenue, rose to be a senior officer there. He was clever with money. He had investments.' Her voice trailed off. Horton sensed a 'but'.

'He played the stock market?'

'No. But he made one or two unsound investments and lost some money that he was hoping would see him and my aunt through their retirement. When Rawly killed himself my uncle went downhill rapidly. He died within a year. My aunt got the life insurance and half his pension but it wasn't much and the house was too big and had too many unhappy memories for her. She lived in one of those large rambling Edwardian houses off the seafront. She sold up and moved here a year after Uncle Edgar died.'

Horton said, 'And now you inherit.'

Patricia Harlow eyed him with something akin to loathing. 'Yes, though that's none of your business.'

PC Johnson flushed the upstairs toilet. He was probably searching under the bath. Horton heard PC Allen climb the stairs. That meant he'd found nothing in the two rooms downstairs or in the cupboard under the stairs. Horton leaned back in his chair and kept his eyes on the stiff-backed woman beside him. 'Where were you and your husband the day Ellie Loman disappeared?' Horton noted that her hands, clasped together on the table, tightened.

'I don't remember.'

'The day your cousin was accused of murder!'

Horton scoffed. 'I'd have thought it would be imprinted on your mind. But let me remind you. It was Sunday 1 July 2001.'

'Then I was at Mass in the morning.'

'And in the afternoon?' pressed Horton, knowing there was something she was uncomfortable about telling him.

She shifted position. One hand reached for a tissue from the pocket of her jacket. 'I went to my aunt's for tea.'

'With your husband?'

'No.'

'Did your husband go to church with you?'

'He's not a Catholic.'

'So where was your husband, Mrs Harlow?'

'I don't see why you should be asking now. No one was interested before.'

Horton said nothing.

After a moment she said, 'If you really must know, he went fishing.'

'On a boat?' Horton asked sharply.

'Where else would you go fishing?' she sneered.

From the beach, on a river, beside a lake. But he didn't say. 'On his *own* boat?'

'Yes. We had a small day boat then.'

'Then?'

'Greg sold it a few years ago.'

Had he, though? 'When exactly?'

'I don't know. You'll have to ask him.'

I will when I find him. 'The name?'

'*Tide's Out.*'

'Did he go fishing alone on that day?'

'I think so. I don't know. Why all this interest?'

'Where did he keep the boat?'

209

'On a mooring in Portsmouth Harbour,' she said with a note of exasperation.

This was getting even more interesting. So Gregory Harlow must have been familiar with Foxbury's boatyard, and he had no alibi for the day of Ellie's death. Horton knew that his expression gave nothing away but Eames had caught on and even though she showed no emotion he could sense her excitement.

He said, 'If it was on a mooring in the harbour your husband would have rowed out to it.' And perhaps he had done that from the slipway at the Tipner Sailing Club. His phone vibrated in his pocket. He ignored it.

'I suppose so.' But her exasperation was tainted with an air of unease.

'From where?'

'I don't know.'

'Oh, come on, you never asked him or went with him?'

'I certainly never went with him and what he did with his boat was his business. I wasn't interested in it.'

Unfortunately that had a ring of truth about it.

Eames said, 'What time did your husband return home that day?'

'I can't remember.'

But Horton wasn't going to let her get away with that. 'Let me rephrase my colleague's question, how long was it after you returned from your aunt's that your husband came home?'

'A couple of hours,' she shrugged, but avoided looking at him.

'And that was when?' persisted Horton.

She looked annoyed she fallen into the trap. 'I left my aunt's at six, Gregory got home around about eight. I can't see why you want to know all this. We had nothing to do with that girl's disappearance. We didn't even know her.'

But she was edgy. 'Was your uncle at home that day?'

'No. He was playing golf on Hayling Island.'

Horton wondered if there was any way of corroborating that after all these years. He doubted it. 'Did he return home while you were with your aunt?'

'No. And before you ask I don't know what time he came in. That surely must be in your files.'

Horton would ask Trueman. 'Did Rawly return while you were with your aunt?'

'No.'

'So he still wasn't back when you left at six?'

'I've just said, haven't I?'

'Who arranged your aunt's funeral?'

She looked surprised at the question. 'I did, obviously.'

'Why did you choose that date and time?'

'It was the only one available,' she said with irritation. Horton raised his eyebrows in surprise, forcing her to add, 'And convenient. With Gregory at the Isle of Wight Festival it had to be then. His boss wasn't very pleased when he asked for the time off.'

'And neither of you asked this woman to your aunt's funeral?' He pushed the photograph of Salacia at her.

She didn't look at it. 'I've already told you, no.'

And the other mourners had confirmed they didn't know her.

'Did you know that Daryl Woodley's funeral was being held just before your aunt's?'

She rolled her eyes. 'How should I have known that? I've no idea who he is. I've never seen him before or heard of him.'

Horton rose. She looked surprised then relieved. But if she thought she was off the hook she was mistaken. 'Shall we go into the front room?' PC Allen entered with a slight shake of his head. With a silent command Horton indicated for him to check outside.

With an explosive sigh of exasperation Patricia Harlow marched out of the kitchen. In the shabby front room she crossed to the window and stood frowning at the police car parked beyond the net curtains. Horton quickly checked his phone and saw the call had been from Sergeant Elkins.

'I wish you hadn't been so obvious. It's most embarrassing,' she said.

'Is this your aunt and uncle?' Horton asked, putting his phone back in his pocket and indicating the faded wedding photograph on the mantelpiece. It, along with a handful of cheap ornaments and a sofa and chair, was all that was left in the room.

She spun round and nodded curtly. Horton studied the young couple in their twenties. She was small with a jolly, pretty little face and looked a bit like a sparrow, while he was tall and slim with a slightly superior expression on his lean face. Losing his money and their son's death must have hit them hard. He thought of the Lomans:

212

a sad thin woman living in a world that didn't really exist and her husband barely alive in one that did.

'Did your aunt ever talk about her son's death?' he asked, putting the photograph back and staring around the faded, chilly room with its worn carpet.

'No. It was too painful for her.'

Horton hadn't read the suicide note but it would be on the case file, if there was one. PC Johnson appeared in the doorway. Horton excused himself and slipped out into the hall. Allen was with him.

'There are only a few bits of furniture left upstairs,' Johnson relayed. 'Everything's been cleared out. There's no correspondence or photographs.'

'Have you checked the loft?'

'Yes, nothing up there but dust and mice.'

Horton told them they could go and returned to the front room. 'Where is your aunt's correspondence?'

'There isn't any except the legal papers.'

Horton studied her closely. It was probably the truth. 'Do you have your aunt's photographs?'

'No. I burnt them.'

'All of them?' Horton asked, incredulous. OK, so photographs of his childhood had been destroyed but his circumstances had been completely different. People usually kept some pictures of their relatives unless they hated them, and he'd had no indication that Patricia or Gregory Harlow had hated their aunt and her family. So why destroy them? Out of shame because of Rawly's suicide? Doubtful. Or because Patricia Harlow was one of those women who hated clutter and wasn't in the least bit sentimental? Probably.

'Except that picture,' she answered, gesturing at the wedding photograph on the mantelpiece, 'and that will go when the last of the furniture leaves. There's no point in me keeping it. It's the past. Nobody wants to look back.'

He didn't but he felt compelled to. Again that shadowy memory connected with Edward Ballard nudged at him.

He said, 'Do you know where your husband is?'

'At work, of course.'

'I've just come from the festival and he's not there. No one has seen him since last night.'

'Then they're mistaken.' She certainly didn't seem worried or concerned.

'When did you last speak to him?'

'I really don't see—'

'When?' barked Horton, making her jump.

Tight-lipped she said, 'Nine thirty last night.'

That looked and sounded like the truth but it didn't mean that she didn't know where her husband was now. She made no further comment and neither did she ask any questions about her husband's vanishing act, which made Horton think she knew where he'd gone and why. Perhaps he still had that boat, or another one.

Eames offered Patricia Harlow a lift home. She looked as though she wanted to refuse but that would mean either walking or catching a bus or taxi so she grudgingly accepted. When Patricia Harlow was in the car, Horton took Eames aside. 'What did you get from Harry Foxbury?'

214

'He was surprised when I told him about the human remains, but he didn't look or sound worried. He remembers Ellie Loman as a pretty, friendly young girl. He also remembered her father but claims he hasn't seen him for years. I asked him for details of the woman he'd been with on Tuesday but he denied being with one. I didn't press him but he's lying. And he again denied knowing Salacia.'

'Did he own a boat in 2001?'

'Yes. He had two. A small motorboat and a small sailing yacht. He gave me their names but said he sold both of them years ago and he doesn't remember when or to whom. He was living at Cosham in 2001 and his house didn't have a swimming pool. I'm still waiting to see if I can get any records on previous employees from 2001.'

He let her go and after she'd driven off he rang Elkins.

'Ballard has made port in Guernsey,' Elkins reported. 'As far as the marina manager in St Peter Port is aware he hasn't left his boat. He's told them he's staying for a couple of nights and the manager wants to know if anything's wrong. I said we were just keeping a discreet eye on him because of an assault on him in Portsmouth and we wanted to make sure he was OK and not suffering any after-effects. I said he didn't want any fuss. I didn't think the manager would buy it but he did. What do you want us to do now, Andy, about Ballard I mean?'

'Ask the manager to notify you if and when he leaves and if he says where he's heading. Then let me know.'

Horton rang off. Heading for the station, he wondered if he should call Inspector John Guilbert, a friend of his in the States of Guernsey police, and ask him to keep a prudent eye on Ballard. But that would make it official, unless Guilbert did it on the quiet, and Horton knew he would if he asked him to, and if he had the time, and without asking the reason why. But perhaps he was mistaken and Ballard had nothing to do with DCS Sawyer or Zeus. But if he did, did Sawyer know where Ballard was? Perhaps he should ask him. His Mercedes was in the station car park next to Uckfield's BMW.

Horton found the Super alone in the canteen tucking into pie and chips. Horton fetched the same and a coffee and sat opposite.

'Waste of bloody time and petrol going to Wales,' Uckfield said, forking the pie into his mouth. 'Stapleton just repeated what he'd told Swansea CID, that he'd never seen Salacia before and he didn't arrange for anyone to give Woodley a photograph of her. He said he wouldn't so much as give that bastard a cold. Sawyer said he'd do a deal with him, information on Salacia or Woodley or both, and a hint of where he'd stashed his money and he'd put in a word to the parole board. Stapleton just laughed and said he'd do his time. Still, Sawyer seemed to enjoy the trip,' he added sarcastically.

'Where is he?'

'With Wonder Boy. Don't know why because I've already given Dean an update.'

'What does he remember about the Ellie Loman case?'

216

'Swears blind Rawly Willard killed her, only they couldn't prove it. He believes that Willard's suicide confirmed his guilt.'

'Ellie went off with someone that day with two bikinis and no towel, which the original investigation didn't pick up, neither did they discover that Kenneth Loman kept a boat and so too did Gregory Harlow, on the trots close to the boatyard and the sailing club. And he was out on it that afternoon.'

Uckfield was looking happier. Horton knew why. Because Dean had messed up.

'Any sign of Harlow?'

Horton shook his head and told him about his interview with Ross Skelton and Geoff Kirby at the prison ending with the search of Amelia Willard's house and his interview with Patricia Harlow. 'I think she knows where her husband is.'

'Then we'll ask her less politely if he doesn't show up soon. Were both the Harlows at their aunt's wake?'

'According to the statements of those who were there, yes.' He'd checked with Trueman.

'Pity. I was hoping Gregory Harlow slipped out and met Salacia that afternoon for sex, lobster and white wine.'

Horton had been hoping the same, but not so it seemed.

'She must have met someone else before meeting Harlow at the quay later that night.'

And that brought them back to Harry Foxbury. He said, 'Foxbury has had a woman on his boat but denies it. Both Eames and I smelt her perfume and he was with someone on Tuesday. It could have been Salacia. She might have arranged to meet him and he doesn't want to admit it because of her body being found at his old boatyard.'

Uckfield pushed away his empty plate. Between mouthfuls, Horton continued, 'Harlow could have taken Ellie out with him. She knew the sailing club and the old boatyard and agreed to meet him there. By the time he brought her back they'd rowed. Perhaps she'd refused to let him have what he considered to be payment for a day out. She threatened to tell his wife. He lost his temper, struck her a violent blow across the back of the head as she made to leave him. Then, seeing what he'd done, and that there was no way back, he pushed her body into the sea. Nobody knew they'd been together and the Harlows weren't even questioned.'

Uckfield took up the theory. 'Then Salacia shows up. She has to be connected with the Willards—'

'Or Harry Foxbury,' Horton interjected, suddenly seeing the link. 'Salacia could have been at the boatyard to meet Foxbury that day. She saw something, kept quiet about it and now Harlow's come into money via his aunt's death, has returned to blackmail him.'

'Sounds plausible.' Uckfield picked at his teeth.

Horton finished his meal and sat back thoughtfully. 'Perhaps she was blackmailing Gregory Harlow before she showed up at the funeral, which was why Woodley had her photograph. Harlow must have got it into the prison and somehow arranged for Woodley to get rid of Salacia, only he realizes he's made a mistake

218

and tries to silence Woodley. He makes a hash of it first time but second time around leaves his body on the marshes. And he decides to kill Salacia himself.' At last he felt they were getting somewhere. There were holes in the theory but perhaps once they tracked Harlow down he'd be able to plug them.

Uckfield was looking more cheerful too. His eyes swivelled beyond Horton and he muttered, 'Here comes her ladyship.'

So Uckfield knew her pedigree? Eames drew level and Horton could see instantly by her heightened colour that they'd got some new and vital information. She flicked him a solemn glance before addressing Uckfield. 'We've just had a call from the Isle of Wight police, sir. They've found Gregory Harlow's van in Firestone Copse.'

'And Harlow?' asked Uckfield.

But Horton knew what was coming. Eames' expression had given that away.

'In the driver's seat. Dead,' she answered.

Uckfield cursed. Horton felt like doing the same but didn't. He felt cheated.

'Suicide?' he asked. Had his theory been correct and Harlow realizing he had gone too far had killed himself?

'They're not sure, sir.'

Scraping back his chair, Uckfield said, 'Then let's find out.'

Sixteen

Harlow's body lay slumped over the steering wheel. Horton's stomach recoiled at the sight of the bluey-pink face and the sign of nesting flies in the eye staring sightlessly at him. The vehicle reeked with the smell of whisky and Horton registered the empty bottle on the passenger seat, the keys in the ignition and that Harlow was dressed in a similar or the same T-shirt he'd seen him wearing when he'd interviewed him on Thursday.

DCI Birch from the local CID addressed Uckfield. 'The doctor says he's been dead for approximately twenty-four hours.'

Horton thought it less than that because Harlow had logged out of the festival at ten thirty-five p.m. the previous night. Driving here would have taken him about thirty minutes and then another hour or so to drink himself to death, less possibly, if he'd taken drugs with the alcohol and Horton was betting he had. He also wondered if those drugs had come courtesy of Haseen Nader.

He said as much. Birch was eyeing him as though he was a nasty smell from the shore of Wootton Creek a mile away but Horton could deal with that. He didn't care for Birch either, a lean inflexibly hard man with sparse light-brown hair above a thin-lipped gaunt face. As far as Horton was concerned Birch had about as much imagination and feeling as the tree he was

220

named after, though to be fair to the plant at least that blossomed once a year, which was more than could be said for Birch the detective. Their paths had crossed several times in the past and had always resulted in friction, mainly because Horton had resolved the cases they'd been forced to work together on and Birch resented that.

Uckfield waved Clarke forward. Taylor and Beth Tremaine waited patiently for the photographer to finish. They'd all travelled across on the police launch, which had moored up on one of the pontoons at Fishbourne a couple of miles away. Two patrol cars had brought them here. Arc lights were in the process of being erected and the undertaker's van was waiting close by, along with the police vehicle-recovery truck. Although this had all the hallmarks of suicide they couldn't take any chances.

Moving some distance away, Uckfield addressed Horton. 'Pity there's no suicide note.'

'He might have left one in the caravan he shares with Haseen Nader. I'll call Ross Skelton to give him the news and tell him that we'll need to search the caravan and question his staff.' And judging by what he'd seen of Skelton he didn't think the quick-tempered boss of Coastline was going to be very pleased about that, or Harlow's death, mainly because it would inconvenience him.

Uckfield turned to Birch. Crisply he ordered, 'Get your officers at the festival to search the caravan and put out a picture and description of the van, asking for any sightings of it. I also want a fingertip search done of this area.' Horton

221

caught a glimpse of fury in Birch's grey eyes at Uckfield's curt dismissive manner. That was not how a detective chief inspector should be addressed. But Uckfield would never forget or forgive the fact that Birch had tried to get him thrown off a case recently because he'd had an affair with someone involved in a murder investigation.

Turning his back on Birch, Uckfield said to Horton, 'We'll break the news to Patricia Harlow.' Reaching for his phone Uckfield added, 'I'll call Dean.'

Birch marched off, rigid and livid. Horton rang Skelton and, as he'd expected, his initial reaction was that of fury. 'That's all I need!' Then he seemed to recollect that one of his employees had died. 'Why the hell would he want to do a bloody stupid thing like that? Who's going to tell his wife?'

'We will.' Horton thought he heard Skelton sigh with relief. 'We'll need to question your staff and search the caravan.'

'Why? I thought you said it was suicide.'

'Routine procedure, sir.'

Grudgingly Skelton said, 'If you have to.'

'Thank you, sir. We appreciate your cooperation.' If Skelton detected his note of irony he didn't comment on it. Horton rang off considering Harlow's suicide. The autopsy would confirm how he'd died and if he'd taken drugs, also what kind, but it couldn't answer why Harlow had killed Ellie Loman or Salacia. And neither could it tell them Salacia's real identity and why she'd been at the crematorium. Perhaps Patricia Harlow

222

would know. And perhaps she'd be able to confirm that her husband had had an affair with Ellie Loman and Salacia. It would explain why she was so harsh and embittered. He wondered how she'd take this news.

Clarke moved away, indicating to Taylor that he had all the photographs he needed. He'd also taken a video. Horton asked Beth Tremaine to empty the dead man's trouser pockets. This she did carefully and without flinching but then she'd had plenty of practice, Horton thought, watching her slender small hands stretch inside the dark blue cotton trousers.

'Wallet with some money, credit cards and a security pass for the festival,' she said before dropping it into an evidence bag. It was brown leather, and well worn. Horton noted that Harlow didn't carry a photograph of his wife around but that didn't mean anything significant.

'There's nothing else in his side pockets, Inspector. Do you want me to check the back pockets?'

Horton did. The body was stiff with rigor. He stepped forward to help her, steeling himself for the ordeal, but Taylor waved him aside. 'We'll handle this, sir,' he said. Horton was only too pleased to let them get on with it. After a moment Beth shook her head. 'Empty.'

Taylor added, 'There's only the usual vehicle documentation in the car compartments.' He handed the keys, which he'd placed in a plastic evidence bag, to Horton. 'As well as the ignition key, and automated key fob, there's a key for the rear door,' he added, walking around to the rear of the vehicle where the two doors were wide open. 'The other two keys look as though they are to his house.'

But Horton thought the smaller key might be to the caravan at the festival. He peered inside the rear of the van. It was empty, which was what he had expected. All the supplies were at the festival, which thankfully they couldn't hear from here.

'Any sign of a mobile phone?' He knew there couldn't be otherwise Taylor would have said. Taylor confirmed this with a shake of his head.

'He could have got out of the van and dropped it, or chucked it away.'

Or it could be in the caravan at the festival. That seemed unlikely, why would Harlow leave it behind? Equally why would he ditch it? The obvious reason was because it contained evidence linking him to Salacia. They would get the number and apply for the phone records.

Uckfield came off the phone. He left instructions with DCI Birch to keep the area cordoned off until they'd finished the search and told the undertakers to take the body to Portsmouth on one of the night-ferry crossings. 'No point in dragging Mrs Harlow over here,' Uckfield said to Horton while unzipping his scene suit. 'She can make a formal ID tomorrow morning before Dr Clayton does the autopsy.' Stepping out of the disposable suit and hitching up his trousers he added, 'Let's break the news to her.'

On their way back to Portsmouth, Horton wondered what Uckfield would make of Patricia Harlow. Perhaps this news would cause that brittle shell of hers to crack wide open.

It was almost ten o'clock by the time they pulled up outside the house, and dark. Horton had wondered if Patricia Harlow would still be up. There was no light shining from the front of the house. A marked police car was waiting for them further down the road. Inside were two PCs. Eames climbed out of her car and handed Horton the search warrant that Trueman had given her. 'It seems a bit insensitive searching her house this late and at the same time we're telling her that her husband's dead,' she said.

'Not if Harlow murdered two women and she's an accomplice,' Horton brusquely replied, recalling Kenneth and Marie Loman. As he headed towards the house, he saw the net curtains twitching at a house across the car-lined street. He rang the bell while Uckfield stood impatiently beside him and Eames waited behind them with the two uniformed officers. He was beginning to think that she must have retired to bed when a light came on in the hall and a few seconds later the door was flung open. Patricia Harlow had discarded the white overall in favour of a lemon T-shirt that stretched across her well-developed chest. She eyed them first with surprise and then with anger.

'What is it now? Can't you leave me alone? This is harassment. I won't tolerate it.'

'Shall we go inside, Mrs Harlow? No need for the neighbours to hear everything.'

She stared at him and each of them in turn before stepping back.

They entered the spotlessly clean hall with its

225

pale pink carpet covered by plastic to protect it from the footsteps of her clients. The smell of antiseptic was as pungent as before. Horton continued, 'We have a warrant to search these premises.' He nodded at PC Johnson, who held out the warrant.

'This is ridiculous—' she began without looking at it.

But Horton interjected, 'I'm afraid we also have some very upsetting news for you concerning your husband.'

'Gregory's on the Isle of Wight,' she declared.

'Shall we go in here?' Horton gestured towards the front room, which he knew to be her surgery. It wasn't the best of places to break the news but it was the nearest and it would allow the officers to search the house.

She entered it with ill grace. Horton nodded at the two officers to begin their search and for Eames to stay with him. Uckfield remained silent but entered the room behind Horton and stood by the door. Nothing seemed to have changed from Horton's last visit.

He began. 'I'm sorry to tell you that your husband's body was found late this afternoon.'

She eyed him with suspicion then her eyes flicked over the small group. 'Dead? But he can't be. You must have made a mistake,' she said hesitantly.

'No mistake, Mrs Harlow.'

Silence. What would she do now?

'I don't understand. If this is some kind of trick—'

'No trick. This is Detective Superintendent

Uckfield. He and I have just come from your husband's body. He was found in his van in a wood on the Isle of Wight.'

Her skin paled. 'How? An accident?' She frowned as though she was trying to make sense of what he'd just told her.

'It appears as though he took his own life; there was a bottle of whisky beside him in the van.'

'Gregory hates whisky. He never touches the stuff.' She said it as though it was conclusive proof that it couldn't be her husband.

'They'll be a post-mortem, which will give us more information about how he died but not why; we thought you might be able to tell us that?'

'Me? How should I know?'

But she knew something. She showed no sign of breaking down, though. That could be because she was in shock or in denial; the news hadn't really sunk in yet. That could take some time. Her eyes shifted at the sound of the officers searching in the room next to them. She turned away to the cabinet where her sterilizer was and began to idly finger some instruments. Her tension filled the air.

Horton said, 'We believe your husband's death might have something to do with the deaths of Ellie Loman and the woman seen at the crematorium at the same time as your aunt's funeral.'

Her hand froze. She stiffened but she didn't turn to face them.

'You know who she is, don't you?' Horton persisted gently.

'No.'

'Mrs Harlow. Your husband is dead. The time for lying is over.'

She spun round, her eyes filled with fury. 'My husband's death has nothing to do with that woman or Ellie Loman. Isn't it bad enough that one person in my family has died because of police persecution? You just couldn't leave Rawly alone and the poor weak soul killed himself, so now you're looking for someone else. Me or my husband. We'll do. Just as long as you get someone for it you're happy. Well, Gregory had nothing to do with her disappearance and neither did I. Do your search and then leave me alone. I've got things to do.' She pursed her lips together and stood erect.

Uckfield jerked his head towards the door. Horton said, 'My colleague will stay with you in here while we conduct the search.'

She made no reply.

In the hall Uckfield raised his eyebrows and gestured for them to enter the kitchen. 'God, she's tough,' he said quietly.

'And capable of killing,' Horton replied. 'Perhaps Gregory Harlow didn't meet and kill Salacia but she did when she discovered he'd had an affair with her. And perhaps she told her husband that and he killed himself, unable to live with it.'

'Yeah, that's possible. I'll poke around in here and the garden. See what they've found in the lounge and upstairs.'

Horton was keen to see the house. He hoped it might give him a greater understanding and insight into Patricia Harlow. He took the lounge first.

'Nothing so far, sir,' PC Allen greeted him. They'd been told to look for any notes or correspondence from either of the dead women or from Gregory Harlow but Horton knew that if such existed it could be on the computer and there was one in the surgery, which they'd take away.

He surveyed the featureless room with its plain cream wallpaper, the same pale pink carpet that was in the hall, and a square cream sofa and two matching armchairs. There was an absence of cushions and rugs and only one picture of a bland country view above a tiled hearth with an electric fire. There was a modern television in one alcove, and a modern sideboard in the other one. He climbed the stairs to the Harlows' bedroom, which reflected the lounge in its neatness. Along with a simple double divan covered by a plain lilac counterpane there was a fitted wardrobe on one side of the fireplace, the latter of which had been removed and boarded over, and a chest of drawers on the other side. A dressing table with a small mirror stood in the bay window but there was no full-length mirror, not even inside the wardrobe. And there was nothing that could provide them with any evidence of why Gregory Harlow had killed himself.

PC Johnson entered with a shake of his head. 'Nothing in the bathroom or the other bedrooms, sir.'

In the hall Horton looked up.

Following Horton's gaze, the officer said, 'I'll find a stepladder.'

'No need, there's a ring on that hatch, which means there's a pole.'

229

'It's in one of the bedrooms.' Johnson fetched it and as the hatch opened the ladder came down. Horton's dread of confined spaces made him want to send Johnson up there but he wouldn't duck out. Facing your fear was the only way he knew how to deal with it, which made him think fleetingly of Zeus.

With a rapidly beating heart he climbed the steps. The memories of being shut in as a form of punishment in one of the many and the worse of the children's homes he'd been banished to following his mother's desertion resurfaced and with an effort he pushed the terror he'd felt then away, determined not to let the bastards who had subjected him to such cruelty get the better of him. Gripping the rail he propelled himself upwards and was relieved to find a light switch to his right. The spacious attic was boarded and contained only one large cardboard box.

PC Johnson followed. 'Wish my loft looked like this,' he said enviously. 'It's full of stuff the missus says she can't bear to throw away but hasn't looked at for years. I said we should have a garage sale, only problem is we haven't got a garage.'

Horton smiled. He peered inside the box. It contained a handful of ornaments, some silverware, an old heavy family Bible and a folder full of documents which, at a quick glance, belonged to the late Amelia Willard.

'Bring it down,' he instructed. They'd take it to the station and go through it but he didn't think it would reveal anything. Too much time had elapsed since Ellie Loman's death.

In the hall he met Uckfield, who shook his head, and together they entered the surgery. From Eames's expression Horton could see that Patricia Harlow hadn't spoken since they'd left her. She showed no signs of grief at her husband's death but that didn't mean she didn't feel it. She could be holding it in. PC Allen began a methodical search. It didn't take long. Horton said they would need to take her computer away for examination.

'I can't see how that will help you unless you think Gregory emailed me a suicide note. He didn't.'

'Could your husband have had an affair with this woman?' Horton nodded at Eames, who again put the photographs of Salacia in front of Mrs Harlow. 'She was originally a blonde,' he added. 'You might recognize her in this picture, which we've had computer-enhanced to show her natural colouring.'

Patricia Harlow didn't even glance at the pictures. Flashing angry eyes at them she said, 'You've just told me that my husband is dead, you've searched my house and now you want to badger me by asking questions. I refuse to say anything more and if you don't leave me this instant I shall call my solicitor and make an official complaint at the highest level about your aggressive, uncaring and abusive manner.'

Uckfield looked as though he wanted to argue but Horton knew they were treading on thin ice by piling the pressure on her now. Gently he said, 'Of course, Mrs Harlow. We understand you have a lot to do and are obviously upset. We'll need

231

you to formally identify your husband's body tomorrow morning. A car will collect you at eight thirty.'

For the first time during their presence in her house she looked alarmed. He wondered if she was going to say she couldn't cancel her appointments. He added, 'Unless there is someone else who could do that, a son or daughter, perhaps?' He hadn't seen any family photographs or evidence that the Harlows had children.

'No,' she hastily answered. 'I'll do it. My son doesn't live locally.'

So there was a child. He wondered what he was like and how he'd take the news of the death of his father. Blotting out Uckfield's impatient manner beside him, Horton continued, 'We are deeply sorry for your loss, Mrs Harlow, and apologize if you found our methods intrusive, but we only want to establish why this woman and Ellie Loman were killed and the reason for your husband's death. In our job we have to ask questions at difficult times.'

She didn't look mollified by his apology but then Horton guessed nothing would soften her.

'We'll see ourselves out.'

They made their way back to the station. Horton was the first to arrive in the incident suite. He had just finished updating Trueman when Uckfield arrived followed by Eames, who put the cardboard box found in the Harlow's loft on a desk near Trueman.

'No suicide note has been found in the caravan,' reported Trueman. 'And there's no sign of Harlow's mobile phone either. SOCO's finished at the scene. Nothing significant found but Taylor will let us have a report tomorrow.'

Uckfield looked as though he was about to say that tomorrow wasn't good enough when Horton quietly butted in, 'It's very late, Steve, we all need some rest, including you.'

For a moment Uckfield looked rebellious but then grudgingly acquiesced.

Before leaving, Horton told Eames he'd like her to accompany him to the mortuary in the morning, thinking it had become something of a habit. Dr Clayton would be giving him his own office next. He returned to his yacht, weary and disturbed by the case. He thought about Patricia and Gregory Harlow's reaction to Salacia's death when first questioned. Both had denied knowing her when shown the photograph but if Gregory Harlow *had* had an affair with Salacia, then why not turf her husband out? Because she loved him?

The images of Harlow's body slumped in that whisky-filled van haunted Horton. How was Patricia Harlow feeling now? Was she alone in that house or had her son arrived to comfort her? Somehow he couldn't see her weeping into anyone's arms but how did he know that? Perhaps that brittle outer shell was hiding her real emotions because showing them would be construed as weakness, making her vulnerable. And perhaps Gregory Harlow had hurt her by betraying her with Ellie Loman and Salacia. Well, perhaps tomorrow, when she viewed the body of her husband, he'd find out. For now it was time for sleep, if it came, and he doubted that very much.

Seventeen

Saturday

'Yes, that's Gregory,' Patricia Harlow said stiffly, before snatching her head away from the body. Horton saw a flicker of bewilderment in her eyes but that was the only emotion she betrayed and her posture never altered. The lines around her mouth and eyes had deepened, though, gouging tunnels into her pale skin. Her face was etched with fatigue showing she'd had a troubled night, like him, and Eames, he thought, because even her blue eyes weren't as clear as they usually were. And in the briefing room earlier Uckfield had looked as though he'd been pacing the floor all night. His skin was grey and his manner agitated and sharp. Dean had appeared briefly with a worried frown on his pixie face, while Bliss looked as crisp and cool as usual and the glint in her eye was steelier than ever. Horton read it as determination to grasp victory on one case at least, the vehicle fraud. He'd heard from Walters that they were building a case against the garage proprietor and there was evidence that the van used to rob Mason's Electricals store could have come from Mellings' garage.

Horton led Patricia Harlow out of the room. He had hoped that her son would have accompanied her not just for her sake but so that they might glean some information from him about his parents and in particular his father. But Patricia Harlow had said without apology or guilt that she hadn't told Connor about his father's death, adding that she would tell him when it became necessary. Horton thought it was necessary now. He could only surmise that she had wanted to make absolutely certain that her husband really was dead before informing him. He wondered what Connor Harlow would say and how he'd feel when he discovered it had been over twelve hours since his mother had first been given the news. Perhaps they weren't a very close family. Perhaps her son wouldn't be that upset? Perhaps Gregory Harlow had been a distant father and Patricia a cold-hearted mother, which had made her son uncaring and detached. It was none of his business but the deaths of Salacia and Ellie were.

Eames offered her a drink but she refused with a shake of her head. Footsteps in the corridor came closer and passed them by. It was hot and humid, the air stifling and oppressive, in total contrast from the air-conditioned room they had just left. When Patricia Harlow spoke it came as something of a surprise because they seemed to have been standing in silence for so long, although in reality Horton knew it could only have been a minute at the most.

'You said Gregory drank himself to death. Is that true?' She spoke crisply but Horton noted the edge of hardness had gone from her voice.

'We won't know for certain until after the post-mortem. At the moment the manner of his death suggests it and that he took his own life.'

235

'But why?' she insisted, eyeing him keenly.

'We were hoping you might tell us that.' He held her stare, seeing the anguish in her eyes; should she tell what she knew or not? He felt a shiver of anticipation. Neither he nor Eames spoke. They both knew the fragility of the moment.

After a moment she squared her shoulders and said tersely, 'Can we get away from here? But not the station. I don't want to go to the police station.'

'OK.'

She slipped into the rear of Eames's car. Horton climbed into the front passenger seat and gave instructions to Eames to pull into one of the viewing spots along the top of the hill, which bordered the northern edge of the city. It was unorthodox and he'd get bollocked because anything she said would be off the record but Horton was backing his instinct. She needed to talk and she couldn't do that, initially anyway, in the confines of the interview room. It happened like that sometimes. This was a big decision on her part. He didn't think she would retract what she told them.

A few minutes later, Eames silenced the engine. Portsmouth lay spread out beneath them shrouded in the heat and smog while beyond it lay the pale silver of the Solent. The hills of the Isle of Wight were barely visible.

Horton said, 'Let's sit outside.' He gestured at the wooden table with a bench seat either side of it. He guessed that Patricia Harlow needed air even though there seemed little of it about. He could do with some himself to rid his nostrils of the smell of the mortuary and death. Eames made to remove her notebook and pen but at a sign from Horton left both in her jacket pocket. She slid onto the seat beside him and opposite Patricia Harlow. They waited. The drone of the cars on the road below them and the throbbing of a Chinook helicopter overhead filled the sultry air. Horton reckoned it must have been two minutes before she spoke.

'She was evil. She deserved to die.'

Horton knew she meant Salacia. He sensed Eames's excitement beside him and found his body responding to it in a way he'd rather not consider. Not now, not ever. She was strictly out of bounds with her rich and influential daddy. He shut out the smell of her light perfume and the knowledge that her thigh was only inches from his. One tiny movement would bring it into contact. He steeled himself to concentrate on the woman opposite.

'She killed Rawly.'

'He killed himself,' Horton answered quietly, trying to follow her train of thought. Her head came up and he saw the anger in her eyes. 'Only because the police hounded him. They thought he killed Ellie, but he didn't, she did. My sister killed Ellie Loman.'

Horton quickly covered his surprise. He resisted throwing Eames a glance and studied Patricia Harlow's face.

'That's who the woman in that photograph is,' she hastily continued, scorn curling the edges of her lips. 'She's my sister.'

The truth at last! It came as something of a shock. The sisters were totally unalike.

237

'Sharon Piper's her real name, or it was. God knows what she calls herself now, called herself.'

'How do you know she killed Ellie?' he asked.

'She hated her. She was jealous.'

Horton was rapidly trying to put this together. 'Jealous that Rawly loved Ellie.'

'No,' Patricia Harlow said bitingly. 'Although Ellie might have fallen for him eventually, but that was before *he* showed up.'

Who, for God's sake? Gregory Harlow? No. Harry Foxbury? Possibly. He could see Eames was thinking the same. 'He?'

'Sharon introduced them. My God, if Sharon had known then that he'd fall for Ellie she'd have killed her on the spot.' She paused then hurried on, the words coming quickly as though she was desperate to get them out before she lost them. 'My aunt and uncle had a party in May 2001. It was their pearl wedding anniversary. Rawly invited Ellie, and Sharon came with Leo. Any fool could see that Leo and Ellie were instantly attracted and my sister was no fool. Although you already know that.'

Horton frowned. Leo, not Harry. Who the hell was Leo? No one by that name had featured in this case, and he was certain he hadn't seen the name on the sailing-club list. And what did she mean about them knowing Salacia was no fool?

He said nothing. This had been a long time coming and he needed to hear it. Thank God Eames was experienced and attuned enough to keep quiet.

Patricia Harlow continued, 'Gregory and I lied to you. We did see Sharon at my aunt's funeral

238

just as we were going into the chapel. I couldn't believe it was her at first. I hadn't seen or spoken to her for years. I didn't even know where she went when she left Portsmouth but I wouldn't have been told anyway and I didn't care.'

Horton wondered what she meant. Why wouldn't she have been told?

'When we all left the chapel after auntie's funeral Sharon had gone. I accused Greg of contacting her but he swore he had no idea where she had been living. It must have been in Portsmouth though because she must have seen the funeral announcement in the local newspaper. It was typical of Sharon to turn up when Aunt Amelia had died, and I knew why; she was after some of her money. There were only two things Sharon was ever interested in, money and Leo. But she wasn't going to get a penny of Aunt Amelia's money. Sharon had her share when Amelia was alive; she certainly wasn't going to get any of it when she was dead,' Patricia Harlow added with bitterness. 'And Sharon had squeezed everything she could out of her husband. She married Marcus Piper for his money. He was a successful businessman until Sharon got her claws into him. She bled him dry. I always wondered about his death, although the coroner said it was suicide. He threw himself off his boat in the Solent, leaving Sharon with the house and boat and a nice fat insurance policy that paid up on suicide. After he died in 1996 she went to live in Spain in 1997, renting a villa, and invited Aunt Amelia and Uncle Edgar over for a holiday and that's when they met Leo.'

Horton noted that her hands were white with tension and her face drawn and harrowed. He wanted to ask her about Leo but he didn't want to stop the flow. There would be time later.

'Then after auntie's funeral Sharon showed up outside our house before anyone else arrived.'

'How did she get there? Did she have a car?' Horton couldn't resist interjecting.

'I don't know. I didn't see. She was standing by the gate. I told her she wasn't welcome. She said she could see that but she thought it would be best for us to talk otherwise the police might learn something about Ellie Loman's disappearance. I asked her what the devil she meant. She looked at Gregory and just smiled. Gregory agreed that he'd meet her at the old Tipner boatyard at ten thirty that evening.'

'His suggestion or hers?'

'Hers.'

'Did she say why ten thirty?'

'No, and I didn't ask.'

'Did you see her leave?'

'No. I went into the house.'

'Did Gregory follow you?'

'After a moment,' she said tightly. 'I was anxious for the wake to end, it seemed to drag on for ever, and when it eventually did, I asked Gregory what Sharon meant by her threat. He said because he didn't have an alibi for the day Ellie disappeared Sharon would fabricate something unless we agreed to her demands, which would be giving her Aunt Amelia's money. She'd make her tale so convincing that the police would fall for it. After all you had before.' She eyed Horton coldly.

He didn't know what she meant and before he could ask she continued.

'I said we shouldn't go. That we should face it out, but Gregory said it would be him that Sharon would accuse not me and he wasn't going to risk that. He thought he might be able to come to a compromise with her. I said, "Sharon doesn't do compromise, she's a greedy bitch." He said that if we didn't meet her then she'd be back. We rowed so by the time he left it was closer to eleven than ten thirty. When he returned home just after eleven fifteen he said she hadn't been there.'

'You believed him?'

'Yes.'

'How was he when he returned?'

'Well, he wasn't covered in blood, if that's what you mean,' she retorted derisively before adding, 'And he wasn't upset. He didn't kill her. He would have told me if he had.'

Eames said, 'Perhaps he wanted to protect you.'

Judging by Patricia Harlow's expression that was clearly something Gregory Harlow had never done. 'He was worried she hadn't been there and so was I. Then you came the next morning and told me she was dead. And now he's dead.'

Was it the truth? He didn't know. And if neither of them had killed Salacia or rather Sharon, who did that leave? Were they back to Harry Foxbury again? But there was the photograph that had been found in Woodley's cell. And there was this Leo.

Eames said, 'How do you know Sharon killed Ellie?'

241

'She must have done.'

Horton said, 'But if Sharon didn't kill Ellie Loman and neither you nor your husband killed Sharon, then someone else did. And it's possible they did so because they also believed that Sharon had killed Ellie.'

Her head jerked up. 'For revenge, you mean?' she said, quickly catching his meaning, making him think she might already have reached this conclusion.

He watched her face as the thoughts raced. Clearly there was someone who could have killed Sharon for revenge, only he'd taken a while to do so, perhaps because he'd only recently discovered that Sharon had killed the woman he'd fallen in love with. Leaning forward and lowering his voice, Horton said, 'Who is Leo, Patricia?'

She eyed him with surprise. 'But you know who he is. You must,' she added, with a bewildered expression, gazing at each of them in turn. 'Leo Garvard was Sharon's partner. He's the man she gave up to the police.'

Eighteen

'Sharon Piper became Carol Palmer,' Trueman said three hours later. 'After grassing on her partner in crime, and her lover, Leo Garvard, she went under the witness protection scheme and was given a new identity. She became Carol Palmer and moved to Spain.'

'Along with all the other grasses and crooks,' Uckfield sneered with his mouth full of food. Sandwiches and coffee had been brought up to the incident suite from the canteen.

Trueman continued. 'It was believed that Garvard was in with some big-time villains and that Sharon Piper wasn't safe once she grassed on him. She dropped off the radar four years ago.'

'Great! So what have we got on her?' Uckfield shovelled in his fourth sandwich.

Horton reached for his second and began to relay what Patricia Harlow had repeated to him and Eames in the interview room and what he and Trueman had subsequently discovered from the case file on Leo Garvard.

'Sharon Piper, as we've already seen on the video, was attractive and totally aware of her sexuality, which she used to trap victims. Her job, after she and Leo had identified their victims, was to help charm them into investing money into fraudulent schemes dreamt up by Leo. One of the schemes was selling false investment policies to clients, the other was land banking. Leo would sell parcels of land, which he claimed had planning permission, and which either never existed or would never get planning permission. He'd then follow it up by selling the investors multiple plots or asking them to pay additional sums in order to liquidate their holdings once they realized they'd never turn a profit. That's how they got Edgar Willard to part with his money.'

Uckfield looked incredulous. 'She stitched up her own uncle!'

Eames answered. 'Yes, which was why Amelia Willard had to move to that small and shabby house. When Edgar died not long after Rawly she found all their savings had gone and that Edgar had taken out a small mortgage on the house without her knowledge in order to fund another of Sharon and Leo's schemes. She had no choice but to sell the house to pay off the mortgage and other debts, and downsize. She lived on her state pension and what she got from Edgar's civil-service pension.'

Horton took it up. 'And I doubt Sharon ceased her wicked ways once she was in Spain. She probably continued with the scams. And as we know victims of such fraudulent schemes are often too ashamed to come forward and admit they've been duped. These are usually successful, clever businessmen, directors or retired professionals.'

Into Horton's mind sprang Edward Ballard. Had he been sucked dry by Sharon Piper? Had he come looking for revenge and got it? When Patricia Harlow had first told them about Leo Garvard, Horton had wondered if Garvard was Ballard but that had been quickly disproved. And, as he'd told himself before, he had no reason to suspect Ballard of being involved. He was about to continue when Bliss interjected.

'We only have Patricia Harlow's word that Sharon killed Ellie Loman and that she wasn't at the boatyard when her husband went to meet her. She's lied once, she could be lying again. Gregory Harlow could have killed Sharon Piper and then wracked with guilt he killed himself.'

Uckfield looked up. 'He could have killed her, yes, but he didn't kill himself.'

Horton froze with another sandwich half poised. 'You've got the PM report,' he said eagerly.

'Came in a few minutes before this conference. Dr Clayton's confirmed it was homicide.'

So bang went Gregory Harlow as a suspect for killing Sharon Piper, but he could have seen who had killed her. 'How did he die?'

Trueman answered. 'Alcohol and barbiturate poisoning, not self-administered. There was bruising inside the mouth and around the jaw area. Someone held his mouth open and poured the whisky down it.'

'A man, then?'

'Dr Clayton thinks it's probable but she can't be absolutely certain.'

'Wouldn't he have struggled?' asked Marsden.

'He was drugged and unable to put up much resistance. Dr Clayton says the toxicology tests need to verify this but she found . . .' Trueman paused to read from his computer screen, then continued, ' "laryngeal oedema in the upper respiratory tract, froth and pus in the lungs and congestion in the brain which confirm alcohol and barbiturate poisoning." She says that Harlow was probably given Nembutal or Amytal. All barbiturates depress the central nervous system causing sleep and in large doses produce coma followed by kidney and respiratory failure, and death. The alcohol was used to speed up the process of death and possibly to make us think he committed suicide. He probably took the barbiturate unwittingly and then someone forced the alcohol down him.'

'Time of death?' asked Horton.

'Between eleven p.m. Thursday night and two a.m. Friday morning. The security officers who DCI Birch's team have interviewed say that Harlow left the festival in his van alone. SOCO have found no additional tyre tracks near or leading to the spot where Gregory's van was parked so either he picked up his killer on the way or he met him there, and the killer entered the woods on foot. DCI Birch has officers out asking for sightings of any vehicles parked near the copse.'

Uckfield wiped his mouth with a large white handkerchief. 'Right, let's bring Leo Garvard in.'

'That might be difficult.' Horton exchanged a glance with Trueman.

'I don't care how bloody difficult it is,' Uckfield exploded. 'He's our killer. He killed Sharon Piper for revenge for stitching him up and for killing his girlfriend, Ellie Loman, and then he killed Harlow.'

'Why?'

'Because Harlow saw him kill Sharon of course. We bring him in.'

'You tell him, Dave,' Horton said.

'Leo Garvard was convicted for fraud in 2002 on Sharon's evidence and he's still serving his sentence.'

'And I'll give you three guesses where,' Horton added.

'Not Parkhurst!'

'Yes, and Garvard is probably responsible for giving Woodley that photograph of Sharon Piper, aka Carol Palmer aka Salacia, but he couldn't have killed her and he couldn't have killed Gregory Harlow, but he could have organized both murders.'

'Then we're back to Reggie Thomas,' Bliss said triumphantly. 'Garvard could have ordered Thomas to get rid of Woodley because Woodley was going to confess.'

'Unlikely,' Horton answered. 'Woodley wouldn't have known the meaning of the word, but he could have screwed up somehow. Or perhaps on reflection Garvard considered Woodley wasn't up to the job. But I can't see Thomas doing it for nothing, or Woodley come to that if he'd gone through with it, which means Garvard must have some money from his scams stashed away.'

'Which Sharon Piper could have been spending,' Marsden piped up.

'Possibly,' said Horton.

Uckfield sat back and scratched his crotch, causing a scowl of disapproval on Bliss's face. Eames appeared not to notice. 'So Reggie Thomas attacks Woodley after he leaves the pub, Sholby's and Hobbs' alibis are false. Woodley doesn't see his attacker so when Reggie offers to take him out of hospital, an unsuspecting Woodley goes with him. But Reggie, in a borrowed or nicked car, drops him at the marshes where he leaves him to die. At the crematorium Reggie manages to speak to Sharon, or passes her a message, asking her to meet him later that night at the boatyard. Maybe he claims he has a message from Garvard. She agrees and he stabs her, steals her car and dumps it somewhere.'

247

Horton said, 'Perhaps he passed the vehicle on to one of his mates, Sholby or Hobbs, or directly to the garage proprietor, Mellings, who recycles it.'

Bliss chipped in. 'That seems highly possible given the intelligence we're gathering.'

Horton frowned in thought. 'That still doesn't explain why Woodley's funeral was arranged for the same day and just before Amelia Willard's.'

'Or why Sharon Piper showed up for it,' added Eames.

But Horton could explain that. 'It's unlikely that she was living in this area, although we don't know that for certain, but if she wasn't then someone from here knew her whereabouts and told her that Amelia had died and when the funeral was being held.'

'Gregory Harlow?' posed Bliss.

'I don't think so.'

'Garvard?' suggested Uckfield.

'Or someone liaising with him,' Horton replied. 'The prison network is very wide.'

'We're not back to Marty bloody Stapleton, are we?' exclaimed Uckfield.

Horton shrugged. 'It could be one of his contacts.'

Uckfield sniffed in disgust. 'OK, with Garvard inside and not our killer, although there's the possibility he engineered Sharon's death, and if we discount Gregory Harlow for now on account of him being killed himself, an unknown hit man, and Reggie Thomas, who could still be in the frame, who else does that leave?'

'Harry Foxbury,' answered Horton. 'There are

248

still the hours of Salacia's life unaccounted for between being seen at the crematorium and arriving at the quayside and I don't think Reggie Thomas would have treated her to lobster and white wine.'

'And nobody in their right mind would have sex with him,' Uckfield sneered.

Horton continued. 'So whoever she met that afternoon could be the person who tipped her off about her aunt's funeral and who dropped her off at the quay and hasn't come forward, because either he's scared of being accused of killing her, or he did kill her. Foxbury could have known Salacia when she was Sharon Piper or Carol Palmer. It's likely he also knew Ellie Loman. Or there might be another motive for Sharon's death that we're currently unaware of.'

'I bloody hope not,' Uckfield growled.

Trueman said, 'We've cleared Kevin Manley, his crew, the boatman Ethan Crombie and the crane operative Bill Shoreham, but it could be a member of the sailing club. Richard Bolton, the sailing-club secretary, was at work at his printing company all afternoon. But now that we've got Salacia's real name, and her most recent one, we can see if there is a connection between her and any of the sailing-club members.'

'Including the Chief Constable and councillor Levy,' Uckfield said pointedly.

Horton thought he saw an expression of horror flit across Bliss's thin face.

Uckfield rose. 'Right. We dig deeper on Foxbury. Eames, you and Marsden find out where Foxbury was Thursday night between eleven p.m. and two a.m. and on Tuesday afternoon and evening. And we want the names of alibis this time and we *will* check them. Trueman, start checking the sailing club members.' Turning to Horton, Uckfield added, 'And as you've already got contacts in the prison, you can have the pleasure of another visit to Her Majesty's Parkhurst and see if this Garvard can tell us how Woodley came to have his girl-friend's photograph in his cell.'

Horton would have preferred having a go at Harry Foxbury, but he was curious to meet Garvard and to find out more about Sharon Piper. He called Elkins and asked him to pick him up from the quay at the Continental Ferry Port. As he headed there he chewed over the new facts that had come to light. They still hadn't traced Sharon Piper's entry into the country. He was convinced she'd come from abroad and it sounded highly probable that she'd come from the Continent. As he swung into the ferry port it suddenly struck him. God, what an idiot, and not just him, it had been staring them all in the face and no one had thought of it. Salacia hadn't flown in and neither had she come by private boat. She'd caught the ferry.

He brought the Harley to a stop at the quayside where the police launch was waiting, retrieved his phone and called Trueman.

'Check the passenger lists of the ferries from France and Spain. I think you'll find Sharon Piper booked on one that arrived some time just before her aunt's funeral. She probably travelled under the name of Carol Palmer, but she might have used her real name. It'll be interesting to see if

250

she came by car and if she booked a return passage.'

'I'll get on to it now.'

Horton headed out of the harbour on the police launch. It had grown overcast but the heat was as oppressive as ever. Elkins foretold a thunderstorm. 'I always get a headache when thunder's on its way,' he grumbled, 'and I've got thumping great one now.'

'And there's me thinking you were some kind of weather guru.' Horton asked if there had been any movement from Ballard.

'Still in the marina at Guernsey on his boat.'

Or at least his boat was, thought Horton. Ballard could be anywhere on that island, which was smaller than the one they were heading towards across a darkening grey and eerily calm Solent. He turned his thoughts to Foxbury. If Reggie Thomas wasn't their killer could it be Foxbury? He couldn't see how Foxbury could have got that photograph to Woodley, unless he knew a relative of an inmate, and that was possible. And the motive for wanting Sharon Piper dead? Perhaps she'd seen him up to some illegal activity in his boatyard years ago; Danby had mentioned he'd once been suspected of smuggling. And perhaps Sharon had returned to blackmail him, especially since he'd come into a great deal of money. But why kill her at his old boatyard? Why not take her out on his boat and kill her in a remote bay or toss her body into the sea?

And if Foxbury had killed Sharon out of revenge for her killing Ellie Loman that meant Foxbury must have been infatuated or in love with Ellie. If so why hadn't Foxbury told the police? Unless Foxbury had killed Ellie because she'd rejected him. Or was there a connection between Foxbury and this Marcus Piper, Sharon's late husband whom Patricia Harlow had told them had thrown himself off his boat? Had he, though? Had Sharon pushed him and had Marcus been a friend of Foxbury's?

Whichever way he looked at it the answer lay in Parkhurst Prison. And although it pained him to admit it, as far as the prison being critical to the investigation, DCS Sawyer had been right after all, it was the key to both Woodley's and Sharon Piper's deaths. He only hoped that Garvard wouldn't be as close-mouthed as Stapleton. He wanted the bugger to talk.

Nineteen

'You'll be lucky. He's not here,' Geoff Kirby said when Horton was once again sitting in his office.

'What do you mean?' Horton cried, annoyed he'd had a wasted trip.

'And I doubt you'll get him to talk because he's in St Mary's Hospital across the road, cancer. It's terminal. He's only days to live.'

Horton cursed. Would the answers to the investigation die with Garvard? He needed to see him. But he curbed his impatience. Kirby could give him some information on Garvard that might help, and it might be all he'd get if Garvard was in no fit state to talk when Horton reached the hospital. Swiftly he told Kirby they'd traced the identity of the woman in the photograph found in Woodley's cell back to Garvard.

'I never saw him with it,' Kirby quickly replied, surprised, 'and he has never mentioned a woman, not even after he was diagnosed with cancer or when he went into hospital two weeks ago.'

'This one gave him up to the police.'

'Ah.'

Horton could see Kirby's mind racing to work out the implications of this piece of news. It didn't take him long. 'You think Woodley was paid to find and kill her.'

'It's one possibility but there's still a great deal unexplained and I was hoping Garvard would explain it.'

'You might not have much joy. He's slipping in and out of consciousness and it's likely that soon he won't come out of it.'

Horton would have to try, though. 'What's he like?'

Kirby didn't even pause to consider his answer. 'Clever, manipulative, shrewd, genial, charming.' After a moment, he added, 'And embittered. Yes, I'd say embittered. And now I know his girlfriend shopped him that explains a lot about his manner.'

'How?'

Kirby's forehead creased in a frown as he seemed to weigh up his answer. 'When I say embittered, I don't mean he went around swearing to get revenge or was outwardly cynical but you got the sense that something was going on inside him that you would never get him to reveal, it was as though he was hugging a secret, and not a happy one. It was a silent bitterness if that makes any sense.'

Yes, Horton thought it did.

Kirby continued. 'Garvard was clever, or I should say *is* clever, he's not dead yet. Outwardly he was no trouble but you got this feeling between your shoulder blades that he was somehow always one step ahead of you, that he knew more than you did and what he knew was far more important than what you'd ever know.'

Horton had known other villains like that. And the profile Kirby was painting fitted that of a con man. 'How did he interact with the other prisoners?'

'He never caused any trouble and they never gave him any trouble, but . . .' Kirby paused again to consider his reply. 'You couldn't pinpoint it but you had this feeling that whatever was going down he was behind it somehow.'

Horton quickly read between the lines. 'The attack on Stapleton?'

'Nobody said anything and there was never any proof that Garvard was behind it, which was why it wasn't mentioned in the report, and of course I didn't know about the woman, but yes, now I can see it is possible. He could have persuaded Stapleton's minders to go AWOL. And, yes, he could have persuaded Woodley to attack Stapleton.' Kirby looked thoughtful for a moment before adding, 'This might sound daft, but it's possible that Garvard could even have persuaded Stapleton to *allow* himself to be attacked.'

Horton rapidly considered this. It wasn't so daft. 'In exchange for what?'

'Money. It's why he didn't want to be let out on licence for his remaining days in his weakened condition, in case some of the villains or victims he stitched up came after him, and it's why we've got a prison officer sitting with him at the hospital. Garvard could have offered Stapleton information on where this money is.'

And Sharon might not have known where Garvard had put all the money from their scams. Perhaps he hadn't trusted her, which would have given her another reason to grass on him. Or was this just another of his cons? Another thought occurred to Horton. 'Could Garvard have been a gang master here instead of or in addition to Stapleton?'

'There's never been any evidence to suggest that, or that he had a power base, but like I said he's a clever, cunning bugger. He must have known that even if we discovered he was behind the attack he wouldn't be moved because he'd been diagnosed with cancer, although there was a time when we were considering transferring him to Kingston Prison in Portsmouth. He stayed in the prison sick bay there while he underwent a six-week course of radiotherapy treatment in June, last year, at Queen Alexandra Hospital Portsmouth, accompanied by a prison officer, of course. It made sense for him to stay at Kingston Prison rather than travel back and forth on the ferry, locked in the back of a prison van. And he *was* ill.'

Thoughts rushed through Horton's mind and

paramount in them was the possibility that he'd found another connection between the Willards and Garvard and a more recent one than 2001. Who had given Garvard his radiotherapy treatment? Had it been Fiona Wright, Dr Gaye Clayton's friend and the woman who had been sailing a dinghy the night Sharon Piper had arrived at the boatyard for her meeting with Gregory Harlow? But he didn't see Fiona Wright as Sharon's killer and he certainly didn't see her as Harlow's murderer.

With a keen interest he said, 'Why did he go to Portsmouth for treatment?'

'There was a problem with the equipment at the hospital here. I don't know all the details but someone from the medical staff can give you that.' Kirby tapped into his computer. 'I can give you the start and finish dates of the treatment but not the exact times of his appointments, the hospital can tell you.'

Kirby handed the printout to Horton. He scanned it briefly before folding it and pushing it in his pocket. 'Has Garvard named anyone to be notified on his death?'

Kirby again consulted his computer. 'No.'

Horton rose and thanked him warmly. On his way across the road to the hospital, he rang Trueman and relayed what Kirby had told him. He asked him to find out if Amelia Willard had undergone radiotherapy for her cancer and if so when. He couldn't see quite how it joined up yet but he was convinced it did.

Trueman said, 'Eames has reported back. Foxbury has an alibi for Tuesday afternoon and evening and

256

for Thursday night. He was with his wife Thursday night. They had some friends over for supper and it sounds kosher. When Foxbury was showing Marsden and Eames out, away from his wife's flapping ears, Eames said he grudgingly gave them the name of the woman he was with on Tuesday, and it's not Sharon Piper. She's checking her out now.'

So Foxbury looked as though he wasn't involved. It was a blow. Into his mind flashed Ballard and as quickly he discounted him. He had no reason to believe that Sharon Piper had been anywhere near a boat, except for the ferry that had probably brought her to Portsmouth, and Trueman was still checking that.

The hospital staff, and the prison officer keeping Garvard company, had been told to expect him. Horton was shown swiftly into the bland single room. It had the smell of death about it. The cavernous man on the bed bore no resemblance to the photograph Horton had seen on the police computer of a dark-haired, rugged good-looking man with a square jaw and blue eyes. Garvard appeared to be asleep.

'He drifts in and out of consciousness,' the prison officer said quietly. 'You might have a long wait.'

As it happened Horton didn't. Perhaps Garvard sensed his presence. Horton pulled up a chair and sat close to Garvard's emaciated body. The eyes flickered open and took a while to focus, when they did Horton withdrew his warrant card and introduced himself. Garvard smiled weakly. 'Took your time. Didn't think you'd make it.'

Horton had to lean closer to the deathly grey

face to hear. He steeled himself not to recoil at the smell of death. 'You could have made it easier,' he answered, 'and saved two people from being killed.'

'Why? She deserved it.'

'Did she?'

Garvard frowned but he was too weak to show too much emotion or reaction. Horton could see that he was drawing strength from reserves that would soon be exhausted. After this last effort it wouldn't be long. He needed to get as much information as he could from him on this visit because he knew it would be the final and only time Garvard would speak.

Horton beckoned the prison officer over. 'Take notes.'

The slim man in his thirties reached for a notepad and pen and Horton silently thanked the heavens that he'd got someone prepared and bright. He nodded to say he was ready. Horton said, 'Tell me about Ellie.'

Garvard opened his eyes. 'Sharon killed her.' His strained voice was barely above a whisper. 'She was jealous. I loved her.'

Horton could see the effort to speak was costing him dear. He wasn't without pity or sympathy, but he couldn't condone what this man had done. He said, 'I'll explain and you can correct me when I go wrong and agree where I indicate.' It wouldn't hold up in a court of law but this man was never going to go before one again, certainly not in this world.

Garvard nodded fractionally to show he understood.

'You met Amelia and Edgar Willard when they were on holiday in Spain staying at the villa rented by their niece, Sharon Piper. You were there working a time-share or property scam.'

'The latter. 1997.'

'Sharon saw through you immediately as you tried to get money from her, her husband having left her with a house, a boat and a life-insurance policy. You were two of a kind, you both had a desire for money and were clever, crooked and cunning enough to know how to get it from people and then invest it to make more for you rather than the people you conned into giving it to you in the first place.'

'Yes.' The word came out as a breath.

'You even managed to get Edgar Willard to invest in one of your bogus schemes, which effectively took all his savings and eventually forced his widow to sell up and move to a smaller house.'

Garvard gave a slight shake of his head. Horton held the man's weary pain-filled eyes. And then he realized what Garvard was silently telling him.

'Or rather Sharon managed to get Edgar to invest in one of your schemes, or was it one of hers?'

Garvard closed his eyes as though to indicate that it was. But was that the truth? Kirby had said that Garvard was manipulative. Perhaps Garvard wanted them to believe Sharon had been the mastermind behind the fraud. The lies went deep in this investigation, just as Ellie and Sharon had ended up, deep under that quay.

He continued, 'You met Ellie Loman at the Willards' house when they were celebrating their

259

pearl wedding anniversary. Rawly Willard, Ellie's work colleague and the man who worshipped the ground she walked on, had invited her. Ellie and you began an affair. She arranged to meet you on Sunday the first of July and you went out on your boat together for the day. Was Sharon with a prospective client tricking him into parting with his money? She was very good at that. A stunningly attractive woman, sexy, convincing.'

Garvard opened his eyes.

Horton knew he'd guessed correctly. So who had Sharon been with that day? Had she managed to con him? And had this man recognized her at the crematorium, or perhaps even before then, when she had arrived in the UK, and killed her for revenge or in a rage when she refused to give back his money? Swiftly he brought his mind back to the man on the hospital bed and the events of that long-ago summer. 'Sharon knew about your affair. And she knew where you would drop Ellie off after your day out in the Solent? How?'

Garvard shook his head slightly.

'You don't know? Perhaps she'd overheard you making arrangements,' but Horton had another thought. Perhaps someone had told Sharon and that someone was Harry Foxbury because he had seen them leave from the sailing-club jetty or from the quayside in his boatyard. On a Sunday nobody would have been working in the yard but Foxbury could have been there. And perhaps Foxbury told Sharon because he fancied her or had had a fling with her. Horton didn't think Foxbury would ever have been one of Sharon's victims because he was too fly for

260

that. But even if he had told Sharon, Foxbury it seemed was in the clear for her murder and hadn't met her on Tuesday afternoon.

He continued. 'Sharon went to the boatyard and waited for you to return, staying out of sight until Ellie got off the boat and waved you goodbye. As she made to leave, Sharon stepped out from where she'd been hiding, hit Ellie violently on the back of the head and then pushed her body into the sea. Maybe you turned and saw it, or perhaps when Ellie didn't show for the next meeting with you, you became suspicious. When Ellie was reported missing you guessed that Sharon had to be behind it.'

Horton glanced at the prison officer, who nodded, he didn't have much to write of Garvard's end of the conversation but he was hopefully noting Garvard's gestures and his summary of the situation.

He said, 'When she betrayed you to the police she knew she was safe from being implicated because if you uttered one word about her killing Ellie, she would tell the police where to find Ellie's body and swear blind you'd killed her. There would be evidence on your boat of Ellie's presence and probably witnesses who had seen you on the boat together or when you had put in somewhere. You'd be done for murder *and* fraud. So you said nothing. Better to be convicted for fraud rather than a longer sentence for murder. You did your time.'

'Die doing it . . . got my revenge,' Garvard croaked. Despite the weakness of his voice Horton could hear the bitterness in it.

Garvard closed his eyes. Horton could see that soon he would drift into unconsciousness, possibly for the final time. But there was still much he needed to know. With new urgency he said, 'How did you get Sharon to come back for the funeral? She was living in Spain. Did you know where?'

Garvard gave a slight shake of his head. Horton thought there was a small smile on his lips.

'How did she hear that her aunt had died?'

Could Foxbury have kept in touch with her and told her? Or had Gregory Harlow known where Sharon was and told her, but why should he if Sharon wanted money from him? No, Gregory and Patricia Harlow had only placed an announcement in the local newspaper to let Amelia's friends know about the funeral arrangements. And then it came to him. There was someone who could have contacted Sharon.

'Fiona Wright.'

Garvard's eyes opened and although the man didn't speak, Horton saw that he was right. Keenly he pressed on, as his mind scrambled to put together the pieces. 'While undergoing your radiotherapy treatment you saw Amelia Willard at the hospital, she was also there for her radiotherapy treatment.' Horton didn't know this for a fact yet, but he was ready to stake his career on it, and the fact that somehow Garvard had got Fiona Wright involved.

'You struck up a relationship with Fiona Wright. You pumped her for information on Amelia.'

He reckoned that Garvard had wanted to know about Amelia's cancer and the prognosis. Perhaps he'd even seen Patricia Harlow with her aunt. 'You extracted a promise from Fiona Wright that when Amelia died she would get a message to Sharon and the only way she could do that – if it's true you didn't know where Sharon was living – was by placing announcements about the death in the national newspapers, or the Spanish ones, or both, hoping that Sharon would see it and act on it.'

'*Telegraph.* Sharon always read it,' Garvard replied falteringly. 'Knew wouldn't be able to resist . . . money involved.'

And that would be simple to check. Horton let out a breath, it was beginning to come together, but he still had more questions. He sat forward on the edge of the chair. 'You had also arranged for Woodley to kill Sharon but it went wrong. Did Woodley refuse once he was on the outside? Did he get a message back to you inside that he'd changed his mind, and that he'd only agreed to it to get Stapleton off his back, the staged attack on Stapleton suited all three of you. So you had to arrange for someone to take him out? And someone to kill Sharon in the same place she killed and left Ellie Loman, because you wanted Ellie's bones to be found. Who did you pay to kill Sharon and leave Daryl Woodley for dead after they'd bungled the first attack on him? Reggie Thomas? Or was it one of Marty Stapleton's gang on the outside?'

Horton saw a smile touch the dying man's face. He'd got it wrong. Damn. He could see Garvard slipping away. Urgently he pressed on, 'Who killed Sharon, Leo?'

Garvard was deteriorating fast, the door opened and an angry nurse hurried in.

'No more. You must leave now.'

Horton was desperate. He glanced at the prison officer, who shrugged. The nurse glared at him. Ignoring her, Horton addressed the dying man. 'Leo, who killed Sharon?'

'Inspector, please,' the nurse demanded.

Horton rose. There was nothing more he could do. He turned to leave when a sound came from the bed. He spun round.

'Got even with her,' Garvard croaked. 'Found Ellie . . . See her soon . . . loved her . . .' He slipped into unconsciousness.

Disappointed, Horton left. Outside he asked the prison officer to sign the bottom of each page of notes and give them to him.

'I didn't get much of what you said, Inspector, but I got a few of the points you made and Garvard's comments and reactions. Hope you can read my writing.'

'It's better than mine.'

He was glad to get out in the fresh air even though it didn't feel fresh. The day had turned sour and the sun was skulking behind a menacing dark sky. Elkins' prediction of thunder looked like being fulfilled any moment. His head was pounding as he called up a patrol car and while waiting for it he paced the busy road chewing over the interview. Something Garvard said, or rather how he'd said it, struck him. It was those last words. *Found Ellie.* Did that mean he hadn't known where her body had lain all these years or that by arranging to have Sharon killed there the police would discover Ellie's remains? It had to be the latter, surely. And he had a sinking feeling that they

264

would never discover who had killed Sharon Piper especially if Garvard had hired a professional killer via Stapleton's contacts to do it. And Stapleton was never going to tell.

He continued to mull this over as the patrol car drove him back to Fishbourne, where the police launch was waiting for him. Garvard had known that Sharon would return for her aunt's cremation and had organized, through Fiona Wright, an announcement to be placed in the *Daily Telegraph* but neither he nor Fiona Wright could have arranged for Woodley's funeral to be held on the same day, and none of the Woodley crowd had any involvement in the arrangements either. So was that just one of life's coincidences? It seemed to be.

Horton knew that Fiona Wright hadn't killed Sharon Piper because Dr Clayton had given her a lift home. So if the killer wasn't Gregory Harlow, Reggie Thomas, Harry Foxbury or a hired hit man then who else could it be? *Think like Garvard*, he urged his sluggish brain. Why would Woodley need that photograph of Sharon Piper? What was Woodley's purpose if it wasn't to kill Sharon? If Garvard knew that Ellie's bones were at Tipner Quay then who else would he enlist to kill Ellie's murderer? Then he had it. Kenneth Loman.

Woodley had never been Sharon's intended killer, he was Garvard's messenger boy. He was to make contact with Kenneth Loman and tell him that Sharon knew something about his daughter's disappearance and that she was returning for her aunt's funeral. Yes, that fitted.

Loman wouldn't have known what Sharon Piper looked like, hence the need for the photograph. Woodley had probably told Loman that he had information indicating that Tipner Quay was significant and was probably the last place anyone had seen Ellie alive. Yes, he rapidly thought. Once Woodley had delivered his message all Loman had to do was scan the local newspaper every day until the announcement of Amelia Willard's funeral appeared, go to the crematorium and tell Sharon that unless she agreed to meet him at Tipner Quay he would go to the police. She agreed but she probably had no intention of telling Loman she'd killed Ellie. Or perhaps she told him it was accident or she tried to pin the blame on Garvard.

Loman, distraught, angry and motivated by revenge, stuck that knife in Sharon Piper's back. He could easily have walked to the boatyard to meet her, not wanting to be seen, and then driven her car away and dumped it, after killing her. And Loman could also have killed Gregory Harlow because Harlow had arrived at the boatyard as arranged with Sharon and seen Loman. That meant Loman would have had to cross to the Isle of Wight by ferry, and perhaps Gregory Harlow had picked him up. Loman could have fabricated some story to convince Harlow they needed to talk. But Horton frowned with puzzlement. It fitted except for two things. He could swear that Loman's reaction to the news that they'd found his daughter's remains was genuine grief. And, secondly, he just couldn't see Loman prising open Harlow's jaw and making him swallow drugs and

266

drink. But if Loman was their killer then the person who Sharon had spent the afternoon with eating lobster and drinking white wine had nothing to do with her death.

On the launch he rang Uckfield. While waiting for him to answer Horton stared out at a muddy and very choppy dark bluey-green sea which the wind was whipping up into angry white spray. Thunder growled out to sea somewhere beyond the Isle of Wight. Cantelli would have hated this crossing. He hoped the sergeant had enjoyed his holiday. He would be glad to have him back on Monday. He wondered if they'd have the answers to this investigation by then. They were close but still it might drag on. And if it did, how long would Eames stay? What would Cantelli make of her?

When Uckfield answered, Horton gave him a concise report drawing a few grunts and 'bloody hells' along the way. When he had finished, Uckfield said, 'We'll bring Loman in for questioning.'

'Go easy with him, Steve. He didn't kill his daughter. I also think that if he did kill Harlow, he would have confessed to it.'

'He still might when we confront him about it,' Uckfield grunted.

Horton reluctantly agreed that was possible. He rang off after telling Uckfield that he'd go to the hospital and interview Fiona Wright. And as the Portsmouth coast loomed closer he turned his mind as to how he'd play it.

Twenty

As it was he didn't have to say much. 'Tell me about the advertisement Leo Garvard asked you to place in the *Daily Telegraph.*'

'He's dead?' she asked, concerned.

'No. But I don't think it will be long now.'

She bit her lower lip and pushed a hand through her brown hair. 'I'd like to be there, but that depends on you, I suppose.' She waved him into a seat in her consulting room, anxiety etched on her tired face.

'If all you did was place that announcement then you won't be detained for long. You might make it in time.' *All you did*, he thought. And that small act had brought Sharon Piper to her death, which in turn had led Gregory Harlow to his.

'I promised Leo I would. It was all he asked me to do. And because of that a woman has died. I'm sorry.'

Leo Garvard must be a hell of a man, he thought. 'Tell me about it.'

'He was two weeks into his treatment last June when he said he thought he recognized an elderly woman as he was leaving. He couldn't approach her even if he'd wanted to because of the prison officer with him and even if he did he wasn't sure she'd recognize him or want to acknowledge him because of his conviction. Leo's appointments were usually timed at the beginning of the day so that he could arrive and leave before too many other patients arrived. Over the following sessions we got talking. Not about his criminal conviction and I didn't ask him. I wasn't here to judge him, just to treat him, but I became emotionally involved and that was wrong, and unprofessional. I'm not sure how we ended up talking about Amelia Willard but we did.'

Garvard hadn't lost any of his charm or his powers of persuasion. Horton remembered what Geoff Kirby had told him and he wondered what weakness Garvard had exploited in Fiona to get her to open up and do his bidding. Compassion, kindness, pity? Or perhaps she'd fallen in love with him.

'Amelia was also one of my patients,' Fiona was saying. 'She was a lovely, gentle, happy lady despite her illness. Leo so desperately wanted to speak to her. Even though he was having treatment for his cancer he didn't believe he'd survive it very long. He told me that he'd been very close to Amelia and her family years ago but they'd become estranged when Amelia's son had killed himself and he'd been sent to prison. It was a great relief for Leo to talk to someone outside the prison service. He told me that he'd been raised in a children's home, he'd never known his father or mother and that Amelia and Edgar Willard were the closest he'd got to having family.'

Bullshit, Horton thought but didn't say. He'd read Garvard's file and he'd been raised in a secure middle-class home by his banker father and his schoolteacher mother, both of whom had died before his conviction.

'Leo had worked hard and built up a successful financial business. But in a moment of madness, he threw it all away. I told him I didn't want to know what he'd done.'

And he wouldn't have told you the truth even if you had asked.

'He asked me about Amelia's cancer and the prognosis. It wasn't good. When Leo came to the end of his treatment he said he wouldn't see me again. I told him I'd visit him in prison but he made me swear I wouldn't. He couldn't bear me to see him there. It was too painful for him.'

I bet. Garvard didn't want Fiona blowing open his little scheme before it had time to hatch.

'He said that if he survived the cancer, when he was released we could be together. In the meantime he asked me to do one thing for him. He didn't make me promise and he said if I decided not to then he would understand. I was to find out when and where Amelia's funeral would be held and put an announcement in the *Daily Telegraph* and I promised to do it even if he died before Amelia. I rang the registrar and asked to be kept informed when the death of Amelia Willard was registered. I knew it wouldn't be long. I thought it might bring the families together. Instead it brought a woman to her death.'

She fell silent for a moment. Garvard had wormed his way into her affections and manipulated her. Even when she discovered the truth about him he knew that she would still see only the best in him.

'I know I should have told the prison,' she added. 'But Leo said it might bring Amelia's family back together following the rift caused by her son's suicide, and I believed that.'

She would, after all Garvard was an expert con man. 'You should have told us about this earlier.'

'But I didn't know that woman's death had anything to do with Amelia Willard. You showed me her photograph but you never mentioned she had been at Amelia's funeral.'

No, they'd been too focused on Daryl Woodley. 'Besides I didn't even know if the announcement had been read, let alone acted upon.'

But Garvard had taken that chance. Sharon might not have read the newspaper or seen the announcement and even if she had she might not have cared. But Garvard was a risk-taker and one more might pay off. Even if it didn't he wasn't going to be around to find out, and he wasn't going to lose by it. He'd played the odds and it had paid off.

'Did you have anything to do with Woodley leaving this hospital?'

'No! I never saw him.'

'Did someone tell you to give Woodley a message from Leo Garvard to say that he wasn't safe here and that someone would meet him outside?'

But Fiona was shaking her head vigorously. 'No. I only placed the announcement.'

He eyed her carefully. Had she taken Woodley to the marshes and left him there, believing someone was going to pick him up, because he couldn't see her deliberately abandoning him and leaving him to die. No, he didn't think so. But someone did.

Horton told her they needed a statement and she promised that she'd go to the station right away. He had no reason to doubt that.

Outside he stood under the shelter of the canopy as people dashed to and from the car park in the pelting rain and the thunder crashed around them. He thought briefly of the festival-goers on the Isle of Wight and the fact that DI Dennings might get a soaking, which brought a smile to his lips. It faded long before Trueman answered the phone.

'The Super is interviewing Kenneth Loman now with Agent Eames. He made no protest when we asked him to come in.'

Horton relayed his interview with Fiona Wright and said that she was on her way to the station. 'Ask Marsden to take her statement.'

'I'll get someone to check out the announcement in the *Daily Telegraph*. And you were right, Andy, Sharon Piper, or rather Carol Palmer, was booked into a de-luxe cabin on the *Pont Aven* from Santander to Portsmouth. She travelled alone and by car. The ferry left Santander at three p.m. on Monday and arrived in Portsmouth at two fifteen on Tuesday afternoon. We've got her vehicle registration. I've put a call out for her car. She was booked to return on the *Cap Finistère* on the midday sailing on Wednesday. We're checking the hotels in the area to see if she made a reservation for the night, but there's nothing so far, and she might not have booked but just decided to take pot luck.'

'And I doubt she would have expected to stay with her sister. She could have arranged to stay with

the man she spent the afternoon with and not necessarily on a boat now that we know she came by car.
It could have been at his flat or house. He hasn't
come forward because he doesn't want to be
involved in her death or is scared he'll be suspected
of killing her.'

'He still could have done.'

'Unless Loman confesses. Does Foxbury's alibi
for Tuesday afternoon and evening check out?'

'Yes.'

So they could rule him out. Horton rang off.
He should return to the station but he felt too
restless for that. If Kenneth Loman was busy
confessing to the murders of Sharon Piper and
Gregory Harlow then that would be it: case
solved, except for Woodley's death, and that had
to be either one of his so-called associates or
someone Garvard had sent. But if Loman wasn't
their killer then who was? This man she'd eaten
a meal with and had sex with? She wouldn't
have picked up any old stranger, unless it was
someone she had met on the ferry on the way
over and had arranged to see him, and that was
possible. But in that case he couldn't be her
killer but if it was someone she had once known
and who'd been fond of her, who she'd previ-
ously had an affair with . . . Several thoughts
jarred in Horton's mind. But how had this man
known she was returning for her aunt's funeral?
The answer was the same he'd reached earlier:
Woodley.

He had to go back to the attack on Woodley.
Why had Woodley been at the Lord Horatio pub
near the waterfront if the message from Garvard

was for Kenneth Loman who lived in the north of the city and close to Woodley's own patch? There were two answers to that question: either Woodley had been told to relay the message to two people, or he'd met Loman on the Hard. Loman could have been there because he'd gone fishing with a friend, or he wanted to be close to where his daughter had worked, the Historic Dockyard. It was tenuous to say the least but as Horton dashed through the rain to his Harley he knew he wouldn't find the answers here and he wouldn't find them at the station.

Fifteen minutes later he pulled up outside the tattoo parlour on the Hard and surveyed the area just as he'd done on Thursday, again taking in the taxi rank, the cafe, the road leading to the railway station and the small ferry which crossed the narrow harbour to the town of Gosport beyond. Then there was the coffee stall, the Net Fishermen's Association Hut, the tourist centre and the Historic Dockyard where Ellie Loman and Rawly Willard had worked. His eyes travelled back to the coffee stall. He read the sign above it and remembered where Eames had bought their lunch at the festival: Coastline Coffee. And here was another connection between Ellie Loman, Rawly Willard and Gregory Harlow. Was it possible?

Eagerly, on foot, he hurried towards the stall oblivious of the heavy rain sweeping in off the harbour. Two of four of the small plastic tables and chairs under the huge awning were taken up by tourists huddled over maps. Horton took his place in the queue behind two tourists and

274

impatiently waited while they ordered burger and chips with their cappuccinos. When his turn came he ordered an americano to go and asked the middle-aged dark-haired lady serving him how long she'd worked there.

'A lifetime, love,' she said smiling. 'And I'm still not appreciated.'

'I'm sure you are,' he said returning her smile. Now for the questions and he hoped some answers that linked in with the theory he had formed. 'Did you work with Gregory Harlow?'

'You know him?' She glanced at him over her shoulder while making his coffee. Her heavy black eyebrows arched in surprise, and there was a pucker of concern on her furrowed forehead.

Horton nodded and brought out his warrant card. As she placed the coffee in front of him she called out, 'Lisa, take over. I've just got to have a word with this gentleman.'

Although he'd hoped for cooperation he hadn't expected it so quickly and readily. His excitement mounted because he could see that she had something to get off her chest and he hoped it was what he wanted to hear.

A blonde woman in her early twenties appeared from the back of the stall wiping her hands on a black-and-white-striped apron and slipped into the older woman's place. Horton stepped around to the back and stood under the rear awning out of the rain, facing the grey choppy sea of the harbour which he could see through the plastic window. The thunder had stopped but the rain was heavier than ever.

275

'I heard that Greg was dead,' the woman, who introduced herself as Iris, said with a sad expression. 'Was it suicide?'

'We're treating his death as suspicious.'

She looked concerned and troubled. 'You mean someone killed him?'

He let his silence do the talking.

'My God! That's awful.' She took a deep breath. 'And that's why you're here asking questions. You want to know about Greg?'

'Anything might be helpful. How long did he work for Coastline?' Horton thought it best to lead up to putting the real questions he wanted answered.

'He started here on the stall in April 2001 just after I did and became a delivery driver for the supplies side after about nine months.' She looked uneasy or rather troubled. 'And he was a delivery driver until last October when Mr Skelton suddenly promoted him to event-catering manager. Biggest leap in promotion I've ever seen.'

Horton eyed her keenly. 'What do you mean?'

Iris hesitated. Horton had seen this before. It was the moment of mental struggle. Whatever Iris had to tell him had ramifications for her personally. He held his silence hoping her conscience would win out, feeling that at last he was on the edge of the truth. Harlow could have got that photograph to Woodley in Parkhurst before his promotion but Horton didn't believe he had.

'Mr Skelton is a shrewd businessman. And successful. He's built this business up from one small coffee stall to a chain of them along the south coast and a big catering company. He makes a lot of money.' She paused. Then lowering her voice still further she continued. 'He's got a big house over the Hamble somewhere, a flashy car – one of those big four-wheel-drive vehicles, looks like a tank – and he has a boat in a marina. Nothing wrong in that but he doesn't like spending money on his staff. He pays the minimum wage and then not always. He has an eye for cheap labour,' she added pointedly.

No wonder she had hesitated. Horton understood perfectly what she was talking about. 'How cheap?'

'Cheapest you can get away with if the people you employ have got nothing to start with.'

'Here at the stall?'

'No.' Lowering her voice and looking out to sea she said, 'Not enough space here.'

Horton followed her drift immediately. He thought of that tent of Skelton's at the Isle of Wight Festival and of Dennings' presence when he and Eames had arrived. Then there was Haseen Nader. He was probably legit, but it didn't take too many brain cells to work out what Iris meant: illegal immigrant workers. Harlow had found out about it and kept silent in return for promotion, or perhaps he'd got his promotion because he agreed to be a party to it. Then his conscience had finally troubled him, especially after Sharon's death when he and Eames had started asking questions. Or rather he'd got scared. He told Skelton he was going to the police, or perhaps Skelton saw he was getting jumpy and decided to silence him. And that made far more sense to him than Loman killing him.

In her normal voice Iris added, 'And to think the poor soul didn't live long enough to spend his bigger wage packet. And not long after his aunt's death too.'

'He mentioned that to you?' Horton asked his pulse quickening.

'No. I overheard that man talking about it. He said Gregory Harlow's sister-in-law was coming home for her aunt's funeral, and he had a photograph of her.'

And there it was. What he had conjectured. And the reason why Harlow hadn't got that photograph into the prison, because this had been Woodley's destination. This was where he had to show the photograph and pass on his message and it wasn't to Kenneth Loman.

Trying to hide his excitement, Horton took out the photograph of Woodley. 'Was this the man?'

'Yes, that's him.'

Horton wondered why she hadn't come forward after all their appeals for sightings of Woodley, but maybe she didn't buy the local newspaper or listen to the local news, or perhaps she'd been on holiday. 'When did you see him?'

'May, early evening it was. I was just going off shift at seven. Well, I've said my piece, it's up to you lot now.'

But Horton had one more question to ask. He already knew the answer but he had to ask none the less. 'Who did he give the message to?' It wasn't Gregory Harlow.

'Didn't I say? It was Mr Skelton. He wanted

Mr Skelton to pass the message on to Greg, I guess, to tell him that he needed to know his sister-in-law was coming back for her aunt's funeral.'

Twenty-One

Horton headed for his Harley, calling Ross Skelton. There was no answer to his mobile. He then called Uckfield and this time got hold of him.

'How did you get on with Loman?'

'He denies meeting Sharon Piper at the boatyard and killing her. Claims he was at home with his wife on Tuesday night and again on Thursday night but says if we ask his wife she won't be much use as an alibi. She can't remember anything after Ellie disappeared.'

Horton knew that.

Uckfield added, 'I don't think he's our killer.'

'He isn't. Ross Skelton is,' and Horton rapidly relayed what he'd discovered from his interview with Iris. 'I believe he's the man Sharon Piper was with on the day of Ellie Loman's death in 2001. Garvard knew this and Woodley's job was to get a message to Skelton to say that Sharon would be coming back for her aunt's funeral, whenever that was. There would be an announcement in the local newspaper and the *Daily Telegraph* – courtesy of Fiona Wright – and Garvard gambled on Skelton wanting to look out for it and wanting to see Sharon

279

again because they'd had an affair. Woodley was probably instructed to tell Skelton that Sharon had been forced to leave the country in a hurry because of the police investigation surrounding Garvard. She would return with a new identity and a new name and would only be in the country for a short time. She wanted to see Skelton but they couldn't be seen together. It was too dangerous for her. There were still some of Garvard's associates who were after her.

'Skelton's the man Sharon met at the crematorium and spent the afternoon and evening with. His company supplies fish and frozen food to the prison on the Isle of Wight and elsewhere on the Island and here on the mainland, so having a lobster tucked away in his fridge at his home or on his boat, and I suspect it's the latter, would have been quite natural. He could have followed her to the boatyard and killed her or he could have driven her there for her rendezvous, killed her and then driven her car somewhere and abandoned it.'

'Motive?'

'Perhaps she had something on him from back in 2001. He's crooked now so he could have been crooked then. Skelton's employing illegal immigrant labour but DI Dennings probably knows that already, or at least the Border Agency do, which is why they're watching his tent at the festival. Garvard knew Skelton was a crook and he judged what Skelton's response would be when he discovered that Sharon was returning. Skelton needed to find out what and how much Sharon knew, perhaps Woodley was even told to hint that she knew something about his current operations. He might not only be employing illegal immigrants, he could be trafficking in them, or drugs. Garvard could have picked something up on the prison grapevine, or from one of the Coastline delivery drivers. He's a twisted bugger and a creative con man, he could easily have made up enough to convince Skelton. Skelton decided it was too risky to let Sharon live. Gregory Harlow saw Skelton kill her or suspected him of it and wanted more than another promotion out of him. Maybe he asked for a big fat pay rise or a bonus. He got killed instead.'

'Right. I'll get the Island police to bring him in and I'll get a unit over to his house, have you got his address?'

'No, but according to Iris it's at Hamble and he has a boat in a marina. Could be Horsea Marina, nice and convenient for Tipner Quay. And he's not answering his mobile.'

Horton relayed the number. It wouldn't take them long to get Skelton's address and locate the boat, and Skelton had no reason to suspect they were on to him and go into hiding. They would have their killer. But what if Skelton wasn't at the festival and he wasn't at home or on his boat?

Horton started the Harley and swung it in the direction of the church which had been robbed of its brass plaques. A short distance after it he indicated left and turned into one of the back streets, retracing on the bike the steps he and Eames had taken on Thursday. He came out by the Lord Horatio pub, which looked worse than normal in the gloomy weather and rain.

His thoughts veered from Ross Skelton to

281

Woodley and Garvard. There was something he'd seen or noted in a gesture from the sick man, or was that just his imagination? He considered what he knew of Garvard and what Geoff Kirby had told him. Where was Ross Skelton now? Skelton and Sharon Piper, he ran it over in his mind. Something was troubling him. It was one small niggling doubt and the image of Garvard on that hospital bed flashed before him.

Before he knew it he found himself heading for the north of the city and within twelve minutes was drawing up outside a terraced house. It took some time for the door to be opened and when it did it wasn't Patricia Harlow who stood before him but a fair-haired, blue-eyed, good-looking man in his early twenties. For an instant Horton thought he was being haunted before Dr Clayton's words at Sharon Piper's autopsy flashed through his mind: *she's borne a child.* My God, now he knew why Patricia hadn't wanted Connor Harlow at the mortuary with her when she had identified her husband's body. And he also knew why Gregory Harlow had stayed with Patricia all these years. Horton showed his ID.

'I'd like to speak to your mother,' he said, knowing that would be impossible.

'She's not here.' Connor Harlow looked anxious and upset, not surprisingly thought Horton, eyeing him closely. 'Is it true that my father was murdered?'

'I'm sorry to say it is. Does your mother know this?'

'Yes. A woman police officer came a couple of hours ago to tell us. Have you any idea who could have done such a thing? Why kill Dad? He never did anything to harm anyone.'

Horton was rapidly thinking. 'What did your mother do after she was given the news?'

Connor looked confused.

'It's important,' Horton pressed as gently as he could while trying to suppress his concern and impatience. He was beginning to get a bad feeling in the pit of his stomach about this.

'She didn't cry, if that's what you mean. She never does.' There was a touch of bitterness in his voice and Horton thought he saw a brief flicker of anger behind the eyes. 'I tried to talk to her but she blanked me out. That's not unusual. She's not the type of person you can . . . she doesn't show her emotions. She went into her surgery. She told me she needed to think and she couldn't do that with me around.' Now Horton heard the pain in the young man's voice.

'Did she telephone anyone?'

'I don't know. She might have done. She went out about ten minutes ago.'

Horton thanked him and hurried away. He felt a slight qualm for being so abrupt and for leaving the man bewildered and upset but time was critical. He told himself that Patricia Harlow could have gone to a friend who was consoling her in her grief, only he didn't think Patricia had any friends. And from what he'd seen of her, and from his brief meeting with Connor Harlow, he doubted she needed consoling over her husband's death. She might even be glad he was dead. From her reaction to the news Horton guessed she'd been working out who might have killed her

283

husband and why. She wasn't stupid, far from it. And there was only one place she could be.

The blue-and-white police tape on the cordon flapped in the wind as Horton drew the Harley to a stop just outside it. The sailing club was still closed, the road was deserted except for the two cars parked inside the boatyard, one belonged to Patricia Harlow and the other was as Iris had described it 'like a tank', a big four-wheel-drive cruiser: Ross Skelton's.

Behind and above Horton the traffic swished and roared along the rain-soaked motorway. The day had drawn in early, the sky was a darkened hue making the sea of the harbour look a muddy grey, flecked with smudgy white foam. Horton tensed and hurried quietly forward through the empty boatyard. He hoped to God he wasn't too late. He could see the two wrecks on the quayside but there was no sign of anyone and certainly not Patricia Harlow or Ross Skelton. Could they be inside the old boatshed?

Swiftly and silently he headed for the quayside, the rain running down his face, his ears straining for any sound. He eased his way around the wreck where Sharon Piper's body had been found and drew up as the crane barge came into view. On it stood the bedraggled figure of Patricia Harlow, looking out across the rain-swept harbour. He reached it before she spun round, sensing his presence rather than hearing his approach, Horton thought.

In an instance he registered her ashen face, her blood-stained jacket and the bloody knife in her right hand before his eyes fell on the body that lay face down at her feet. It was Skelton. The back of his head was a mess of blood, flesh and bone but there was no knife wound. He rapidly theorized that she must have stood in front of him and stuck the knife into his guts taking him totally by surprise and then hit him over the head with a piece of metal piping he could see lying close by. And he didn't think she'd acted in anger.

'It's over, Patricia. Put down the knife,' he commanded with authority, while his heart was hammering fit to bust. Keeping his eyes on her he made to climb on the barge but she quickly stepped away from the body towards the edge and closer to the sea. The rain was drumming against it like a hundred stones being flung at the flat steel surface. Edged with a flimsy piece of wire strung out by poles not even knee high it wouldn't take much for her to topple over.

'I need to check if he's still alive,' Horton insisted, climbing onto the barge alert to the fact that at any moment she might step further back. But this time she remained still. She showed no signs of relinquishing the knife though. He didn't like the fact that she was still holding a weapon which she could plunge into him while he was crouching over the body, but he assessed that he could dodge out of her way by the time she reached him and then he'd be able to easily disarm her.

He pressed his fingers against Skelton's neck. There was no pulse. He tried again, his eyes flicking downwards for an instant. There was a movement to his right but she had edged further away from him rather than closer. Skelton was dead. Straightening up, Horton said, 'Patricia, you need help. Let me get it for you.'

'No!' she shouted and seemed surprised that she could speak. It seemed to invigorate her. 'No,' she repeated now more self-assured. He saw something of the former Patricia Harlow reasserting itself. She pulled herself up and tossed back her head. 'He killed Gregory. He was going to kill me. I had to do it. I had to get him before he killed me.'

There was no pleading in her voice. She had spoken as if it was a matter of fact and that anyone would understand why she had done what she had. Maybe Skelton *had* tried to kill her. Perhaps the knife had been his. But if so how had she got it from him? Horton couldn't see him giving it up willingly and she could never have taken it from him by force. Skelton had looked to be a fit and agile man. Had he put it down for a moment while waiting for her to show and she seized the opportunity to grab it? Skelton had then spun round but too late she'd plunged it into his stomach.

'Give me the knife, Patricia,' he repeated firmly, stepping towards her and holding out his hand.

'No. You'll arrest me for murder.' She snatched the knife behind her back as though afraid he would steal it from her and took another step towards the edge of the barge. If he moved again he might force her over the side and if he rushed at her she'd turn and either jump or fall in accidentally. And he didn't want to go in after her with that knife she was wielding. He had to get her to give herself up and more importantly give up the knife.

Almost conversationally he said, 'Why was he going to kill you?'

'Because I knew about him employing illegal immigrants, of course,' she scoffed as though he was stupid for not realizing it. 'Gregory told me. When the police said Gregory's death wasn't suicide then I knew Ross Skelton must have killed him.'

But why would she have agreed to meet her husband's killer? Rapidly he replayed what Connor had told him. It was probable she had made a call from her surgery, they could check that, and if she *had* made the call then it had to be to arrange this meeting with Skelton and not the other way around. *She* had come here with the intention of killing *him*. Why? Revenge for her husband's death? Somehow that didn't ring true. So it must be because she suspected him of knowing something that could damage her, and there were only two things it could be.

He said, 'If Skelton had planned to kill you then he'd need to make your death look like suicide, which means he didn't come here with a knife. Perhaps he intended knocking you out, making it look like an accident and then pushing your body into the sea.' He saw her eyes narrow and her mouth tighten. 'But you came here with a knife. Is it the same knife you used to kill your sister, Sharon?' He wanted to provoke a reaction.

'I didn't kill her. He did.' She jerked her head at Skelton's recumbent body.

Evenly Horton said, 'Why would he do that?'

287

'Because Sharon was with him the day that Ellie Loman disappeared. He saw her kill Ellie. And he was with Sharon the day Aunt Amelia was buried. Gregory recognized his car parked just outside the crematorium as we were turning into it. She must have arranged to meet him there.'

No, that was Garvard's doing. He'd had a long time to plan this.

'If he saw Sharon kill Ellie Loman then she was more likely to kill him to silence him.'

'Maybe she tried and it went wrong,' Patricia Harlow leapt too readily at this.

There was one very big flaw in her story and at last he was beginning to see exactly what must have happened. He thought he caught a movement to his left behind the crane but dismissed it as the wind swinging the rigging. 'Why didn't you come to us when you suspected Ross Skelton of killing not only your sister but also your husband?'

'I couldn't. You wouldn't believe me. You'd try and blame me like you did poor Rawly.'

'And we'd be correct. Because you did kill your sister, Patricia, and Ross Skelton discovered that while he was killing your husband.' He saw instantly that he'd got it wrong. There was a flicker of smug triumph in the back of her eyes. He eyed her steadily and closely, rapidly recalling all the interviews with her, the times she'd lied and twisted the truth. Then he knew.

Calmly he said, 'Sharon didn't kill Ellie, Patricia, you did.' He held his breath keeping his steady gaze on her. Would she continue to deny it or would she finally crack? Only the wind howling through the crane rigging and the rain lashing against them punctuated the silence which seemed to stretch on for ever. Finally it broke.

'It was an accident,' she said in a rush. 'I only pushed her. She fell and knocked her head on the cleat.'

He let out the breath he didn't realize he'd been holding. That was consistent with the injuries to the skull that Dr Clayton had pointed out to him but there was more to Ellie's death than that. With barely disguised disgust he said, 'But you then dumped her body in the sea and left her there to rot.'

'What else could I do?' she said as though she'd had no choice.

'You could have confessed,' he said, with bitterness. 'You could have saved Rawly Willard from taking his own life, and spared his parents, your aunt and uncle, from years of suffering.' Not to mention the heartbreak and anguish she'd caused Kenneth Loman.

'The police killed Rawly with their persecution of him,' she said dismissively and defiantly. 'That had nothing to do with me.'

'And that's what you've told yourself all these years.' Horton held her hard stare. 'No, Patricia, you killed Rawly as surely as you killed Ross Skelton and Ellie Loman. And Sharon knew what you'd done. She'd always known, hadn't she?'

He saw instantly that he was correct. And Sharon had kept silent because it suited her to have it over Garvard. 'Does Connor know who his real mother is and that he's the result of an affair between your husband and your sister?'

She flinched but the knife stayed firmly grasped

289

in her hand pointing at him. He didn't doubt that he'd be able to disarm her, but still she was perilously close to the edge of the water.

Stiffly she said, 'I agreed to bring him up as my own.'

And you never let Gregory forget his affair. Seeing Connor every day was a reminder to Gregory of his infidelity. How Gregory Harlow must have been tempted to tell him over the years. But his silence was the price he had to pay for having had an affair with Sharon while married to her sister. And silence was his guarantee that the boy would have a family upbringing rather than be abandoned to a children's home or be put up for adoption. If Gregory wanted to see his son growing up he would have to stay with Patricia and keep silent. And he did.

Despite the body in front of him, the woman holding the knife and the relentless rain, which was the least of his worries, Horton needed the answers to a few more questions, and he needed to get her into custody.

He said, 'Why were you here when Leo Garvard dropped Ellie back on that Sunday after she'd spent a day on his boat?'

'Can't you guess?' she said scathingly.

'You wanted Sharon to see them together. You wanted to hurt her as she had hurt you by sleeping with your husband.' Patricia had thought that Sharon was in love with Leo, but she wasn't. Sharon had probably had a string of affairs aside from Skelton and she had used sex many times to trap her quarry. Garvard knew this and went along with it. But Patricia hadn't known that.

'I overheard Leo arranging it with Ellie. I was by chance at the coffee stall on the Hard when I saw them together. Ellie was on her coffee break, she always took it at the Coastline Coffee stall. They didn't see me. I told Sharon that I had to meet her at the boatyard. I had something to tell her about Leo. I knew that would bring her here. I came here that Sunday after I'd had tea with Aunt Amelia. Gregory was out fishing all day. The boatyard was closed on a Sunday, but we all knew how to get into it. Harry Foxbury was always lax with his security, besides there was nothing to steal except old boats and bits of metal that weren't worth much.'

Not then maybe but now worth a fortune, thought Horton, remembering those metal thefts. 'They came back early.'

'Sharon was late. I waited out of sight until Leo left on his boat with Ellie touchingly waving him goodbye. I had to stop her leaving before Sharon got here and before Leo's boat was out of sight. I confronted her. She said she loved him and that he was going to leave Sharon for her. I said she was a stupid young fool.'

'And you told her what Leo and Sharon did for a living. She didn't believe you.'

'She got upset, hysterical. I grabbed her. She tried to get away. I pushed her and she fell. Before I knew it she was dead. Sharon saw it all.'

And had Leo Garvard looked back and seen Patricia Harlow and mistaken her for Sharon or had he only seen Sharon? But Horton considered a third option and knew it was the truth. Garvard had known all along that both sisters had been here and had had a hand in Ellie's death and cover up.

The clang of metal against metal from the crane dimly registered with him as the wind whipped through the rigging. He said, 'So you and Sharon struck a bargain. It suited Sharon to say nothing about you killing Ellie because she wanted Garvard out of her life and she wanted all the money from their fraudulent scams, or rather as much as she could get her hands on that they'd secreted away. When she shopped Garvard to the law he knew he couldn't tell the truth about dropping Ellie off and seeing you kill her because you and Sharon would swear blind that each was with the other and that in all likelihood he'd be done for murder as well as fraud. And Sharon would keep quiet about your part in Ellie's death because she wanted wealth and a chance to get away.' And had Gregory Harlow known this? If he had then he could have used it to get Patricia out of his life by giving her up to the police. But that would have involved Connor's real mother and disrupted the family life he had desperately wanted his son to have. So they had all kept silent until Leo Garvard had found a way to break that silence. His cancer and the chance sighting of Amelia Willard at the radiotherapy department had sparked an idea that had eventually led to three more deaths, and to bringing Ellie's body up from her watery grave. How fortunate then the timing of raising the sunken barges. Garvard must have read about it or heard about it on the news. But Horton knew that even if the barges hadn't been raised Garvard would have found another way to bring Ellie's killer here and expose her remains.

'It's over, Patricia. The truth has to come out now. Hand me the knife.'

'No.' She stepped back.

'There's nowhere to go.'

She spun round and within seconds was clambering and stumbling over the deck of the barge towards the seaward side in the dark. Shit! He turned setting off in the opposite direction around the crane to head her off praying that she wasn't going to throw herself into the sea or trip over something and fall in and that neither would he. He could hear her faltering footsteps, then there was a cry and nothing, not even a splash. He rounded the crane and drew up sharply. Kenneth Loman was standing over the prostrate figure of Patricia Harlow. Horton swiftly glimpsed Loman's harrowed sodden face, his wet dishevelled clothes and the heavy piece of piping he was holding. The knife was on the deck and the side of Patricia's face a bloody mess of mangled flesh.

His breath caught in his throat as Loman raised the hand carrying the piping; his eyes were full of hatred directed at the body at his feet. Horton knew what he was thinking, she'd put him through a living hell and he wanted to vent his anger. He wanted to obliterate her and the pain he had suffered all these years. But he would never be able to, not even if he beat Patricia Harlow to a pulp. Sharply Horton shouted, 'Killing her won't bring Ellie back.'

Loman hesitated.

Horton stepped forward and repeated firmly but

293

more quietly. 'Leave her, Ken. Ellie wouldn't want this.'

Loman froze. He seemed to consider Horton's words then he exhaled, the piping fell from his hand and clattered onto the barge. His body slumped. Horton could see he was close to collapse. Stepping forward he took his arm. 'Let's get away from here.'

Loman made no protest. As Horton steered him towards the quay he wondered if Patricia Harlow was still alive.

Climbing off the crane barge, Loman said, 'It's all right. I won't run away. You'd better call the ambulance.'

The man was spent. Horton watched him ease his broken defeated body onto the giant cleat, where he stared across the black expanse of the water. Horton doubted he saw the lights across the harbour. It had stopped raining. He remained close, half afraid that Loman might throw himself in but then he guessed that Loman would want to see this thing through to the end.

He called first for an ambulance for Patricia Harlow. Ross Skelton was beyond help, and for all he knew Patricia could be too. Then he called Uckfield. While he waited for him to answer, Horton wondered if the cleat Loman was slumped on was the one that Ellie had fallen and struck her head against, if Patricia Harlow could be believed, and Horton wasn't convinced by that given her track record.

Swiftly he gave Uckfield a potted version of what had happened and that they'd need SOCO and some patrol units here. They wouldn't have far to come. He crouched down to face Loman; his wet hair was clinging to his dirty, exhausted face. 'How much did you hear?' he asked gently.

'All of it. I was behind the crane.'

'You saw her kill Ross Skelton?'

The image of Garvard's gaunt, grey face on the hospital bed flashed before Horton's eyes along with Geoff Kirby's words. Garvard was cunning, clever, manipulative. He knew a man's weakness and how to exploit it. Garvard had pulled the strings from his sick bed and had taken pleasure during his dying days in imagining how it might work out but had he ever imagined this?

Loman said, 'When they let me go at the station I knew the boatyard wasn't far away and I couldn't go home. I just wanted to be where Ellie had last been alive. I heard them arrive and dodged out of sight. I didn't know who they were, I just didn't want to see or talk to anyone. I was angry and upset because I had wanted to be alone. I didn't think they'd climb onto the crane barge but she did and he followed. Then she spun round and stuck a knife in him. I was shocked, confused. I didn't know what to do. She hit him over the head and dropped the weapon and then almost immediately you showed up. Is it true what she said, that she killed Ellie?'

'Yes.'

'Then I hope she dies and I'm convicted for her murder. Prison can't be much worse than the hell she's put me through all these years.'

No, thought Horton, and it wasn't over yet. There was still the matter of Sharon Piper's murder.

Twenty-Two

'Congratulations, sir,' Eames said, knocking and entering his office an hour later. He cut her short.

'Did you look up those statements?'

'Yes.' She seemed taken aback by his abruptness. Quickly recovering she said, 'The mourners at Amelia Willard's funeral you asked me to check. There was only one man who said he didn't see the woman with the large black hat because he had to go to the toilet.'

Horton's pulse quickened. 'And he is?'

'Lawrence Sanderling. Flat 1, King Charles Court, North End. Is it important?'

'Oh, it's important all right.' Horton reached for his sailing jacket. He'd changed into a set of clothes he kept in his office: cargoes and a T-shirt, socks and shoes. He'd learnt over the years that they'd be needed on many occasions and not only because someone had thrown up over what he had been wearing but that they might end up covered in blood. This time it was because his other clothes were soaked through.

'Let's talk to Mr Sanderling.'

'But what about the interview with Kenneth Loman?' Eames asked, surprised.

'Uckfield can get someone else to take Loman's statement.'

Uckfield was reporting to Dean, who was at home. So too was Bliss because there was no sign of her at the station. But then it was nearly ten thirty.

'You can always go home, Eames,' Horton added, heading through the CID office.

'No,' she said quickly, plucking her jacket from the coat stand and following him.

He remained silent as Eames drove through the glistening wet streets to the north of the city. His thoughts took him back to Patricia Harlow. The initial prognosis was that she would recover but that she'd be permanently scarred and there was the possibility of brain damage. A car had been sent to take Connor Harlow to hospital. Soon he'd discover the extent of his birth mother's and his adoptive mother's crimes. He wasn't sure how Connor was going to handle that but he knew there would be pain and bitterness. Ross Skelton's two daughters, aged twenty-three and twenty-one, might feel the same along with shock when they discovered their father had murdered a man and was a crook. His estranged wife might gloat over it, though, or was that his view of how Catherine would react? DI Dennings had reported that he and the Border Agency had found six illegal immigrant workers in Coastline's operations at the festival and now they and Her Majesty's Revenue and Customs would be trawling through Skelton's business operations like a prospector looking for the smallest glint of a diamond that could change his fortunes.

A message on Horton's desk and another on his voicemail from Sergeant Elkins had said that Ballard had left St Peter Port, they weren't sure when. He must have slipped out. No one had seen him go.

Eames pulled up outside a shabby block of flats not far from the leisure centre in the north of the city, and close to where Woodley had lived. It also wasn't far from the old boatyard. Eames pressed her well-manicured finger on the dirty intercom, while Horton noted the peeling and scuffed paintwork, the rubbish lying around in the forecourt and the rotten windows. She hadn't asked why they were here and he could see that she had been rapidly trying to work it out. Perhaps she had by now.

A man's wary and wavering voice answered. Eames quickly introduced them and added, 'We are quite happy to wait here, Mr Sanderling, while you call the police station to verify who we are and to push our identity cards through your letter box or put them up against your window.'

'No. Come in.'

The buzzer sounded and they stepped inside. Horton registered the dirty hallway, scratched paintwork and the smell of urine and rubbish.

A door to their right was opened by a grey-haired, well-built man in his late seventies dressed in a petrol-blue cardigan over a check shirt and grey trousers. Horton made to show his ID when the elderly man forestalled him. 'I know who you are and why you're here.'

They followed Lawrence Sanderling through the tiny vestibule into a small living room with old-fashioned furniture and a threadbare carpet. Seeing and interpreting his glance, Sanderling said, 'Not much for a man who once used to run a company, live in a large house not far from Edgar and Amelia near the seafront, own a boat, privately educate his daughters, and was married to a lovely woman.'

'Sharon Piper and Leo Garvard,' said Horton sadly.

'Yes.' Sanderling waved Horton into an ancient chair with a sagging cushion in front of the electric fire. Sanderling drew up a hard-back chair and gestured Eames into it, before pulling up one for himself.

'It was my own fault,' Sanderling said, once settled. 'I was stupid enough to believe them and greedy enough to fall for their lies, but I wasn't the only one and I thought if it was good enough for Edgar then it was good enough for me. Sharon was his niece, for God's sake.'

'You saw her when you came out of the toilet at the crematorium.' Because this was the man Horton had stepped aside for when he, Uckfield and Marsden had followed Woodley's mourners to the front of the crematorium.

Sanderling nodded sadly before a spark of life and anger flashed in his grey eyes. 'There she was dressed to the nines looking well and wealthy. Living off my money and other fools like me, laughing and tucking her hand under the arm of a man. I nodded at her and she blanked me. She didn't even remember who she had once fleeced.'

'Even if she had I don't think she would have cared.'

'No.'

'You should have come to us.'

Sanderling lifted a shoulder. His body seemed to be curling up in itself. 'I couldn't stomach going into Amelia's funeral after seeing her. I decided

299

to follow them.' He glanced up at Horton. 'I had no idea why or what I was going to do. I was on some kind of autopilot and very, very angry, not a showy sort of violence but something deep inside me had snapped. It was eating away at me, driving me on. She got in a car parked in the overflow car park where I'd left mine. I always park there when I go to funerals at the crematorium, and there seem to be a lot of them at my age, it's easier to slip away. He got into a big silver four-by-four, Toyota Land Cruiser. I didn't know then where he went but I followed her to Gregory and Patricia Harlow's house, where she sat in the car. When the funeral car arrived she climbed out and crossed to them. There was a brief exchange between them and then Sharon got back in her car and drove to Horsea Marina. I saw her get on this boat with the man she'd met at the funeral.'

Horton had been correct about that. Skelton's motor boat had been impounded. On it was a RIB that Skelton used as a tender and Horton had been told that, like Foxbury's, it had a powerful Suzuki 300hp engine on it, or rather twin engines, powerful enough to whip him across the Solent in fifteen minutes. Horton was betting that Skelton had returned to the mainland from the Island then used his RIB to cross back to the Solent, he'd moored up in Wootton Creek or at Fishbourne and walked to Firestone Copse, where he'd arranged to meet Harlow. There he'd killed him, walked back to the RIB and returned to the marina or moored up outside it and returned to the marina the next day or Saturday. All this they would painstakingly check.

Sanderling was saying, 'I had no idea how long she intended to stay on the boat with this man. It might be all night. I wanted just one glimpse of recognition from her, or one sign of remorse.' He gave a hollow laugh. 'I certainly wasn't going to get that. The longer I sat there the more I thought back over my life, remembering how it had once been. I thought too of Edgar and Amelia and poor Rawly and the anger grew. It was a cold, calm sort of rage, as though everything had suddenly became very clear. I knew what I had to do.'

He took a breath. In the silence Horton heard the rain start up again, thrashing against the window, and the solemn ticking of the clock on the mantelpiece, where there was a photograph of a couple that was clearly Lawrence Sanderling and his late wife. In the flat above a dog began barking incessantly and a baby started crying.

'Then just as I thought I'd be in the car all night she came down the boardwalk and got into her car.'

'What time was this?'

'Ten fifteen. She headed for Portsmouth. For a moment I thought she must know where I lived and was coming to see me. See how stupid I am,' he said with a bitter laugh. 'But she turned off and headed for the old boatyard at Tipner. I stayed well back because there are no street lights there and I didn't want her to see me. I knew there was no other way out except that road, or by sea. So after a while I followed her, dimmed my lights and pulled up at the sailing club.'

Eames interjected. 'Were there any cars there?

'No. And it was in darkness. I had a torch in the car. I saw her waiting on the quayside. I headed for her. She must have heard me because she swung round. Perhaps if she hadn't spoken I wouldn't have killed her.'

Eames interrupted. 'Sir, I should warn you that—'

'Oh, don't bother with all that now, you can caution me or whatever later. Besides even if she hadn't spoken I guess I still would have killed her. After all, what have I got to lose? A prison cell has got to be better than this dump and I'll be fed and kept warm.'

Eames flicked Horton a sad glance.

Sanderling continued. 'Besides I didn't only have a torch in my hand, as you well know. I also had the knife I use for gutting fish, which I keep in the car along with some other bits for fishing, when I get invited out. She said, "Who are you? What do you want?" I said something like, "You don't remember your victims, then?" But why should a woman without a single shred of conscience, an evil wicked woman, remember the people she had destroyed? She told me to go away. And that if I didn't she'd call the police and have me arrested for pestering her. I said, "Go on then call the police and I'll tell them what you and that boyfriend of yours did to me, Edgar Willard and countless others." That pulled her up sharpish for a moment then she said she didn't know what I was talking about, and that obviously I was confused, suffering from some kind of dementia, and that people like me should be locked away in a home. She turned away. I grabbed her, caught

302

the chain of her handbag on my arm, it broke and fell. She made to turn. I still had hold of her and I plunged the knife in her back and thrust her into the sea. I remember staring down at the water thinking, Good, now you won't destroy anyone else's life. I put the handbag in the boot of her car and drove it to the multi-storey car park at the ferry port. The car had a foreign number plate and I thought it was the natural place for it. It must still be there, unless you've found it.'

They hadn't because they'd only recently got the registration number and no one had thought to check a legitimate car park for it. They'd been looking for it abandoned or flashed up somewhere.

Sanderling said, 'I returned to the boatyard, got in my car and came home.' He looked at both of them in turn. 'I've been following the investigation on the news. I've been waiting for you to come. I didn't know there was another body down there. Is it connected with that wicked woman?'

Horton answered, 'We believe it to be the remains of Ellie Loman.'

Sanderling's eyes widened with surprise. 'Was she murdered?'

'Yes.' Horton knew he shouldn't say anything about the case but Sanderling, although a killer – and Horton couldn't condone what he had done – should know. 'But not by Sharon Piper, although she knew about it. Patricia Harlow killed Ellie.'

'My God!' A veil of sadness touched his eyes.

Eames rose. 'Would you fetch your coat, sir? Is there anyone you'd like to call? Your daughters perhaps?'

'No. There's no one.' At the door he said, 'When you're old people stop noticing you.'

Yes, and that had been Horton's mistake. He had thought nothing of the man going to the toilets in the crematorium until less than two hours ago. And if had recognized the significance of him earlier perhaps he could have saved two lives.

Twenty-Three

Sunday

Horton stepped out of the station and gazed up at the pale pink sky in the calm, fresh morning. The streets were silent. It had been a long night. They'd taken statements from Loman and Sanderling, both had refused to have a solicitor present, neither man seemed concerned about what would happen to him. Loman would probably receive a suspended sentence unless Patricia Harlow died but even then he would in all likelihood escape prison given the circumstances behind the attack, unless he was very unlucky with the Judge. And Sanderling? Horton simply didn't know.

He took a breath. Uckfield had been bouncing around the station with a big grin on his craggy face, elated at clearing up one of Dean's failed cases and disappointed that there was no one around to hear him crow about it. Monday though would be different. Horton thought they would hear about it on Ben Nevis. Uckfield would get his revenge on Dean for pulling in DCI Bliss to review one of his cases. He'd gone home about an hour ago along with an extremely tired Trueman and a weary and relieved Marsden because Uckfield in his joy had forgotten all about the press debacle. Only Eames remained inside the station. Horton thought he should call Mike Danby and tell him about Ellie Loman's murder. Or perhaps he'd delegate that to Eames. Danby was staying in one of her family's properties, after all.

He heard footsteps behind him. Eames.

'Thought you'd like to know, sir. A call's just come through from the hospital. Leo Garvard died this morning at three thirty-three.' She looked as tired as he felt. Fatigued she appeared vulnerable, more approachable, and even more beautiful. He experienced a strong yearning to wrap his arms around her and hold her, which he quickly nipped in the bud, not without some difficulty. What was the point? She was out of his reach and she'd be returning to The Hague on Monday. He knew that wouldn't have stopped other men from trying and might even have made seducing her more attractive but he wasn't most men. He didn't want a one-night stand. He wasn't sure if Eames would want that either. God, he didn't even know her first name.

'Did they tell him what had happened?'

'Yes, but whether he heard . . .' She shrugged. 'He was unconscious.'

Horton knew though that hearing was the last sense to leave a person. So perhaps Garvard did know, and knowing, he had finally let go.

Eames continued. 'We might discover who left the photograph of Sharon in Woodley's cell now that Garvard is dead. I'm assuming that Garvard had the photograph all the time.'

'Probably, but I don't think anyone's going to admit to putting it in Woodley's cell.'

Eames considered this for a moment before saying, 'And Ross Skelton attacked Woodley and because he made a hash of it first time he picked Woodley up from the hospital and took him to the marshes where he left him to die.'

It was the conclusion that Uckfield had drawn and the timing of Woodley's visit to the coffee stall seemed to match it, although they didn't have the exact date for when Iris saw him. Uckfield's reasoning behind it was that Skelton had been planning to join forces with Sharon. 'He *was* a crook and a killer,' Uckfield had reiterated. 'Woodley must have told Skelton, under Garvard's instructions, that Sharon had a scheme he'd be interested in that would make him a great deal of money but that no one should know about it. That would have been enough for Skelton to silence Woodley. He proved himself a killer with Gregory Harlow's death. He followed Woodley to the pub, waited until he came out then attacked him but he botched it. Then he picked Woodley up and took him to the marshes.'

'How did he know Woodley was going to leave the hospital?' Horton had thrown in.

In exasperation Uckfield had answered, 'Skelton telephoned him or visited him and spun him some yarn about someone being after him and that he'd help get him away.'

It was the theory that Uckfield was clearly going to stick to, and one which would never be disapproved. It meant the clearing up of another case, and a notch on Uckfield's proverbial promotion belt, but Horton said to Eames, 'Skelton didn't attack Woodley.'

She frowned. 'Lawrence Sanderling couldn't have attacked Woodley and neither did Patricia or Gregory Harlow, so if Skelton didn't, who did?'

'When we catch our metal thieves we'll ask them,' Horton said.

She looked at him in surprise.

'Whoever struck Woodley was disturbed doing it. Our metal thieves were in the area that night, not at the church, but the date matches that of when they stole that bronze statue from a garden in Old Portsmouth and a fountain from the wine bar. They cut through the back streets in their van and prevented Garvard's instructions from being carried out. Woodley was expendable, a messenger boy. He'd delivered the message and needed to be eliminated.' His words suddenly conjured up Edward Ballard. Several thoughts galloped through Horton's mind but he was too tired to even grasp one of them as they flashed past.

'So who killed him, or rather left him at the marshes to die?' Eames asked baffled.

'Ask Marty Stapleton, although I don't think he'll tell you.'

'Shit!'

He smiled. 'That's not a very nice word for a girl like you.'

307

'I know a lot worse. So Stapleton *was* in on it.'

'Yes, in letting himself be attacked by Woodley in prison, and in providing someone to take Woodley out after he'd delivered the message. Garvard probably didn't know who Stapleton ordered to do it and didn't care, just as long as Skelton was on the hook.' And the person who had attacked Woodley could have been in the pub drinking, watching and waiting for Woodley to leave, knowing that he had finally delivered his message to Skelton. Either that or he had waited outside, and it wasn't Reggie Thomas because Thomas like Woodley would finally blab. Garvard had wanted someone who had no connection with Woodley and who would never be traced. For a second Horton's mind leapt back to Edward Ballard before he continued, 'Garvard had no idea that Woodley's funeral would coincide with Amelia's Willard's.'

'Gambler's luck.'

'Bad luck for Gregory Harlow and Lawrence Sanderling.' He should also say bad luck for Patricia Harlow and Sharon Piper but he couldn't bring himself to do so. 'Woodley had only the one message to deliver and that was to Skelton. For all Garvard's planning he hadn't foreseen Lawrence Sanderling.' Or had he? He had known that by bringing Sharon back for the last of the Willards' funeral, and assembling those still alive from the time of Ellie's death, something would happen. And it had.

Eames, clearly following his train of thought, said, 'So who did he plan to kill Sharon? Or is "plan" too ambitious?'

'Maybe. He knew that Sharon would see Patricia and that they were both involved in Ellie's death. Perhaps he thought that Patricia would kill Sharon. And he judged that Edgar and Amelia's friends would be at her funeral; friends he and Sharon had conned, so one of them could do it for revenge.'

'And they did,' she said sadly and quietly.

'Yes.' There was a moment's pause before he continued. 'Or perhaps Garvard thought Skelton might be prompted into doing it because he thought Sharon knew too much about him employing illegal immigrants and perhaps even assisting in bringing them into the country. Maybe Woodley delivered more than the message Iris overheard.' Horton shrugged.

'And in return for organizing Woodley's death, Stapleton gets whatever money Garvard has stashed away.'

'Well, it's no good to Garvard now.'

'We might find it,' she said optimistically.

Horton doubted it. 'I don't think that will be of much comfort to Lawrence Sanderling and Kenneth Loman.'

'No.' She sighed before adding more brightly, 'Buy you a coffee, guv?'

It was the first time she'd called him guv. He looked at her clear-skinned face with its dark smudges under her intelligent blue eyes and his heart quickened. He'd like to have said yes. He'd liked to have talked to her and not about the case, but what did he have to say to a woman like Eames from a background so totally opposite to his? 'Think I'll give coffee a miss for a while.'

309

'I'll see you tomorrow, then.'

He thought she sounded disappointed but perhaps he was only hoping she was. He eyed her surprised. 'I thought you'd be returning to Europol.'

'I'm waiting instructions and there's no one to give them to me at this ungodly hour or should I say godly hour seeing as it's Sunday.'

He watched her climb into her car and drive away. Cantelli would be back tomorrow and he'd be very pleased to see him.

Despite what he'd said to Eames about not wanting a coffee he headed for the Hard not knowing if Coastline Coffee would be open. It wasn't but the cafe serving the taxi drivers was.

He waited while the taxi driver in front of him ordered a big breakfast and chatted with the cafe proprietor. He was in no hurry. Mentally tuning out the radio music his thoughts turned to Edward Ballard and the idea which had occurred to him earlier. He knew that Ballard had had nothing to do with Sharon Piper. Ballard was a messenger boy, just like Woodley. He'd delivered the message and had left. But what message? And why? Even more importantly, whose message? Sawyer's words came back to him: *We believe that someone connected with Zeus will try to make contact with you.*

Had that been Ballard? Did Sawyer know that? Was that why he'd arrived at the marina before Horton, because he had been tracking Ballard's movements? Had he known Ballard had arrived and would try to make contact with him? Had the gang member Europol apprehended in

Stockholm, who had died of an allergic reaction to aspirin, told them about Ballard? Had Eames really come from the Netherlands? Even if she had, Horton wondered if she'd been in Stockholm before that. Maybe he should ask her.

We don't believe you're in imminent danger because Zeus needs to know who you are and how much you know first. Had Ballard reported to Zeus, or someone connected with him, who was living in Guernsey and now that he had done so he was on his way back across the English Channel? To where, though? And what could Ballard have told Zeus about him? He'd said nothing worth relaying and there had been nothing on his yacht about Jennifer Horton, not even her photograph.

'What can I get you, mate?'

Horton brought his weary, troubled mind back to the cafe proprietor and ordered a black coffee to take out. He was exhausted and his head was thumping. He was too tired to think, but snatches of Sawyer's conversation continued to play in his head.

Do you remember Jennifer talking about any one man more than the others; or someone who called on her or she met or who took you out?

Could that have been Ballard? Maybe Sawyer had access to Jennifer's history. Yes, that made sense. Sawyer could have discovered that Ballard had worked with or known Jennifer, perhaps even been her lover.

Horton paid for his coffee and took it along the Hard. He couldn't get Ballard out of his mind. He thought of that can of Coke he'd sent for DNA

311

and fingerprints. Ballard had hardly touched the drink and after accepting it he'd been keen to get away. Was that the message that Ballard had delivered to him? Ballard had wanted to leave his mark in order for him to investigate. To discover who he was. Perhaps fingerprints and DNA would tell him who Ballard was. But he had a suspicion neither would. He knew it wouldn't be that simple. He again thought of Sawyer's offer to go in with him; should he take that secondment to the Intelligence Directorate? It could be a short cut to the past and the truth, as well as a promotion albeit temporary.

He was convinced there had been a purpose to Ballard's visit and he was equally convinced that the attack had been phoney designed so that Ballard could make contact with him. Then there had been that farewell gesture which niggled away at the back of his mind. He'd seen it before . . . Suddenly and sharply the picture snapped into focus. My God! Of course!

He'd come home from school early, he couldn't remember why. He might even have bunked off. A man had been talking to Bernard, his last foster-father and a policeman. They'd been standing just outside the house. Horton had seen the man hand something to Bernard, a small tin. The man turned, walked towards his car where he'd turned, looked back and raised his hand in farewell. Bernard had nodded and gone inside the house. Then the man had looked around and his eyes had alighted on Horton where they had lingered for some moments before he'd climbed in his car and driven away.

Ballard! Horton saw him quite clearly now,

fit, muscular, blond. Several questions jostled for space in Horton's head as he stared out to sea. Did that mean Ballard was connected with Zeus? If so then had Bernard been? But no, he couldn't believe that. But why not? Maybe Zeus had wanted to take care of his son, or Jennifer had made him finally promise to make sure that her boy was OK and that was why he'd been fostered with Bernard. But surely he couldn't be corrupt?

Horton swallowed his coffee not tasting it and threw the paper cup in the bin. He knew very well that coppers could be bought or got at, or be basically unsound, but gentle, kindly Bernard? No. His chest felt tight with emotion and his brain whirled with questions. Why had he been fostered with Bernard and Eileen Lichfield? Who had placed him there? Where had Ballard come from? Who had he been working for? But two questions clamoured in his brain refusing to be silenced: why had Ballard given Bernard that tin – and Horton knew it was the one that had contained the photograph of his mother and her birth certificate, both of which had been destroyed in the fire on his previous yacht – and why had Ballard visited him now?

With sudden clarity Horton knew the answer to the latter question. Hastily he climbed on his Harley and raced to his yacht. There he hurried down into the main cabin and lifted up the seat cushion where Ballard had sat. He tensed. Staring at him was a black and white photograph. Holding his breath and with a thumping heart he picked it up. In the foreground was a group of six men;

313

two were sporting beards and untidy long hair which touched the collar of patterned open-necked shirts while the other four were clean shaven with short hair that reminded Horton of the Beatles. All were sitting on the floor and had their arms around each other smiling into camera while behind them was a small crowd of mainly men with a few women. He turned it over. Written on the back in neat black ink was a date, 13 March 1967. Ballard had delivered his message, and although Horton had no idea what it meant yet, he'd find out. And whereas the photograph of the late Mrs Stanley wearing a brooch that might once have belonged to Jennifer had drawn a blank, he knew with absolute certainty that this one wouldn't.